I0717517

The Isdralan Chronicles

Micah and the Candles of Time

Prodigy of Flame

The Golden Gull

This anthology bridges the 'pond' and revels in the grammar and spellings of two distinct dialects of English. Here, you'll journey through U.S. stories where wizards 'realize' their potential, and U.K. narratives where witches "realise" their destinies.

Keep in mind, the collection isn't a battleground of 'traveled' vs "travelled" or 'favorite' against "favourite". It's a vibrant excursion where 'pants' can morph into "trousers", and 'trucks' transform into "lorries" just as you turn the page.

Whether you're whisked to a U.S. 'harbor' or a U.K. "harbour", each story weaves its own tale So, dive in, dear reader, and remember, whether you're 'gotten' lost in the U.S. or have "got" lost in the U.K., the charm of a captivating adventure remains universally enchanting.

The
Golden Gull

The Isdralan Chronicles

Wolf Grove Media

The Golden Gull

Published by:
Wolf Grove Media, LLC
13110 NE 177th Pl #1038
Woodinville, WA 98072

Typesetting: JB Drew

Additional Art: Illustration in in "Brave Soft Hearts" by Irularts
Biplane, Propeller, and Pilot images in Balloon Buster courtesy of macrovector on Freepik.com
Illustrations in The Red Diamond by Nathalie Velasquez

A CIP record for this book is acailable from the Library of Congress Cataloging-in-Publication Data

ISBN-10: 1-958329-10-8
ISBN-13: 978-1-958329-10-8
Printed in USA

"The past is but the beginning of a beginning, and all that is and has been is but the twilight of the dawn." - H.G. Wells

Without you, our readers, this anthology would merely be a dream. Your fervor for the creative arts and dedication to supporting artists, writers, and creators have made this dream a reality. Wolf Grove Media wishes to express profound appreciation to these extraordinary individuals for their pivotal role in shaping our shared world.

In the words of Maya Angelou, "You can't use up creativity. The more you use, the more you have." Your continuous support fuels our creative fire, inspiring us to weave words and craft stories that ignite imaginations. This anthology is a testament to your belief in our craft. Thank you for joining us on this journey.

Acknowledgments:

Haley Drew "Look within. Within is the fountain of good, and it will ever bubble up, if you will ever dig." - Marcus Aurelius

Jamie Pica "Of all the paths you take in life, make sure a few of them are dirt." - John Muir

Ian Wambua "Reading is an act of civilization; it's one of the greatest acts of civilization because it takes the free raw material of the mind and builds castles of possibilities." - Ngũgĩ wa Thiong'o

Karen L Franklin "You can never get a cup of tea large enough or a book long enough to suit me." - C.S. Lewis

Glen Cooper "One day I will find the right words, and they will be simple." - Jack Kerouac

Jason Lovero "Writing, to me, is simply thinking through my fingers." - Isaac Asimov

Michael Pica "Any sufficiently advanced technology is indistinguishable from magic." - Arthur C. Clarke

Patricia Gagne "The more that you read, the more things you will know. The more that you learn, the more places you'll go." - Dr. Seuss

Ric Lancaster "It is what you read when you don't have to that determines what you will be when you can't help it." - Oscar Wilde

Sika S. "We are responsible for our dreams. This is the ultimate lesson of psychoanalysis - and fiction writing." - Ama Ata Aidoo

Emily Lancaster "A writer only begins a book. A reader finishes it." - Samuel Johnson

Ruby Mason "The arts are not a way to make a living. They are a very human way of making life more bearable." - Kurt Vonnegut

Robert Lancaster "A reader lives a thousand lives before he dies. The man who never reads lives only one." - George R.R. Martin

Elizabeth Boyd Graham "I have always imagined that Paradise will be a kind of library." - Jorge Luis Borges

Sean McNicholl "The world is full of magic things, patiently waiting for our senses to grow sharper." - W.B. Yeats

Amber Beauvais "To learn to read is to light a fire; every syllable that is spelled out is a spark." - Victor Hugo

Isabella Ramirez "A writer only begins a book. A reader finishes it." - Samuel Johnson

Table of Contents

Prologue: The Golden Gull 1

To Lugh 50

Balloon Buster 84

Brave Soft Hearts 92

The Raven's Descent 170

Deep Breath 228

The Red Diamond 282

Trading on Vanir 340

Epilogue: The Golden Gull........................ 396

The Golden Gull
By Steve Drew

W ANTED FOR MURDER! 1000 GOLD REWARD," read the announcement on the town crier board. It went on in less intrusive lettering, "Half-elf boy, answers to Raama. Also guilty of maiming, destruction of property, warmongering, and theft. Reward for information leading the Citadel of Mages to his capture." Conveniently, below was a picture of Raama. They clearly constructed it with a spell they had not taught him in his brief time at the Citadel of Mages. It showed his face as it was right now. He realized he should not be standing right next to a wanted poster of himself for so long and stopped making expressions just to watch the picture change. Fascinating spell, though. While bypassing the rest of the town and continuing his journey to the nearest harbor city, he had already started puzzling out how to do it.

As he walked, he thought back to the announcement and how unfair it all seemed. Murder. Him, a murderer. He had sealed a teacher in an air-tight bubble, but he hadn't killed him. The bubble would have released teacher Marcus the moment he admitted what he had done. A confession that he, himself, was worse than a murderer. Instead, the teacher had attempted magically burning his way out of the bubble and roasted himself alive. Perhaps Raama was guilty of assisted suicide? Alright, fine. Without the confession, Raama had to concede their point on murder. He put a mental tick mark next to the murder claim.

The maiming, he assumed, referred to Khurd. Khurd was a fellow student and toady of Marcus. Raama assented a couple burst eyeballs would qualify as maimed. Of course, this was in self-defense, as Khurd was attempting to rip Raama's soul from his body. As badly as he was weaving his spell, Khurd would have destroyed all the living souls in the area. Raama supposed you could not very well put "hero" on a wanted poster. Raama's attempt to stop Khurd's casting had resulted in a clash of magics leveling the entire top of the mountain that housed the school. Thinking about it, Raama suspected that the friends of Khurd that were blown to particles in the explosion were probably on the murder list as well. Perhaps that one was appropriate too, then. Tick.

Destruction of property. Probably the same incident. Although there was also the chunk of the school missing where Raama blasted it away from the mountain in order to escape the teachers. No arguing that one. Tick.

Warmongering. Such a harsh term. He never actually declared war. He just said he would if they didn't change their ways and remedy the situation which the teacher had created. The poster made their decision clear though. He supposed honoring his word meant he was now at war with the Citadel of Mages. Tick. Raama sighed audibly as he walked.

Theft! At least that one was a plain lie. He had left the school with literally nothing but the robe he had been wearing. Was the robe school property? Drat. Tick.

Raama pressed on without sleep until he reached the city. Of the two ships in port when Raama arrived, the Golden Gull left the soonest. He did not even bother filing away the name of the city they were traveling to. Raama just needed to get far away from here as quickly and quietly as he could. He negotiated a rate with the captain of the Golden Gull by offering half of the captain's initial rate. The anger on the captain's face worked as a gauge to a more appropriate offer. The haggling began and finally they settled on a number. Raama even got the captain to agree to sending a ship-boy to fetch the supplies Raama did not have time to go gather himself. Raama boarded the ship and spent the next few days in his cabin. The exhaustion, lack of sleep and poor diet while coming to the city had left Raama feeling queasy. The rocking motion of the ship was not helping and Raama could only hope that ships stopped rocking once they were underway.

The swaying did not go away as the ship unmoored. Instead Raama spent the first several days in a state of pain and amusement. He felt the pain as everything he had eaten for the past few ten-day seemed to come out one end or the other. The amusement was his unintended gift to the crew. They laughed as he alternated between running to the rail or to the closet with the bucket. They offered comments on foods that would help settle his stomach and laughed raucously when he looked about to vomit again.

One of the ship-boys, a girl named Aanee, eventually took pity on Raama and brought him some leaves of White Hellebore to chew on. By the end of the first ten-day, Raama was walking around without feeling the motion of the ship in his stomach. The crew clapped him on the back and congratulated him on getting his legs under him. He even felt well enough to help with the tasks above deck when he was not getting in the way.

When Raama requested permission to explore the ship, the captain brimmed with pride and responded. "Of course, lad, explore away. She's a beauty on her maiden voyage. She'll be the fastest merchant class afloat for quite some time. Should even be fast enough under load to outrun a pirate on open water."

Raama didn't know how he should respond, but nodded politely and excused himself to go look around.

"Have the boson give you a quick tour and show you the off-limit areas, then explore the rest anytime you like," the captain said to his back.

Raama liked the sound of that. Both because he was curious and because he enjoyed listening to the boson. The boson was a half-orc with a high-pitched voice that reminded Raama of a goblin teacher at the Citadel. That teacher habitually over indulged in the wine served with dinner. Raama loved listening to both of them speak. He also noted that, as much as the crew loved to laugh at other people, Raama had never heard one mocking word about the boson from any of them.

The boson showed Raama the crew quarters, cook's quarters, galley, captain's quarters and the reserves. All of those were areas passengers could not go without accompaniment from the crew or specific instructions from the captain or boson. The boson continued the tour with brief stops everywhere else and then started to head back to his duties, leaving Raama to explore. Before he left, Raama pointed at the water seeping through the side of the ship and asked if they had a leak. The boson's look made Raama aware of his naivety. As Raama was about to apologize for, and withdraw his question, the boson smiled and explained that ships leaked from time to time.

"T'ain't buck'ts, t'ain't nut'n," he said. "Oak'm didn't dry right there," he said. "Add oak'm if feel bet'r'."

The boson pointed to the oakum bucket and mimed dabbing it in for Raama. As the boson walked away, Raama grabbed the bucket, which smelled like a mix of day-old campfire and rotting leaves. Motivated by the image of water flooding the ship, Raama spent the rest of the day dabbing oakum into the room. He reinforced the oakum by weaving thin strands of air through it as he dabbed it between the boards. This provided a tighter seal and helped the oakum dry quicker. Raama's mental image of how easily these boards could buckle motivated him to weave some earth into the boards to provide extra strength. That he was so far from safe land and was now trusting a few pieces of wood and this stinky substance for his safety hit Raama anew. He wondered if his earlier sea sickness had been his body's way of telling him how stupid he was to leave the land behind. His body was right; perhaps he had been hasty in his decision to escape by ship.

A few crew members came through as he was working. They smiled at him and went about their business. Word must have gotten to the captain of what he was doing. At full dark, just as Raama used the last of what was in the bucket, the captain came in and started inspecting the work. He ran a finger along the seams, poking and prodding.

"Dried fast. You didn't use flame, did you?"

"No, captain."

"Nice work, mister Raama. Ship masters in the yard could take a lesson from you. We typically apply oakum to the outside, except for emergencies, but this seems to work quite well. Having a mage aboard could have advantages." At Raama's startled face he continued, "no denying it, lad. I saw the posters going up just before we set sail. Fortunately, I think I am the only one that did, but I can't swear to it. I fancy myself an excellent judge of character and I doubt you're the murdering, thieving type. Are you?"

"It depends on your perspective, captain," Raama replied truthfully. "People are dead and disfigured because of my actions."

The captain seemed surprised at the candor and was thoughtful for a long moment. "Seems a tough business, learning to be a mage. I suspect all kinds of things can happen. And the thieving?"

"The robes on my back when I left, I would guess."

The captain nodded and asked quietly, "mister Raama, are you going to cause trouble on my ship?"

"No, sir."

Then, with more steel, "and, do you realize how far the swim is back to land if you cause trouble on my ship?"

"Yes, captain."

"And can you use your magic to make this oakum resistant to fire?"

Raama thought for a moment before nodding. "I can make the entire area not burn, but I prefer not having word spread about my abilities."

"Boson!" the captain bellowed back the way he came. In moments, the boson stuck his head in.

"Aye, cap'ain," said the squeaky voice.

"How much pitch do we have on hand, boson?"

"One daily. One disas'er. Full up."

The captain nodded. "Two full barrels. Mix up mister Raama a bucket of oakum anytime he needs it until we have only half a barrel left. We'll buy more at the next port, please."

"Aye," said the boson, before disappearing.

"I'll keep your secret, lad. If you'll keep fixing up rooms like this, I'll return your fare when we reach port. If you make it unable to burn as well, I'll pay you a good bit more. Deal?"

Raama simply nodded. He enjoyed the work and was going to get his coin back. Life was looking up for Raama.

Raama still spent part of each day on deck learning whatever the crew had time to teach. Often he spent hours learning to tie knots of all varieties. It amazed the crew how the half-elf could sit on deck, tying and untying knots again and again. Raama focused so intently on the knots that he failed to notice the wagers going on behind his back. Crew betting on how many attempts it would take before the half-elf mastered the knot. Eventually, the crew wagered on whether they could tie the knots faster than Raama and lost as often as they won.

Each afternoon, he would get his assigned bucket of aromatic sauce and head to the area assigned by the captain. After testing the fireproof nature of Raama's work with a lit torch, the captain had assigned fire risk rooms like the galley first.

Raama had a crew member assigned to be present when he worked in crew rooms. The captain had explained that he wanted a witness if someone claimed a theft, but Raama did not mind. The ship-boy assigned was Aanee, the same one that had given him the White Hellebore during the start of the voyage. Despite the name ship-boy, only girls held the position on this ship. Aanee was present anytime Raama was caulking an area that required him to have supervision. She enthralled Raama with stories about her life as an orphan, roaming the streets of the city.

"There were twelve of us that tried out for this position. All of us from the street," Aanee told him. "We had to climb poles, learn to tie knots and beat up straw dummies to compete. At the end, the captain offered me the job and told me to report by the next dawn for the sea trails. Denita, that spawn of a trampy alley rat, tried to lock me in a shed and take my spot.

"Less gawking, more dabbing," she said, pointing. Raama started and realized he had stopped working as he listened.

To cover his embarrassment, he asked, "what did you do?"

Aanee's soft laugh sent shivers up Raama's spine. "I crept aboard before we sailed and after we left the docks, I threw her scrawny ass over the side. The captain laughed and told me not to be late again, and that was the end of that. Now I am never going back."

"Will you live at sea forever, then?"

"A captain lives her life on the water, and I will have a ship of my own someday. Maybe even this one."

When she started talking about being a captain, Raama kept his eyes focused on the work. She could get touchy about anything she took as criticism, and she could take even a look as criticism. That belaying pin she fiddled with seemed like something Raama would prefer to avoid being hit with.

Crisis avoided her tone stayed light. "And, who knows, maybe there will even be a spot for an oakum smelling half-elf that knows how to plug holes."

Raama missed Aanee's presence when he did rooms he could visit alone. While lost in his work, he was keenly aware how much death lay beneath his feet. Aanee's stories had a way of keeping things shoved into the back of his mind that he would rather not think about. Such as exactly how much water was on the other side of these boards or how a partially trained mage was going to wage war with the school of mages. As Raama completed a room, the captain would carve a fancy-looking R on the third board from the bottom of the floor. The captain would tell Raama that he would note the work in the ship's logs. When Raama's mental image of what that meant slipped out in conversation, Aanee howled in laugher. She gasped for air between laughs and explained the logs were the captain's journals of the ship's journey. This impressed Raama, and he re-solved to keep a log of his own once he could gain one. The laugher, he ignored. The pieces of flotsam Aanee left in his cot for a ten-day in case he wanted to start his own log, he also ignored.

With the work of the day complete, Raama lay on-deck, weather permitting. The open sky and the stars fascinated him while he listened to the crew joke, sing, and tell stories. Raama had never felt this sense of belonging, even in his own village. His favorite were the diddies. Raama often whistled them throughout the days while working. Other songs were lude tales of women in far-away lands that did things that seemed somewhat improbable. The crew favorites involved references that Raama did not understand. They still seemed to light his face on fire. His discomfort did not go unnoticed. Aanee noticed his blushing and began teasing him, quietly, when the crew were singing.

"Did you need me to tell you what they are singing about, Raama?"

Raama would try to change the subject. "No, Aanee. Look at those stars and tell me another story."

Aanee would look at the stars. Sometimes she would tell him more about her life in the city and sometimes she would just lie close by and stare at the stars as well. Always though, she would end by watching him out of the corner of her eye while smirking. "Did you need me to explain why they sing about those things, Raama?"

"No, thank you. I think it's time for me to get some sleep, anyway."

Raama had grown to love sleeping aboard the ship. He was usually exhausted by the day's activity, and the rocking of the cot lulled him into a deep sleep and held him there until the first shift change of the morning. Tonight, though, Aanee was following him below. As he entered his room, she started to come in.

"Perhaps I should make sure you can git in the cot safely," she said with a mischievous grin.

"I've been doing it fine for several ten-day now, Aanee. Good night." And he gently closed the door in her face, only to hear her laughing on the other side.

Sleep was tougher after that. Each night, she began doing the same thing. Escorting him to his room and asking if he needed to learn how to git in his cot. He would lie awake for a while with his heart beating quickly, imagining what her auburn hair would look like if it were not in a ponytail.

Then, one night, before he could shut the door, she slipped into the room and said, "Enough of this. You prove you know how, and I'll stop bothering you."

Raama went and climbed onto the cot, nearly falling for the first time in a long while, but recovering quickly and slipping under the blanket.

"We'll call that a maybe," Aanee said while rolling her eyes. "Are you telling me you sleep with your clothes on?"

"Well. No, but…"

Shaking her head, she held out her hand. "Hand them over. I'll hang them up for you."

Raama slipped out of his clothes under the blanket and handed them over. "Really, this is unnecessary."

Aanee put the clothes on the peg and turned for the door. "I'll get the lantern for you before I go."

"Ok, thanks Aanee," Raama said, sighing in relief. This was almost over.

The light went out and Raama heard steps going towards the door, then the sound of the door closing. Then a rustle and a padding of feet. Before he could say anything, cold feet touched him under the blanket.

"AANEE," he squeaked in startlement. Then he stopped breathing, because he felt her skin against his.

"This is how you 'git in a cot', you stupid, oakum smelling, goon of a half-elf."

The next morning, all the crew seemed to know what he had done. Most slapped him on the back and said, "Well done" or some such thing. Raama wanted to explain that he hadn't done it. Really, Aanee should get the praise. However, he was a bit too shy to say anything. Instead, he set about his day, settling into his routine and hoping there would be a new routine added to at least some of the night times.

* * *

When the captain told Raama that they were about halfway to their first port, Raama felt a twinge of melancholy. He was not ready for life aboard ship to end and experienced trepidation about starting over. He reminded himself of his mentor's words. "Be curious, Raama. Curiosity overcomes anger, fear, and sadness. A life of curiosity won't lead you astray." He worked to embrace the curiosity about where this change would take him, but still felt sad at the thought of life onboard ending. Until the storm hit.

The ship had weathered many foul nights, but the storm was Raama's first experience with waves that were taller than the ship. The captain and crew were tense while they went about their business, which scared Raama the most. By this time, Raama had worked in all the rooms, sealing them. He busied himself below decks, checking on how the caulking was holding. The creaking of the planks eventually drove him back on deck. No matter how many times the captain told him ships were built to creak, the sound sent shivers of fear through him and the storm had the creaking at a new height.

As he arrived back on deck, the darkness was absolute. The crew had stowed all lanterns out of habit to avoid problems in a storm. Fortunately, his eyes had adjusted to the dark below decks, where he used his fingers as his primary sight source. Above deck, he could see the darkness that was empty and the darkness that was a shadow moving. The blurring in his eyes as the salt water stung them helped not at all. Raama grabbed a guard rail and followed it to the stern where the captain would be. He made the captain aware he was there and then waited in case of need.

The captain acknowledged his presence. "She'll blow out quickly, Raama, don't you worry. We just have to stay afloat until she does."

Raama knew the words were meant to be comforting, but found them somewhat lacking in that regard. Instead, he focused on the surrounding waves and the dark shapes they seemed to create at the top. If he squinted hard enough, it almost looked like another ship was atop the wave while this ship was near the bottom. After a few wave cycles, Raama realized it was another ship.

"Ship above, captain," he shouted, but it was too late. The ship was bearing down on them rapidly.

"Brace," the captain yelled moments before the other ship landed on them. The bowsprit of the other ship punctured the Golden Gull's hull midship on the port side. The impact would have knocked anyone off their feet and potentially into the ocean.

Raama engaged his mage sight and shielded his eyes from the rainwater, while he scanned for the circling orbs that indicated life. He could sense a few beings floating in the water.

"Man overboard," Raama yelled and pointed at each location in succession as he called out the bearings. Crew by those rails tossed lines, coated in a bright yellow substance that was visible in the water, in the directions he had called out.

Raama focused on the ropes for a moment, at a loss for how to help his crewmates in the water. Then his mage sight saw the tiny orbs that made up the rope. He added weaves of air to each rope, encircling them and creating a cone of air around the rope with the open end of the cone facing the crew in the water. With a deft motion of his hand, he moved those cones most of the distance towards the end of the line before hardening the air strands. He could feel the rope's orbs bouncing harder and harder against his air funnel as he strengthened it. By adjusting the funnel, he could make the bouncing orbs move the rope towards the crewmate. The ropes snaked out as though the rope and crew were attracted to each other. Quickly, all beings in the water had seen and grasped the ropes. The yellow substance acted like a glue agent, and a similar substance at the ship's end started glowing green.

"Haul," came the simultaneous voices from the captain and other crew members scattered around the deck as the colors changed.

Minutes later, the waters were empty of crew members. The air, however, was full of shouts of "boarders" and "pirates" and the clanging of metal on metal under toned by the splintering of wood.

The captain turned to a crew member standing nearby. "We get that ship off us or we will both break apart. Tell the mariner to get an axe crew over there."

"I can help with that, captain," Raama said meaningfully.

"Belay that order," the captain said to the crew member that was already moving away. Turning back to the dark spot where Raama's voice had come from, "do what you can lad, we'll deal with the secret if we survive."

Raama nodded, already losing himself to the mage sight. In the darkness, those looking Raama's direction could only see forks of lightning from the shadows where his eyes were. Whether his eyes reflected the lightning rushing down from the sky, or the lightning reflected his eyes, was uncertain. The result was the same. Multiple strikes of lightning flashed down in rapid succession. They struck the pirate ship, blasting through it as if rushing to contact the sea water underneath. Raama reveled in the feel of contact with lightning again, and realizing how much he missed this feeling. He kept deluging the pirate ship with strike after strike.

Lost in revere, Raama did not know how much

time passed before he heard the captain bellowing. "Boarders that don't surrender go over the side!" More softly to Raama, the captain said, "we're free, lad. Let it go."

Raama, still savoring the contact, continued to watch the lightning racing towards the salt water. The way the light spread from the strike point fascinated him. He felt a hand on his shoulder.

"Lightning at sea is a dangerous thing, mister Raama. Best if you can stop it now, please."

Raama smiled with chagrin and released the lightning. He turned around to find the captain and helmsman close enough to see. The helmsman staring at him, mouth agape. The captain cuffed the helmsman on the back of the head. "Mister Raama just saved this ship. The lightning also seems to have encouraged our boarders to surrender faster."

Raama looked along the ship, but the lightning had destroyed his night vision. He sent a streak of lightning across the sky to light the deck below. There he saw the pirates, tossing their weapons on the deck and sitting down while some crew members encircled them. Those that weren't surrendering were entering the water either by choice or with help from crew members. Raama released the lightning.

"We've got flooding!" The words Raama least wanted to hear. His fear of drowning took hold of him and he ran towards the voice. Grabbing a five-foot section of rope, he deftly tied one end around his waist. He lashed the other to an unbroken section of railing and leapt over the side. As he smashed into the side of the ship and got crushed between the ship and a wave, he thought he might have been hasty. He had salt water in his eyes and lungs, and started coughing fiercely. Another wave crushed him and he panicked.

"Is this how I die," he thought? Then the muscle memory kicked in. First, he wove a shield of air around himself. The waves and ship still buffeted him, but now they did not affect him as much. He gave himself a moment to cough out the seawater he had inhaled. "Breathe air, drink water." He repeated the mantra Aanee had mockingly used every time he got it wrong. Usually because she had timed a joke for just as he was drinking. He laughed at the memory and inhaled more water, forcing himself to start the mantra over and shove Aanee from his mind.

Next problem, the jostling. He could feel the side of the ship as it smacked into him repeatedly. He focused on his shields, extending them outward into a bubble around himself, then made the bubble larger until it covered the hole in the ship's side. As his tears cleared the salt water from his eyes, his mage sight returned. Now he affixed the shields to the ship at the edges of the damaged area which was slightly larger than prow width of the pirate vessel. This effectively sealed the breach and gave him a bubble to work in that wasn't moving constantly. No matter how the waves and ship moved, he was now moving with them. It should also stop the flooding, while he figured out how to repair the ship.

He reached out and put his hands on the wood of the ship. Staring intently at them with his mage vision, he could see the tiny orbs that made up each plank. The orbs were combinations of even smaller orbs that he thought of as air, fire, earth, water, heat, cold, and others he did not have names for. He sensed more of the same pattern in the water and realized that he would need some pieces of the ship in order to repair her. Flows of air pulled the wood debris from the waters and pinned it against the ship as resources. He started smoothing out the orbs and stretching them towards the orbs on the other side of the breach, pulling from the debris as needed. For those watching, tendrils of wood from both sides reached towards each other, twining together and flattening into a whole plank. The debris stuck to the side seemed to just melt into the ship. There was another pattern to the wood that did not seem to fit. Raama broke those pieces down and reformed them as the same type. They seemed to have more earth and fire in them, which Raama intuited would strengthen them. He went back and added the earth and fire to the rest of his work.

When he was done, he released his mage sight and pushed away from the ship to admire his work. He found himself encased in a tarp of some sort and yelled. The tarp was quickly pulled away and replaced by bright sunlight beating into his eyes. Raama adjusted his sight and then looked at his work. The planking was solid again, as if nothing had happened to it. Oddly, there were impressions on the side that matched his hands and cheek. Where he had rested against the ship, he had left a permanent indent in the wood.

The noises above settled, and he heard the captain's voice. "Ready to come up then, mister Raama?"

"Aye, captain."

In moments, he was back on deck and having food and grog pressed into his hands. Aanee and the captain took turns explaining that Raama had been on the side of the boat for over a full day, not responding to anyone.

The tarp had been Aanee's idea.

"Either keep your frail skin from getting burned or put up with you whining all the time." He seemed to have a slight sunburn on his neck and she punctuated her sentence by lightly slapping him there. She smirked at him and then hugged him.

Raama noticed everyone observing him while they went about their work. The captain turned to go below deck, beckoning Raama. "I want to show you something," was all he said. As they walked, he continued, "clearly your secret is a secret no longer. We had a ship's meeting about ya, lad. I explained what I knew and that for as long as you want to sail on this ship, I consider it the ship's good fortune to have you. As you can guess, there was a mixed reaction to the news."

Raama imagined so, though only one reaction was on his mind at the moment. He had told Aanee over the pillow about his life, including his time at the Citadel of Mages. He was not sure if she believed him or thought he made things up to impress her. She had never asked him to cast for her. She just teased him as her own private mage and continued to enjoy his 'fanciful tales.' How had she reacted to finding out they were real stories? He wasn't sure why, but he felt grateful that he had told her instead of letting her find out from someone else. It felt more natural.

He felt an elbow. "She took it best of all, lad. Almost like she knew. Now, pay attention." The captain said it with a smile but also with the tone of one not accustomed to repeating himself.

"As I was saying," he continued. "I am not concerned about the ones that were angry or elated. All have spent time at the rail watching you save the ship, so none doubt your intentions. Good or ill, those that speak are the ones I trust. It is the ones that will not speak either way or at all that worry me. Those have always been the ones most likely to do something stupid." Approaching a door, the captain stopped. "Here we are. This is what I wanted you to see."

The captain opened a door to one of the crew's quarters. Inside the room, a shipwright was working over a cone of wood that came through the room at an angle, taking up most of the livable space. The wood seemed to be the same material as the planking, but the shipwright was hitting it with a heavy mallet and not making a dent.

"No progress, James?"

"None captain. We might have to cut off the whole side at dry dock to get this out," replied the heavy breathing shipwright.

The pirate bowsprit, which had speared their hull, now looked like a support beam, albeit at an odd angle. It fit as though built with the ship, intentionally out of place. Raama ran his hand over the cool, smooth wood.

"I think it's petrified, captain," said James. "No reason for them to use a petrified piece of pine for their bowsprit, but seems that's what they did. Maybe they intended to use it as a backup for their ram instead of tying sheets down. If so, why not tip it in metal?"

The captain eyed Raama. "James, have you tried smashing a hole in the wood around the bowsprit?"

"You want me to hole the hull, captain?"

"I want you to try," replied the captain wryly.

The shipwright gave a tentative hit with his mallet against the ship wall. When it bounced back, he set his stance and gave five more heavy blows in rapid succession. Then he, too, turned to look at Raama, anger clear on his face.

"That'll do. You're excused." Whatever the shipwright had been about to say died with the captain's dismissal. He closed his mouth and left the room, the unmarred wall mocking him as he walked away.

"First, thank you for the repairs, mister Raama. We are only afloat now because of your quick thinking. However, you have turned my ship into a sea cow that lists so badly to port it'll take us months longer just to make it to a safe harbor with a dry dock. Can you undo what you've done?"

Raama ran his hand over the bowsprit. "I'm sure I can, with time. Perhaps I can take this room and study the bowsprit for practice."

"That leads me to my next question, then. I have a choice to make about the crew, but before I do, I need to know your intentions. The quiet ones are trouble-makers brewing. If you are leaving at the next port, I'll keep them on long enough for you to get out of the area before I put them off my ship. If you're staying, I'll drop them ashore at the next port."

They spoke at great length about Raama's options. He appreciated the candor he could provide to this captain, how the captain listened, offered what he knew, but never spoke of what Raama's decision had to be. While a mage had high value to any ship, this captain was more interested in what was best for Raama. In the end, Raama decided he would rather stay and become part of the crew. The two men agreed on a rate, shook hands, and exited Raama's new quarters together.

Over the next month, through experimentation, Raama got the ship to stop listing. He slowly solidified the hull on the other side until it leveled out. Then, at the captain's urging, he solidified all the parts of the ship where other ships might strike with their ram. Unfortunately, this made the ship so heavy she sat low in the water and barely made speed with full sails.

Raama and the captain experimented with ideas until finally they found a solution. Raama could weave small bubbles of air amongst the middle of the planks. The pockets of air seemed to help the buoyancy and after another month, the ship sailed her original speed again.

In his room, he left the bowsprit so that he could study it, though he molded it enough to allow him to hang a cot in the room.

With full speed restored, it was not long until the Golden Gull made port. Her first of her maiden voyage. Raama walked along the docks, only to find that now the ground made him seasick all over again. He supposed it was groundsick? Regardless, he did not enjoy the sensation. Nor did he fancy the thought of being seasick when they sailed again. So, after a quick stop to buy a journal to use as a log, and a few gifts for Aanee, he returned to the ship and stayed aboard.

The captain let his crew go on shore leave in groups, while he bartered goods and stocked up provisions for the next leg. The tales the crew told in the taverns had the Golden Gull pegged as a ship of good fortune. Sailors came by daily to see if there were berths available. The captain spent a full ten-day docked. Their final night before setting sail again, the captain sent word out to the new hires and put off the trouble-makers. Dawn saw the ship well underway with a crew that knew they had a runaway mage onboard and considered him family anyway.

* * *

The next five years were a content time for Raama. He and Aanee found they enjoyed each other's presence, even after the nightly visits had lost some of their newness quality. While she applied herself to climbing the ship's ranks, Raama learned the ways of the ship and found many ways to make the vessel both more durable and faster. Raama had infused every part of the ship with his magical essence.

It was a prosperous time for the ship as well. The ship made more per cubic inch than any other two merchant ships trading the same routes. Due to both her spreading fame and the inability of pirates to dampen her profits. She made runs in record times, commanding the highest fares and cargo rates. She collected bounty after bounty for pirates that tried to board her. More than once, she had sailed into port with a pirate ship in tow to claim the prize for the captured ship. Despite the crew's urging that the captain take the ship privateer and hunt pirates, Raama insisted they only deal with pirates that attack them. The captain agreed. Keeping a mage secret from those not on the ship was difficult enough with the fame the Gull had gained. The crew convinced others in the ale houses on shore leave that it was all rumors. They spread rumors that Raama was a master swordsman, single-handedly battling pirates. At another port, a spy, infiltrating the pirate ships and killing the pirates while they slept. Each port heard a different story to drown out the story of mage. The crew was as fiercely protective of their mage as he was of them. When a pirate ship dared to attack the Golden Gull, their mage was coldly efficient in using lightning to empty that ship of her pirates. This avoided any harm to the crew of the Gull and caused minor damage to the pirate ship, elevating all the stories equally. The lack of bodies as evidence helped keep all stories in play. Coming up with new outrageous tales to share in port became a favorite pastime of the crew.

Raama knew it had to end someday, but he was still unprepared when the day came. The evening before their last sailing, a party of visitors approached the ship from the dock. Word about the odd group quickly traveled through the ship and all hands were on deck as a Mage in full regalia stepped forward. With a calm, snide voice that traveled easily along the dock and deck, he spoke.

"I, Dataku Oriss of the Citadel of Mages, declare that this ship, the Golden Gull, has been harboring a fugitive wanted for crimes against the Citadel of Mages. I thereby impound this ship and claim all aboard as property of the Citadel of Mages."

"Like hell you do," replied the captain, equally calm. "You have no authority over this ship or its crew."

As the captain spoke, Raama finally reached the railing near Aanee and peered at the group below. He could identify five mages of varying level and recognized the bearded man as teacher Marcus's mentor. They rarely saw Headmaster Oriss in the student section of the Citadel of Mages but he was still recognizable to all students. In studying the orbs around the human, he could discern that he did not differ from

Marcus. Two of the other mages had the same foulness about them. The junior-most two seemed awkwardly uncomfortable with the confrontation.

"That's him," Raama heard from the docks as someone pointed his way. All eyes turned to him and he and Oriss locked gazes. Raama could see the casual death of this ship in Oriss's eyes.

"James! Well hello there, you smarmy little spawn of a sewer rat!" The captain's disgust for his former shipwright was clear.

An elbow took Raama in the ribs. "I taught him that one," said Aanee excitedly! "He used my insult! I told you I will be a captain one day!"

Raama smiled without turning towards her as he considered the options.

"Bataku Raama," Oriss greeted, using the title of Outcast Mage which Raama had granted himself upon leaving the school. "Surely you did not think you could hide from us forever," he said in a tone that implied Raama's cowardice.

"Dataku Oriss," Raama spoke loudly, "if I surrender and come with you, will you let this vessel and her crew sail free?"

"Stow that, mister Raama!" The captain shouted, more angry than Raama could remember. Simultaneously, most of the crew mumbled in protest to Raama's question as well.

The captain turned to Oriss. "Your outcast has saved the lives of each member of this crew more times than we can count and been a valued and beloved member of this crew for over five years. You'll not take any crew member of mine by force. And if you interfere with my ship business, I and the Captains Guild will see that no member of your precious citadel sets foot on a vessel again. Nor your cargo, either."

Raama could not tell which inflamed Oriss more. The clear slight in the way the captain did not say the full name of Citadel of Mages, or the implication that he would interfere with the Citadel of Mages' sea traffic. Raama also noted, curiously, that even this many years later he could not think of the Citadel of Mages without using the full, proper name.

A small ball of fire shot from Oriss's hands towards the captain. Raama, while mulling his inability to be less than proper with the name of his former school, had noticed the telltale signs of the weaving. He had a shield of air thrown in front of the captain before the ball of fire left Headmaster Oriss's hands. The impact of the two knocked the captain off his feet, but dissipated the fire and heat away from the ship. Raama could see the other mages reaching for the lei.

"One point, 'taki," he said quietly, invoking the friendly term for casters. He saw them pause and look his way. "If war between us is inevitable, and it would seem that you yearn for nothing less, then remember this. The last time I had to stop a fellow mage from casting a spell resulted in the loss of the entire top of your precious Citadel. Of Mages." Damn. He wished he had been able to leave it at just citadel. Damn.

"I promise you that you will not harm a member of this ship," he continued calmly. "I cannot promise you I will be able to stop you without reducing you, the dock, and everyone standing on it to particles." At this point, he looked directly at Oriss.

Oriss, clearly enraged and on the verge of ordering the assault, was suddenly struck on the side of the head by a belaying pin. As he collapsed, Raama looked to his side to see Aanee, who had slunk along the rail and taken the mage leader down by surprise.

"Even a mage can't survive a blow to the head," crowed Aanee, smirking.

He noted movement on the docks and saw two

mages preparing weavings to throw at Aanee. Of course, it was those two. With barely a gesture, he sent two thin forks of lightning their way and tied the weaves to their dead bodies. The blast knocked everyone on the docks off their feet but left them otherwise unharmed.

Raama saw a flash of light, heard the word "traitor" and saw a dagger thud into James's chest.

"Belay!" Raama bellowed, in his best impersonation of the captain, who was still working to regain his feet. He turned to the junior mages.

"We are at war. There is no mistaking that. Your leadership has led you astray enough to attack non-mages just because they impede you. Take your precious leaders back to the Citadel of Mages and tell them I will come for them. Leave the three bodies as reminders of where hate can lead you. I did not start this, but if you attack me or the Golden Gull, we will finish you all."

He heard quiet cheers and assent behind him and noted that the crew, still supporting him, was supporting him from a further distance back. Only Aanee and the captain were within arm's reach. He smiled fondly. As the dock party dispersed and Raama released his lightning, the captain spoke softly to Raama and Aanee.

"This will not be the end, Bataku Raama. They will be back."

Taken aback at the captain's use of his title, and the respect behind it, Raama took a moment before responding. "Let's figure out our next steps when we are through the straits, captain," Raama replied.

The Golden Gull set sail at first tide.

The Strait of Siren's Teeth were a narrow waterway separating the two vast bodies of water that the Golden Gull traversed. As those two forces collided in the rocky passage, they tossed the ships about. Therefore, the ships' captains had a longstanding arrangement of order so that one ship at a time traversed it. There was a high volume of traffic this morning for the straights, but ships were used to waiting to enter. When it was the Gull's turn, she sailed confidently to the teeth as she had so many times before. Unobserved were the five ships at each side of the straights that took position, turned sideways to the straits and had mages on deck that started casting.

"Raama, she won't steer straight!" The captain's cry held no panic. They had been through this many times before. Safety through the straits was one of Raama's contributions to the ship.

Raama shifted to mage sight and started looking about. He could now see the mages' casting fore and aft affecting the water, the ship, and the rocks. It appeared as if some castings were lashing the ship and rocks together, making spinning orbs on the rocks and front of the ship seek each other out. The surrounding water was spinning slightly on each side. Two mini whirlpools formed and encouraged the ship along the course to the rocks. Clearly, the mages had thought this out.

Raama lifted his shields and reached out with his mage senses, trying to reverse the spin at the rocks and repel the ship. The weight of the ship was working against him. The Gull, responsive to his magical touch, did her best to comply, but could not avert from the collision course. He focused instead on the air orbs around him and tried to make them lighter. As he did, a few shot upward away from him. He needed to contain them. Running below deck, he brought a shield up along the deck and hull, encasing the area below to hold the air in. He then started lightening up the air inside the shield, watching the air bump into his shield and press, trying to get free. Knowing time was against him, Raama converted more and more air, as quickly as he could, and felt the drag of the ship reducing. He was now keeping it away from the rocks with less effort. He distantly heard banging in the distance and the crew talking in what sounded like high-pitched voices. Almost as if they were imitating the boson. Filing that away for later, he pushed upwards with the air as much as he could and felt the ship break its magical mooring to the rocks. As the ship broke free, it lurched and shot upwards so fast it knocked Raama to the floor, banging his head. Much as he tried to fight it, the darkness reached out and drug him down. His final waking thought was recent advice that even a mage can't survive a blow to the head.

Raama awoke, muddled. Unsure how long he had been out, he sat up, carefully touching his head and tasting a metallic taste in his mouth. He noticed immediately that his breath was making fog in the air, like it was winter. In fact, he could see a slight sheen of ice on the floor. That worried him. He was glad his shield had not dropped while he was unconscious. He opened the hatch to the deck with some trouble, but stepped out to find darkness. When he spotted the crew, they were all still, as if frozen, some floating gently above the deck. Raama quickly lashed them to the deck as he tried to figure out what was happening. Above him was the clearest night sky he had ever seen. Over the side of the ship, it was as if he was looking at an enormous map. Was he flying like a bird? The ship was flying! The air Raama tainted must have caused the ship to fly. He released the shield that had been holding in the light air and watched it all race by towards the stars. Then the ship, feeling heavy again, started descending. Quickly. Raama saw flames cresting around the side of the ship, and a few crew mates that had been outside the ship exploded. He quickly warded the ship against fire and got to a position on the deck where he could watch himself approach the sea again. He would attempt to lighten the air again as they got close, so he could soften the landing. If he went up at the straits, he would come back down at the straits. He just had to be careful not to land too hard. Perhaps he could even guide the ship away from landing inside the straits? He had spent a lot of time looking at maps of the region he traveled. But the area below did not fit any map he had seen. Why did it look so different? And the speed. They were picking up such speed as they descended. Raama was weaving some air shields to slow the ship down when the wave of darkness took him again.

He awoke on a sandy beach, with the taste of salt lingering on his lips. The rhythmic sloshing of the waves was the only sound as he blinked the confusion from his eyes. Struggling to his feet, he brushed wet sand from his clothes. The raw scent of the sea mixing with the earth assaulted his nose as he dragged his body forward to inspect his surroundings.

Before him loomed a jagged cliff with a dark indentation at its base. Rocks stood guard at the cave's mouth. Just over his left shoulder, he saw the ship, or what remained of it. Its fore, impaled by a large column of rock, looked as if a giant's finger were poking right through a toy.

Mouth agape, head bleeding, he ran to the ship, nearly passing out again as a wave of nausea tore through him, and looked for Aanee. The few bodies he found on the ship were frozen, shattered, burned or otherwise broken, and Raama realized he had killed his entire complement of crewmates. He spent days in a daze, exploring the area for their bodies and carting them back to the ship, intending to make a pyre. Raama was bereft and rudderless for not the first time. Each corpse, by name, received an apology for his mistake. None offered a single word of forgiveness.

He spotted Aanee's body wedged in a furrow of the spire. The strength left his legs, and he collapsed in the sand. The tears shock had held that back started flowing, as he looked at her lifeless body, stuck out of reach. Time seemed slower here. Raama was distantly aware of each tear as it rolled down his cheek and fell. Each tear's minor explosion against the sand created a small eruption. His brain did not even register the steady assault on the sand.

He could not leave her body there, but it also felt wrong to use magic to retrieve her. He would have to blast the surrounding spire to release its hold on her. While he had no concern for the spire, Raama could not bear the thought of marring Aanee's body further with his magic. He had done enough damage.

Instead, he forced himself to his feet and walked to the side of the spire. He grabbed the rock and started pulling himself up along it, scrapping his knees and elbows with each climb. He didn't bother to care. His focus was on one spot where he needed to be to free Aanee. Reach, hold, pull. That was his entire world. His body screamed at the abuse, but his brain paid no heed. He must free Aanee. His only love. Whom he had killed. Instead of making him weaker, that thought fueled him. He must free Aanee. His only love. Whom he had killed. The pain was nothing. He wanted the pain. He deserved the pain.

When he finally reached the alcove, flaps of skin hung from his arms and knees and blood flowed freely. He reached in and gently unwedged her body, cradling it in his arms. Having her pressed against him again and feeling cold where once it had been warmth, something inside him snapped. He was unaware of summoning the cushion of air that lowered them to the ground. Nor of how each tear he had dropped on the sand flew into the spire with a force greater than the ship that crashed into the Golden Gull. The shrapnel that dared approach Raama and Aanee was reduced to sand before it even got close. By the time Raama's feet touched the sand, the spire had been severely punished for its crime. A dune of sand, at the base, showed the path of Raama's descent from the spire.

He walked the beach, lost in madness, with each tear rolling off his face dashing to the spire. When he had no tears left, small drops of blood replaced them. The spire, whose only crime was to have been in the spot the ship landed, ceased to exist above where the ship rested.

A familiar voice, on the edge of his perception, brought Raama back to awareness. Thinking it was Aanee, he realized his surroundings. It wasn't Aanee, of course. Her body lay in front of him, just inside the cave where he had apparently set her. He noticed the throbbing in his arms and legs where scabs had formed. Raama shifted to mage sight and scanned the area for the source of the noise that had disturbed him. He saw unusual orb particles floating around the cave, which he had never seen before. The noise came from those orbs.

They gave off a vibrating hum that sounded like speech coming from far away. He could see the orbs, but his magic could not feel them. Fascinated, he wove strands of air around them to see if he could move them. They bounced along the air weaving, almost as if they were excited to see other magic. On a whim he stretched the weave of air towards and around Aanee's body, hoping the orbs would stay as a sort of memorial to Aanee. As the orbs spun around her corpse, they picked up speed, and she quickly turned to dust in front of his eyes.

He cried out in shock, madness encroaching, and released the weaves. When her body did not return, he tried to undo what he had done. He reversed the flows of air so the orbs traveled the other way. At first, nothing happened. Then Aanee's body uncrumbled from dust and returned to its form. No matter how long or fast Raama left the orbs spinning, her body would not change any further than when he had first laid it on the floor of the cave.

First laid her on the floor! The ship! Her body had existed on the ship.

It can be said that what Raama did next was not well thought through. In his defense, he was desperate to save his love and his family in any way possible. Desperate, bordering on madness.

Ignoring the protest of his under nourished and heavily abused body, he gathered Aanee's body and put it onboard the ship with the others. He wove air into and around the ship in a reversed pattern, which he hoped would allow the ship to reverse its history. He would connect it to the time orbs and then board quickly to ride the ship back on its journey to a safe spot where he could let the time orbs go.

He wove a strand of air into the cave to connect the time orbs with the air waves floating through the ship. He watched the orbs slowly approach down the weave and crafted a flow to help lift him aboard the ship. As the orbs made their first circuit of the ship, they stopped following a predictable pattern. Something in the magic running throughout the ship seemed to suck the time orbs away from the flows of air and into the planks of the ship itself. They wove faster and faster through the weavings layered throughout the Golden Gull over the past five years. In moments, they were moving so fast that the entire ship seemed to glow with a soft blue light.

An explosion blew Raama backwards into the embrace of his only remaining friend. Darkness. When he came to the beach was as it had been before the ship crashed here, he assumed. The spire was intact, with no ship impaled on it. It seemed to smirk in triumph at him. His friends and ship were gone. The only reminder of them, the journal laying in the sand a few feet from him, with a few pages torn out and floating away along the beach. He saw smaller time orbs floating gently in front of him. In each orb, he saw a different version of the Golden Gull. If he focused on an orb, he could see the fine details moving inside them. Each version of the Gull looked different from the others and sailed with a different crew. Yet Raama knew them and, somehow, their stories. He went from orb to orb, seeking the one with his captain, crew, and Aanee. He hoped to get back to them. As he walked from orb to orb, they led him into the cave. He disappeared into the cave, clutching his journal as he followed the orb trail, not to return for over 30 years.

48

Raama's existence hung suspended, delicate as a leaf floating to the ground. He wandered aimlessly, wrapped in a blanket of memories and lost in the haze of shared laughter and intertwined fingers. That is until he woke each morning, shivering, on the cold hard ground of the cave. He would follow the orbs, hoping to glimpse his Aanee, but it never came.

On this morning, one particular orb caught his attention. Inside it, a majestic-looking man stood on a boat, the wind playing with his chestnut hair as he gazed ahead. The currach seemed to cut through the water, undisturbed by the swift currents swirling beneath. Above, the sky and sea looked like twins, with the sun's reflection creating a beautiful dance on the water.

As Raama watched the scene, his mind raced, and he wondered if these orbs could help him find what he had lost? Would one of them have the answers?

Part One

To Lugh
By Seán McNicholl

Manannán stood to the front of the boat, hands clasped behind his back, the whip of the wind blowing his brown locks over his shoulder. Deep within his chest he felt the call - To Lugh. And the closer the ship sailed to the land, the louder the call keened.

The little boat split the water, carving out its own course, oblivious to the currents beneath her. The sky overhead mirrored the ocean; a blue canvas smattered with pillows of foamy white here and there, as the rotund sun watched over all, its orbed reflection jilted and staggered by the lap of the water.

"Are you alright there, Aonbharr?" he called to

the horse that ran atop the waves, hooves clipping and splashing the water as she ran. Aonbharr whinnied and shook her head without breaking stride, the sunlight dancing off her silvered mane.

The splashes of water kissed the golden scrawl along the ships wooden planks, inflaming the name etched there; Sguaba Tuinne.

"Have we far to go?" Manannán asked. The little boat groaned in answer, satisfying him, and he breathed the sea air, the salt stinging from the tip of his nose to the depths of his lungs.

His mind flitted like a sparrow on the wind, fractions of thoughts appearing in the foam of his mind before being dragged to the subconscious abyss; the fury on face of Lugh the last time they parted, his own father's warning to stay clear of the land, and the new inhabitants of that land—the humans.

"Leave them to their own devices," his father had said, "they do not understand our ways, they cannot understand our ways. You could teach a salmon to sing quicker."

"But we would be like gods to them!" Manannán had argued.

"But we are not gods. The Greeks thought themselves gods and look what happened. It ruined every last one of them! Do not be so foolish as to fall into the same temptation. Leave the humans to their own devices, nothing good can come from mixing with them. There is nothing on the land that is not perfected here in Tír na nÓg; our grass is more lavish and greener, our waters bluer and clearer. Our animals are our friends. And enemies are none. My son, heed my words. Leave them be."

"But what about the others who are still on the land?"

"There is few of them left. And they too shall come to Tír na nÓg, in time. It is where we all must go. And it is where we must stay."

But the call to Lugh had been too strong, gnawing at his bones by day, and stalking his dreams by night. And this morning, he followed the call. Lugh had remained on the land, and so to the land Manannán was going.

His face broke into a smile as the land broke the horizon, rising out of the water like the great sea beast of old. Aonbharr snorted, diving herself into the foam and back out again upon seeing it, whinnying to the blue sky. Even Sguaba Tuinne seemed to shudder with excitement, the gilded gull on her stern seeming to flap its golden wings.

Manannán threw his arms wide, as though to embrace the land, the little boat never slackening pace, the horse still thundering alongside.

"Éire," Manannán breathed, palms still raised to the sky. He could see the yellow stump of a beach, swiftly rising a green land mottled with brown heather behind. Both ends of the beach were encased by the grey thunder of cliffs, their faces battered and scarred by the lash of the sea.

The boat never slowed and the horse never broke stride as they breached the beach, moving from water to sand to mossy heather, the boat parting the land as easily as it parted the sea.

The horse snorted.

"I know," replied Manannán, "It feels like home."

As they crested the top of the first hill, the boat slowed, Aonbharr cantering beside it. Before them rolled out green valleys and hills, rising and falling, washing over and into each other, pillows of white now floating in the sky-blue sea above.

"Now where?"

The boat and the horse both gave a shiver.

"Alright," he said, "I guess we go north."

And the boat and the horse dipped down the far side of the hill, into the waiting valley.

The sun was beginning to tire when the trees became dense, moving from the sparse long-reaching shadows it a blanket of gloom wrapping itself around them. Deeper and deeper they went, thicker and thicker the forest, until both Sguaba Tuinne and Aonbharr were moving at a slow weave between the trunks and the growing darkness. The rays of the low sun were barely able to fight through the thicket overhead when Manannán called for them to rest.

"Because it's dark, and we don't know where we're going and we don't know how far we have to go," he answered as the boat shuddered.

Aonbharr snorted.

"I agree, we should head north tomorrow. Lugh

usually likes hanging out up north."

He hopped from the boat onto the forest floor, twigs snapping and leaves rustling. He reached back, lifting a small tan leather satchel from the boat's belly and, reaching within its depths, pulled out an impossibly large cloth covering and several long, polished wooden poles. With them quickly erected into a tent, he peered into the bag once again, chewing his lip as he did so.

"Barley? Oats? Hay?"

The horse threw her head left and right.

"You can have an apple after your dinner. Oats it is." And he pulled a large sack of oats from the bag, pouring a healthy amount out onto the forest floor.

He returned the sack to the little bag, and withdrew a handful of chopped firewood, arranging it carefully at the entrance to the tent, before taking from the satchel a burning torch with which he set the firewood alight. Its warm glow pushed the shadows behind the trees, where they watched the three enviously.

"I think I'll have chicken tonight," he announced, taking from the bag a pre-plucked raw chicken, which he foisted over the now-roaring flames. The succulent scent perfumed the air, dripping off the leaves as the branches leaned closer.

Sitting alongside the boat, he and Aonbharr ate in silence, only the smack of lips rising over the crackling of the fire as the flames and shadows danced in step. As the night moved in, Manannán retired beneath the folds of the tent, Aonbharr resting herself within the fading glow of the fire.

He dreamed restlessly, ghosts of images haunting his sleep; swords clashing, his father crying out to him, Lugh's fierce blue eyes piercing him. His body writhed amongst them, pulling the tent from its pole, ensnaring him within its fabrics as his mind conjured up images of the great sea beast of old grabbing him and pulling him to the depths.

His screams awoke the horse who leapt to her feet, ears pinned forward, nostrils flared, eyes showing white. The boat wobbled heavily in its place.

"Sorry, I—" he muttered, pulling himself free from the fabric, but his apology was cut short, his attention caught by the torches moving amongst the trees.

"Who goes there?" a gruff voice called from the darkness, flame held before him.

"That depends who it is that is posing such a question." Manannán smirked at his own pithy reply. The smile had not faded when the torchlight caught the glint of a blade being withdrawn, and one by one all the torches reflected blades.

"You are to identify yourself immediately, by command of the High King."

The swordsmen drew nearer, the heat from their torches bruising Manannán's face.

"And if I don't?"

"Seize him!" The cry startled Aonbharr who feared on her hindlegs, thrashing the fore and connecting with any of the men she could. Strong hands grabbed at Manannán, each pulling and hauling in a different direction. He offered no resistance, drifting from pull to pull, like driftwood in the tide. Other men surrounded and reigned Aonbharr, at least those still standing. Six men were not so lucky, having received the blunt end of the hoof.

The men pulled Manannán and Aonbharr into the trees with them, the light of their torches dancing among the shadows, bringing the forest to life. From behind, someone called, "Take the boat." Others murmured among themselves as to how Manannán had hauled the boat this far in land alone.

The company walked until the sky lightened, bringing pinks and oranges to the gloom, just before the sun rose. Manannán had attempted to make small talk, but only received a blow to the back of the head in response. He didn't try again.

They broke through the last line of trees that ringed a gentle slope of verdant green, down to a small lake, its waters still. A fort protruded into the lake, standing on stilts.

The sun peered over the horizon and winked on the water's face.

"Move." A sharp jab into his lower back pushed Manannán down the slope.

The fort was surrounded by a tall wooden fence, with sharpened tops. A footbridge over the water stopped beneath a lookout tower, and the squad passed over it, into the awaiting courtyard. Beyond arose a thatched dwelling, a mountain of rush and reed, pressing hard into the now-pale-blue morning sky. The soldiers gathered in a semi-circle, with swords drawn, around him and Aonbharr, who grunted and snorted in derision. Manannán smiled warmly at each of them, but all that was returned were sneers and scowls.

From the darkness of the doorway in the centre of the thatched building emerged a man, swaddled in heavy fur, a golden broach upon his breast. Beside him lumbered a lanky boy with the first shoots of stubble marring his cheeks.

"What do we have here?" The man declared, brushing back a swathe of peppered black hair from his brow.

"My lord, we found him trespassing in the woods. He refused to identify himself. We think he's one of Méabh's spies. Probably sent down to steal cattle again."

The king eyed Manannán, then admired Aonbharr, his nose scrunching at the sight of Sguaba Tuinne now being hauled through the gate.

"A spy? Why?"

"Well, my lord, he's dressed… differently. He's not one of our lot. And we lost another two bulls this week."

The king nodded gravely. The lanky boy watched on. Both stared at the gilded bird at the head of the boat.

"Who are you?"

"Manannán MacLir, king," he said, stepping forward with a hand outstretched. A blade under his chin stopped him from advancing further.

"Calm down, Binnian," the king ordered and the blade was lowered.

The king flicked his eyes up and down, searching every inch of Manannán. "You're Manannán MacLir?"

"I am indeed."

"The son of the sea god? The Manannán MacLir."

"That's me. But please, Manannán is fine."

The king laughed mirthlessly. "Manannán is fine, he says! Did you ever hear the like of it? Well, Mr MacLir, I'm afraid I've got bad news for you, we don't want your sort round here. We drove the rest of your lot underground and we'll bury you beneath it! Take him! Hang him! Roast the horse!"

Hands beat, pulled and assaulted Manannán. Hair was pulled, skin was pinched, a rope was fastened around his neck.

"Should we burn the boat, my lord?"

"No, keep it. But get rid of that awful name. Call

her The Golden Gull. Get her into the water, I'll test her after breakfast."

Somewhere beyond the huddle of hand and arms, Manannán heard Aonbharr rear up, whinnying loudly. A heavy thud, a groan, and a lighter thump told him she had hit the mark again.

The rope tightened around his neck and he was hoisted above the hands, swinging from the gatehouse rafters. Whoops and cheers were carried up to him.

The king looked on and sneered.

"Yes, king, it's best to drive the magic folk underground, isn't it?" Manannán said in the kings ear.

"Yes, it is," the king replied, turning to address him. His face paled and jaw swung wide. "But—but—but you—you are up—"

The king flashed up to the swinging body, long lanky limbs swaying, face a vibrant purple.

"My boy!" The king squealed. "Cut him down! Cut him down!"

The boy fell heavily on to the ground, gasping and panting, and the purple eased to red.

"Hang him now!" The king thundered, stopping to

embrace his son, and once again the rope was fastened and Manannán was hoisted over the crowd. A lesser cheer accompanied him this time.

"King, you really should have these furs washed."

The kings eyes bulged and he spluttered again, his arms embracing Manannán to his breast. Over his head, lanky limbs and a purple face swung again.

"Cut him down!" The king squealed, his voice piercingly high. Again, the boy fell, gasping and gulping the air.

They all stood back from Manannán, swords drawn but lowered. He whistled and Aonbharr dunted her way through the huddled mass, nuzzling her nose into him.

"Now, I believe I had a bag with me?"

Blank faces stared back, tremoring slightly.

"My bag?" He repeated, smiling at them.

"In—in—in the boat."

"Thank you, sir. Alright, then if there's nothing further, then I shall take my leave. Come on Sguaba."

The boat created the soil and followed the pair through the gate, several soldiers collapsing at the sight.

"Well, that was an eventful morning."

The horse whinnied and the boat tremored as they passed into the trees, not bothering to check to see if they were being followed. They knew they wouldn't be.

"And what have they done to you?" Manannán halted, running his fingers over the deep scores in the gold lettering along the hull. Beneath it, written in crude primordial etchings was the name Golden Gull.

"Ugh, how crass!"

The boat shuddered.

"You like it? Really? You want me to call you Golden Gull?"

The boat tremored again and Manannán raised his palm. "Alright, on your hull be it!"

It was still early morning, and the sun was just stretching itself into the day, warming up its rays. They petered through the thicket of branches overhead, casting long shadows upon the forest floor.

"So do we still continue north, GG?"

The boat shuddered again. Manannán nodded. Aonbharr snorted. And the three continued through the tangle of branch and brier. Movement was slow, but the three kept company; Manannán helping the other two through the denser parts, they slowing for Manannán in the clearings.

It was approaching evening, the sun exhausted and starting to recline in the sky, when the first settlements came into view. They had left the trees and had been walking among fields of wilting and sickly crops for a little while.

The houses were of the same style as the kings dwelling, though on a much smaller scale. Their thatched roofs lay the span of a hand from the ground, rising up cone shaped, thin smoke weaselling into the sky through the hole at the summit. Gaunt looking men stood guard, as haggard women clutched skeletal children tight. All eyes watched the land-dwelling boat.

"Hello there!" Manannán called, arm raised in salutation. No one responded.

"Hello there!" he repeated, another few strides closer. A few arms rose in response.

"I wonder if yous can help me," he said beaming, now standing before them. They still eyed the boat. "I'm looking for Lugh Lamhfada. Have you seen him?"

"No," came a solitary response.

"Do you know where I might find him?"

"North."

Manannán sighed. "Still north. Always north."

He looked to each of the people standing around, haunts of humans, their skin thin and papered, bones protruding at every angle.

"This your land? Your farm?"

"Is."

"I suppose you could do with a new plough? To till the land properly, bring out fresh crops?"

"Suppose."

Manannán rolled his eyes. "You lot are real talkers. Well, anyways, I can help you there. I have just the plough."

He leaned into Golden Gull and withdrew his bag. He emphasised the emptiness of his hand before burying it deep within the sack, rummaging around, before straining into a heave. He pulled and hauled until a wooden handle appeared at the mouth of the bag. He pulled harder, the mouth opening impossibly wide, beams and blades escaping to the evening sun, until before all their hanging mouths stood a plough, larger than any had seen.

"So," he encouraged, "What do you think?"

"Big."

"Oh for goodness sake! Listen, this plough moves by itself. You just line it up and tap it — away it goes! Here, try!" He grabbed the nearest man by the arm, hauling him beside the plough. The man flicked his gaze between the plough and Manannán, who nodded eagerly. The man tapped at the plough twice. It lurched forward, its blades piercing the ground, soil spraying into the air. It moved seamlessly, unhesitatingly, into the lowering sun, turning at a the end of the field and returning towards them.

"See! A thing of beauty!"

"Thanks."

"You are most welcome sir!" Manannán declared, slapping his thigh, all eyes now firmly fixed on him. "Your fields will be finished before midnight and then — oh no."

A mighty crash stole everyone's attention, and they

turned to see the plough crashing straight through their settlement, tilling the thatched roofs and wattle walls with it, not a single dwelling surviving its wake.

"Damn."

"Yes," Manannán agreed, "Damn. Alright, alright. I can do this the easy way."

He clapped his hands twice. The plough halted. The earth tremored. Rocks, rushes, reeds and roots flew into the air, whirring around as though carried on the wind, before arranging themselves to build new houses, their walls squared with pitched eaves. Before each door lay an assortment of fresh vegetables, healthy, plump and ripe. From the long grass chickens bawked and pecked at the newly turned soil. Manannán grinned.

"Well, that should sustain yous for a while."

"Should."

"Alright then, I guess we'll continue north. Take care now."

"Bye."

Manannán clapped his hands lightly, throwing a look to Aonbharr, before he, the horse and the boat moved off into the growing gloom.

Thanks followed them as they left.

The trio pitched camp that evening in the bend of a river, not far from the settlement, the river babbling to itself as it watched Manannán struggle to erect the tent.

"Because I don't need magic to do simple things," he retorted to Aonbharr's snort. "I am more than capable of putting a tent up—oh for goodness sake!"

The poles collapsed into each other, the fabric falling with a frump. Aonbharr neighing and frolicking on the spot, the Golden Gull rocking on the bank.

With his face scowling, Manannán snapped his fingers, the poles jumping to life and the awning billowing over them, coming to a placid rest.

"I don't want to hear it."

Manannán stormed into the tent to the wild whinnies of Aonbharr, the boat almost keeling over it rocked that hard.

He threw himself down upon the puffed feathered bed sighing. The shadows hugged him and his eyes closed.

He drifted upon the tide of sleep, allowing it to pull him further from the shore of reality, out to the ocean of dreams.

He found himself coursing waves, the spray mingling with the rain, wetting his skin. Peels of thunder chorused upon the howling wind, as the lightning danced across the grey clouds. His mind conjured the image of a sinking ship amongst the waves, just visible through the pelts of rain. He saw again the man clinging to the ever-shrinking hull, strong arms holding tight. His fierce red hair covered most of his head and face. Somewhere deep within himself, Manannán felt the pang of familiarity, both of scene and man.

"Grab my hand!" He called, arm reaching out as they drew near.

"Would you ever leave me alone, Manannán?" The stranger replied, his long red hair matted to his skull.

"But—what—how do you know who I am?"

A wave crashed over the boat, wind battering the rain into them.

"Just leave me alone Manannán, don't make me visit your dreams again."

And with that the red haired stranger sank into the abyss of the ocean.

In the soft bed, Manannán churned, throwing himself into another dream.

He was sitting at the head of a long table, a banquet laid out before him. The smell of roast boar perfumed around him, wetting his mouth. All seats at the table were filled, royalty decked in gold and jewels, all eyes patiently watching, smiling at him. His right hand seat laid bare.

He jumped as a trumpet sounded, all rising to their feet and addressing the great door at the far end of the room. Manannán arose, hesitating, eyes darting from the guests to the door, which heaved itself open.

The red haired stranger walked through, eyes fixed on Manannán.

"You!" Manannán exclaimed, hand pointing.

"Leave me alone!"

The stranger rushed to the table, eyes reflecting the flames of the torches that lined the walls, grabbed the boar from the central platter and hurled it at Manannán. The force of the hot, juicy flesh knocked him into another dream.

He was standing in a sprawling field, ringlets of mist swirling around. But the grass was glistening red, dripping red, and the mist was hung with moans and cries. He stepped into the mist, the grass squelching beneath his feet. Through the billows of grey a huddled mass appeared; a man propped against the stump of a tree. His red hair was caked with mud and blood, and a deep wound pierced his side.

"I told you, Manannán!" He cried, sword clasped in his hand. "Leave me alone!"

"But—but—who are you? How do you know me?"

The strangers eyes rolled. "Manannán, seriously. It's me. It's—"

Outside the tent, an owl hooted into the night, breaking the dream and rousing Manannán into a semi-slumber.

He rubbed his eyes and cursed under his breath.

He sat up, stretching, his mind clutching at the dissipating dream that melted in his mind, like wisps of smoke on the breeze. The face surfaced to his mind.

"Lugh."

The name vanished into the night.

Manannán followed it, leaving the tent and stepping into the night the anaemic moonlight that attempted to mimic the sun. Shadows loitered around the camp, wrapping themselves around Aonbharr and Golden Gull. The river, now a gurgling black, snaked past.

He walked to its edge, his knees sinking into the soft mud as he peered into the darkened water. He breathed into the water, stirring it with his hand, a blue spark shimmering from the depths. He stirred faster, the vortex pulling the light closer, brighter, and he squinted into its core.

"Lugh." His voice reverberated back to him. "Please. We need to talk."

"Leave me alone!" A voice emerged from the water.

"Lugh."

From the bright blue light appeared Lugh's face, fury carved into it. "No! Leave me alone!"

A fist flew from the light, breaking through the surface and turning into water, splashing across Manannán's face. He spluttered and wiped his face, the light in the water vanishing, and the blackness returning. The moonlight mocked him, shimmering like a dancer on the water's surface.

Manannán knelt by the waters edge until the sky was smeared with pinks, and reds and oranges. Aonbharr nuzzled at his side gently, rousing him from his reverie.

"He won't even speak to me, Aonbharr. What do I do?"

The horse dragged her hoof across the mud, pulling a crevice through it, then shook her long silvered mane.

"You're right. Of course. Let's go."

He rose to his feet, wiping down his legs, clearing the mud and drying them simultaneously.

He rustled a quick breakfast for himself and Aonbharr, both consisting of oats and berries, and then set off along the course of the river.

They followed the river, Aonbharr and the Golden Gull switching from land to water without hesitation, as it wound its way northward, through valleys and fens, to its consummation with the sea.

Sprawling out before them lay the wide arms of

sandy beaches, trying to embrace the ocean that extended to the horizon.

"Which way now?" Manannán asked. The Golden Gull shimmied and moved forward, the other two following in its wake.

The sand was soft beneath his feet, pulling him down, slowing him.

"Hold on, I'll hop in," he called to the Golden Gull, throwing his leg over the hull and hoisting himself in.

The three moved on, the boat parting the sand with ease, the hooves of the horse clipping and spraying the air with motes that fell silently to the ground.

The call within Manannán's chest yearned stronger, the need to find Lugh keening within him.

He stood at the front of the boat, allowing the breeze to wash over him. He closed his eyes and filled his lungs with the bitter sea air. His mind flitted back to his dreams, churning like the waters of the river, images sinking and surfacing and being swept away. He saw the boat sinking, Lugh clutching to its hull. It was how they had met. Manannán had been sweeping the sea, running through the storm, feeling that exhilaration of

flirting with the lightning. He had heard Lugh's desperate cry, just floating above the surf. Lugh hadn't rejected
his hand then, he had been pulled aboard amid coughs
of water and gushes of appreciation. Their friendship
had started then.

And the banquet hadn't ended with Manannán
covered in the juices and flesh of the boar — they had
laughed and drank and sang all night; Manannán, Lugh
and the Ard Rí, the high king of the land. Manannán
had been the guest of honour, Lugh at his right hand.
The good times.

Manannán sighed, opening his eyes to the blis-
tering sunlight, that burned upon the golden sand. The
beach was coming to an end, encased by jagged grey
cliffs that rose out of the water. His heart stuttered as
he saw a lone figure on the cliff edge, watching out over
the sea. Every fibre told him it was Lugh, and without
being told Aonbharr and the Golden Gull increased
their pace, leaving the beach to the waves of grass that
lined the dunes. The land reared steeply up to the cliff
top but neither boat nor horse slowed on the incline. As
they drew near, they could see the long strands of red
hair flowing in the breeze.

"Lugh."

"I told you to leave me alone." Lugh didn't turn, still staring out to sea.

"We need to talk." Manannán approached slowly, walking on the balls of his feet, ready to move.

"I have nothing more to say." Lugh crossed his arms, puffing his chest.

"But Lugh—"

"Nothing!" Lugh roared.

Manannán sighed, shoulders sagging, and turned to Aonbharr. She nodded her head and flicked her mane. Manannán set his jaw and nodded back.

"Alright Lugh," he addressed, turning back to face the sea, "then I challenge you to a glam dicin!"

Lugh turned, eyebrow crooked. "A transformation battle?"

A grin broke across his face, and with a step forward his body morphed and shifted, turning into a huge black bull, eyes blood red, snorting and stomping. The bull lowered his head, horns angled, and took charge, soil taking flight from its hooves. Manannán charged toward the bull, diving into the air, his body swelling and contorting into a gargantuan wave, crashing into the bull and washing it over the cliff edge.

The bull plummeted, surrounded by swirls of water. Just before it hit the sea's surface it churned and morphed once again, piercing the water as an over-sized salmon. The wave, falling in torrents, twisted and writhed, and fractured. The waters darkened and solidi-fied as it fell, sprouting feathers. They swooped, appear-ing as a flock of sea eagles, that kissed the waters edge. The salmon, with its powerful fin, burst through the water and leapt into the air, colliding with a few birds, knocking them into the depths. The remaining birds dived, bracing talons, and sank them into the soft flesh of the fish. Fins and wings clashed, the birds hauling the thrashing fish back to the cliff edge, where it floun-dered momentarily before swelling into a griffin — a great beast, it's body like that of a lion, with the head and wings on an eagle.

The birds retreated amidst the swipes of claws, merging themselves together in a mass of feathers. The ball contorted, ballooning out until its shadow darkened the land. The feathers hardened and darkened. It's body was black and scaled, gigantic wings beating, its head horned. It roared, flames billowing out.

The griffin craned its neck, taking in the fullness of the monster before it, and tremored slightly.

"Alright, alright," said Lugh, mutating back into human form, "you win."

The great monster shrivelled and shrank, back into Manannán, who stood grinning.

"I knew I would," he teased.

"What was that thing anyway?" Lugh enquired, hand gesticulating wildly.

"They call it a dragon. They have them over the water. Impressive beasts." Manannán shrugged and looked sheepish.

"Dragon," Lugh repeated, rubbing at the wet tangles of beard that hung from him. "It's a scary looking beast. But here, you didn't need to go so deep with your claws!" He lifted his shirt, revealing small puncture wounds down the length of his torso.

"How do you think I feel after being battered by that fin of yours?" Manannán retorted, and the two laughed, the familiarity of the old times washing over them. From behind them, the Golden Gull and Aonbharr approached slowly, trying to catch the words.

"Can I apologise now?" Manannán asked. Lugh nodded. "I'm sorry about what happened with Clíonadh. But it was a long time ago. And you had said yourself that you two weren't actually a couple."

"You still shouldn't have—"

"I shouldn't have," Manannán agreed. "And I am sorry. Do you still speak to her?"

Lugh shook his head. "Nah, she went over to Tír na nÓg to see what it was like and never bothered coming back. I ended up marrying a mortal, would you believe. Have a son now, Setanta. Fierce warrior, like his Da!"

"How could he not be?" Manannán laughed. "How's your wife?"

"Oh, she died, you know how mortals do. And Setanta went off to war, started calling himself Cú Chulainn — the Hound of Ulster. Honestly, children these days…" Lugh trailed off. The silence weighed heavy.

"And what have you been doing?" Manannán asked.

"Just… nothing, I guess." Lugh shrugged.

"What about—"

But Lugh cut him short. "Don't even mention Tír na nÓg, I'm not going. So if that's what you're here for, you can forget it."

Manannán sighed and relented. The yearn within him pulled harder. Lugh fixed him with a heavy stare, his red brows knitting together. The Golden Gull moved up beside Manannán and rocked gently. The realisation dawned on Manannán.

"Take the boat," he said.

Lugh stared, the sun filling his widened eyes. He opened and closed his mouth a few times without words coming out.

"Are you turning back into a salmon?" Manannán laughed. "Seriously though, the boat, take it. That's what you need to do."

"And—and go where?"

"Anywhere!" Manannán exclaimed, throwing his arms wide. "She can go any where or any time or any place. You know that. She'll take you where you want to go."

Lugh's mouth floundered again for a few seconds. "But—but—it's yours. What will you do? Where will you go?"

"You say Clíonadh is in Tír na nÓg?" A sly grin creeping across Manannán's face. Lugh's brow knitted briefly before he broke out into peels of laughter, it rolling out of him like thunder in a summer storm.

"She is, aye," he said. "But, will you be alright?"

Manannán checked his chest. The yearn was quelled, quieted, rested.

"I will," he said, nodding. "This is how it's meant to be. And I have Aonbharr." He gesticulated to the horse who stomped on the spot, relieved at not being forgotten about.

Lugh let out a low whistle as he took in the boat, running his hand gently along the hull. The boat rumbled from side to side.

"The Golden Gull?" Lugh said, running his fingers over the hasty black paint.

Manannán shrugged. "That's the name now, won't let me change it back."

Lugh slapped the belly of the boat gently and chuckled. "Golden Gull it is! Manannán, I don't know what to say. What if you need it back?"

"Then you'll know. Trust me. Now, do you know where you want to go?"

Lugh lowered his head, pushing a foot into the soil. "No. But I can feel where I want to go."

"Even better," Manannán laughed.

"Does that make sense?"

"It does to me!" Manannán reassured. Trust that instinct. Golden Gull will do the rest. Hop in."

Lugh threw himself over the hull into the boat, the wood creaking quietly beneath his weight. He took his place at the front, the breeze catching his hair and casting it out behind him. He smiled and looked down at Manannán and Aonbharr before him.

"How do I look?"

"Like you belong," Manannán answered, Aonbharr whinnying her approval. "Now, go on."

He gestured to the cliff and Lugh nodded. The ship lurched forward, parting the ground, heading toward the cliff edge where the sun overhead. The Golden Gull breached the cliff edge, passing on into the air, as though moving across the water. Up and up the boat rose, Lugh standing in command.

Manannán walked to the edge of the cliff, smiling up at the pair, as they approached the sun and passed within its rays to the other world.

As the tale ended and father and son faded away, Raama remembered a bond he had once shared. Under Dataku's tutelage, he had learned to understand his magic. Now, he yearned for that guidance once again.

A new orb interrupted his reverie, demanding his attention. This one contained an oddity, a machine like a bird, its wings outstretched in flight. He'd never seen such a contraption before, yet it fascinated him. In some ways, it reminded him of his own Golden Gull, but this machine held a unique magic, one he hadn't encountered before.

A sense of intrigue washed over Raama as he considered the endless forms magic could take. He watched, studying the energy around the contraption, eager to delve into this mystery.

Balloon Buster

By RD Lancaster

The lieutenant stared across the valley, straining to see the balloon. High in the sky, the sun hid behind a curtain of smoke and dust, making it seem more like midnight than midday. He squinted, but still could not get a clear look at the deadly dirigible they called him here to deal with. Rubbing his eyes, he tried to refocus. Six days of dodging bullets and flak was taking its toll.

"They got us pinned down, sir." Corporal Jones handed him a canteen. "Lost three planes trying to take that blimp out so far. Four more barely made it back, all full of holes."

The lieutenant took a long drink, then lay prone

and brought his binoculars back up for a look. A small window opened in the haze. "There you are." He scanned under the balloon all the way to the ground. "Corporal, do we have incendiary rounds?"

"We do, sir." He waved over two soldiers. "Which one is yours?"

"The SPAD with feathers painted down the sides." He went back to the binoculars. "The Golden Gull."

"You heard him. Get that plane ready to fight." The men started for the airstrip, then turned and came back. The corporal gave them a glare. "What's the holdup?"

"Sorry, Corporal. Is that Frank Luke?" the dark-haired private asked.

"That's Lieutenant Luke to you!" the corporal barked. "Now stop wasting time and get to it!"

"Who's Frank Luke?" the other private asked.

"Only one of the best fighter pilots in the war! Already racked up seventeen kills. They call him The Balloon Buster."

"Seems awful young to be a lieutenant, or a fighter pilot."

"Well he is," came the reply, "and if anyone can

take out that blimp, it's him!" The private jogged back. "Lieutenant," he held out his hand, "could I shake your hand, sir?"

Frank sat up, giving the private a smile. He held out his hand. "Sure Private,"

"Bryan, sir," he gripped the lieutenant's hand enthusiastically, pulling him up so fast that Frank almost left his feet. "James Bryan, and this is Private Richardson." Private Bryan beamed at him.

"That's quite a grip you got there. Glad to know you, men. Where are you from?"

"Texas, sir. Born and bred." He continued to shake Frank's hand.

"Great state," the lieutenant worked himself free of the private's grip, "did my ground training there. James, could you do me a favor?"

"Anything, sir. You name it and consider it done!"

"Could you put this in the side compartment?" He handed the private a pistol. "I like to keep a spare where I can reach it."

The private took the gun from Frank as if it were a piece of fine china. "I will, sir." He snapped to attention and gave a salute. "Not that you'll need it, sir. No one can bring you down."

Frank returned the salute. "I appreciate it, James, and the confidence."

"All right, private! Stop wasting the lieutenant's time and get it done!" Corporal Jones yelled. He turned to Frank, "Sorry, sir."

"No problem, Corporal." He smiled and waved at the men as they left.

"Did you hear that?" Private Bryan smiled. "He called me James."

The corporal shook his head and turned to Frank. "Hope you can take that thing out, sir. We really need a break."

Lieutenant Luke held his gaze on the balloon. "The Gull is the best there is. We'll get it done or die trying, and take a lot of them with us."

He had to attack from above. Coming at the balloon from the side would leave the plane vulnerable to the gunner in the basket, and the nets and cables hanging below made it impossible to get underneath. He worried that flying at that altitude would leave him open to anti-aircraft fire. The big guns were too slow when he flew low, but now he would be right in their sweet spot.

Frank climbed and banked, readying for his first pass. He dove, flak exploding in black clouds around the Gull. Something tore through his shoulder, but he held tight and stayed on course. The balloon came into range, and the lieutenant fired the twin machine guns. The incendiary rounds found their mark, but did little damage. He climbed again. Coming down for his second pass, he pushed the Gull hard. He was losing more blood than he realized, and he wasn't sure how many more passes he could make. He fired again, this time with better luck. The rounds ripped a hole in the side of the balloon. Frank had his target now.

More flak exploded around him, forcing him to dive. He used the maneuver to strafe the enemy landing strip, then climbed away. The enemy pilots scrambled for their planes. They were coming after him. Lieutenant Luke reached altitude and circled, waiting for them. His shirt was soaked with blood and he felt light headed. Closing his eyes, he forced himself to focus.

The sound of bullets against the Gull snapped him back to the moment. He saw three planes bearing down on him. Frank climbed hard and went into a power stall, and the Gull dove down past the enemy planes. As he flattened his line to come in under them, they rolled and followed, gaining speed. Machine gun fire tore at the wings, but he held the plane on a steady course toward the balloon. The enemy planes closed on him.

He was in range now. His vision blurred and he fought to keep his eyes open. He let loose another round of bullets, hitting the side of the balloon and igniting the hydrogen. Luke rolled left and barely avoided impact, but the plane behind him was not able to pull away. It slammed into the balloon and caught in the burning fabric. The weight of the plane pulled everything down on top of the ground crew in a fireball.

Lieutenant Luke raced with all he had toward the mountain range at the far end of the valley. Six enemy fighters followed. He knew that he would have to make a hard landing and fight his way out. Frank checked the weapon at his side, then reached into the compartment for the spare. Inside he found two pistols and an extra box of rounds. He smiled, giving a salute as he pointed the Golden Gull into the sun.

"What's he doing?" Richardson pointed at the planes.

"Leading them away!" Bryan answered.

"But, he won't have enough fuel to get back if he crosses the mountains."

Bryan smiled. "They won't either. Makes it easier for our boys to advance."

"He'll be on his own behind the lines." Private Richardson shook his head. "He won't stand a chance."

"Maybe, but I'll bet he won't make it easy on them." Private Bryan came to attention and saluted the lieutenant as he flew away. He patted the empty holster at his side. "Give 'em hell, sir."

The image of the strange airborne contraption lingered in Raama's mind, stirring up memories of his own foray into the magic of flight. His misguided attempt that had brought only sorrow. The thought served as a bitter reminder that dangerous magic came at a cost he wasn't willing to pay again.

A new orb interrupted his thoughts as it floated into view. It was a scene he recognized well—a ship gracefully navigating the waters. There was something captivating about the way it bobbed on the surface, gliding through the waves. His fingers reached out, longing to touch, to feel the vibrations of another tale. For a fleeting moment, the harsh lessons of the past faded away, and he found himself lost in the sea's call.

Brave Soft Hearts
By Riel Rosehill

We had once shared a dream. A dream of returning home after the war had passed, a dream of a simple life, away from the city. The kind where we'd grow vegetables and farm sheep among rolling green hills, bathed in birdsong and sun. We'd make our home there in a small cottage, warm with the scent of freshly baked bread and love.

Where we wouldn't have to meet in the dark to kiss.

Both Aland and I had been discharged from service before we'd lost the war over fertile lands, further nourished with blood. Leaving old and new parts of ourselves in the bloodied mud of the camp among fallen soldiers —my mind, his arm, our future— we'd gone separate ways. And whatever force had held my heart in one piece had been left behind too.

My knees buckled as the memory washed over me, hitting me with a tidal wave of nausea as the deck moved beneath my feet. Grabbing onto a sun-warm mast, I steadied myself. Over the railings, the tranquil ocean stretched sparkling aquamarine under the azure sky, bobbing the boat in the summer breeze. It was hard not to lose the ground, riding the sloping waves and the storm inside my head.

I'd been struggling to pay attention lately. To my —or others'— actions since my last days in camp. This wasn't the first time I found myself somewhere, unable to recall how I'd gotten there and what reason for. Only this time, I found myself on a carrack, with no idea when I'd boarded it—nor where it headed.

Around me, jars, barrels and crates lay scattered on the ground, filled with light and gold and antiques and something resembling fairy dust labelled hope. A busy crew worked moving them below deck, whilst a short, round-faced woman with a headband checked the labels and made note of each item in the thick leather-bound book she carried.

Before I could gather the strength to let go of my support, she stepped in front of me.

'Mind your step.' She put her hand on my arm and pushed me away from the mast half a step. Broken glass crunched underneath my boots. A coltish teenage boy jumped next to us and swept around my feet. The woman pulled a piece of cloth from her satchel and patted my temple with it before putting it in my hand, blood-stained. 'Name?' she asked as she reached out towards me, lifting a small, shiny locket on a golden chain I wasn't aware of wearing around my neck. It wasn't mine—I'd never seen it before.

'Cillian Hale,' I gave my puzzled reply and wiped the blood trickling down my fingertips from another cut. The woman checked the inside of the locket and made a note in her book.

'Aye, Cil-li-an.' She scribbled my name on the page before meeting my eyes. 'Sorry about the cuts. Welcome aboard The Golden Gull!'

She flashed me a confident grin and held out her hand, squeezing mine without mercy when I accepted it. 'Jamie Black, quartermaster.'

I pressed the cloth over the newfound cut on the back of my left hand. 'How did I get these?'

'The jar for you was too small,' she said, as if that was supposed to explain it.

Still disorientated, I reached for the curious locket resting on my chest and clicked it open, hoping what was inside would clear my confusion.

I didn't expect its hidden words to tear right into my soul.

Happy ever after?

'What's this?' My words bled, voice cut on the shards of my shattered dreams.

'Just a way of keeping things organised.' The quartermaster shrugged. 'Make sure to keep it on as long as you sail with us.'

I shifted my weight from one leg to another.

'About that,' I said, turning the words with reluctance and hoping a memory would pop back into my mind to save me the embarrassment. But I had to admit, 'I don't know where I'm going.'

'That's to be expected,' Jamie said, matter of fact. 'You're part of the cargo.'

Once Jamie pointed me in the right direction, Captain Blair Dixon was easy to find. Standing behind the figurehead on the prow, stealing its golden wings for her own, she observed the open waters ahead. Even her shadow on the deck wore the wings of the carved seabird, making it look like an angel captained the boat. An angel in worn boots and men's clothing. She puffed a wooden pipe, and beaded braids fell to her waist from under a wide-brimmed hat, a contrast against her linen shirt like strands of seaweed and shells on the white shores.

'Captain Dixon?' Her name sounded like an accusation as I approached her.

She regarded me with cool eyes for a moment, then, blowing out the smoke, returned to squinting at the horizon.

I took a deep breath. 'I'm Cillian Hale.' My voice sharpened. 'Part of the cargo…?'

'That's right,' she answered, without sparing me another glance.

The queasiness worsened in my stomach. 'I'm not sure I understand.'

'Hm.' The captain smiled, but it didn't quite reach

the crow's feet of her eyes. 'Do you smoke?'

'Maybe I should,' I said, averting my gaze as she offered her pipe to me. She was missing two fingers. 'Why am I on your boat?'

The captain snorted and took another drag.

'We trade in dreams'—Her husky words floated towards the sky, dressed in hot smoke and foreboding—'wishes that were granted for the future. Dreams that would've come true, but the person who once dreamed them, for one reason or another, swapped them for something else. It's usually either out of greed or desperation. Some would trade their future health for fortunes, and some would exchange all the gold they would've found to be blessed with a child. For a fee, they can exchange their dreams for the ones others left with us.'

'What's that got to do with me?'

'Dreams come in many shapes, Cillian Hale. Look at them.' With her pipe, she gestured towards the few items still on the deck. 'Sometimes they aren't a tangible thing, it's like putting air in a jar. Sometimes, they are an artefact. Some rare, magical thing: a pocket watch with enchanted clockwork that gives you more time, or a pendulum that always swings towards the right choice;

a dream can manifest as anything. It can be anything.'

'But that doesn't explain–'

'Sometimes, like in your unfortunate case, the dream is attached to, or simply is a person. In those instances, when the dream is traded, we end up with the likes of you.' She sized me up, unimpressed. 'You are here because you were once somebody's dream, their "happily ever after." You were their wish, granted—but there was something they wanted more.'

I didn't need to ask Captain Dixon whose dream I used to be—my life, my heart, my future had belonged to Aland. Learning we had still had the promise of a dream come true, made losing it to a trade more painful. But it didn't surprise me he had given it all away.

'I would've done the same,' I said, biting my tongue before the selfish "But what about me?"

It was my dream too, this dream that would never be.

The captain raised an eyebrow. 'You would've traded the life you wished for?'

'For his sake.' I turned my gaze from her amused eyes to the bright-blue waves, hiding darkness below. 'Sometimes a dream turns into a nightmare.' And even if it would over time become the sweetest of dreams again, maybe I would rather wake up too. Especially if I knew it would resemble that nightmare.

Blair's eyes rested on me for a long while before she spoke. 'Maybe that's what he thought when he gave you up. And maybe it is the truth, but you wouldn't be the dream you are if it mattered. No kind of happy ending will erase a hard past; it can only contrast it.'

'Are you saying his trade was a mistake?'

'No. It was simply a decision. I can't tell you whether it was right or wrong, only that it was made.'

Hoping it could be changed, I swallowed my pride. 'Can it be reversed?'

'Not unless he comes back for you. But I wouldn't get my hopes up.' Blair shook her head. 'He was already granted another wish.'

'What wish?' The words tumbled out before I could even consider if I wanted to know the answer. Maybe if he had asked for something that would make things right. Perhaps a new arm, or a different happily ever after to replace ours. I would've been happy for him.

At least that's what I told myself.

But Aland's choice promised him no better future; in fact, he received nothing.

He wanted just to forget.

My eyes were still adjusting to the dimness of the hull as I stood in the door of the small cabin which barely fit the two hammocks hanging inside of it: one made with a blanket, the other, which would be mine, filled with the belongings of a roommate I had yet to meet. Pushing aside the worn maps and a brass spyglass thrown over the pile of clothes in the hammock, I picked up a single left boot, lonely and abandoned by its other half. 'I guess we have something in common.' I sighed.

'Hey, roommate.'

Startled by the low voice, I stepped back from the hammock and turned to the man leaning on the doorframe, wearing a smile both honest and forced, the sort kind people muster when they are either tired or aren't thrilled to meet you. I couldn't blame him for it—I didn't know a soul who would want a surprise roommate, let alone one who talks to their shoes.

He stepped inside. The little light cast by the porthole behind my back reached his tall frame in timid rays; soft, but not shying away from touching his bronze skin under his half-buttoned shirt. It stroked highlights into his dark hair, down the waves brushing his round shoulders and guiding my eyes to his inked arms, strong enough to steer a ship caught in a wicked storm.

'Are you looking for something?'

'No.' I dropped the boot back into the hammock and cleared my throat. 'Sorry to intrude.'

'It's fine, as long as you don't snore. Hope that's not the reason why you got dumped?'

'No.' I blinked. It would've been nice if it were that simple; if I had been just dumped, and for something so trivial. I would've picked that over the war. 'Are you also here because of a ditched dream?'

'Don't let your eyes fool you.' He smirked. 'I'm not some wish waiting to be fulfilled.'

The dim light caught the mischievous glint in his storm-blue eyes as he offered his hand.

'Haider Wright. Sailing master.'

Unlike the quartermaster, he didn't squeeze my

hand hard. His warm, calloused hold was the perfect balance of firm and gentle, one I couldn't immediately let go.

'Cillian Hale,' I replied, out of breath after only two words. Maybe it was how our handshake lasted longer than what's polite, maybe it was the roughness of his skin or the playfulness in his voice that both scared and intrigued me, but something about his touch reminded me of Aland's. My nose pinched. He would never hold my hand like that again.

The hammocks swung with the rocking of the boat over larger waves as I pulled my hand from Haider's, but his eyes didn't let me go.

'What are you?' He glanced over me while putting his hand on the wall for balance.

'What?'

'What kind of dream?' He got hold of my locket before I could step away and clicked it open. His eyes flicked to mine over the words of happily ever after, lips parted.

Snatching the locket from him, I dropped it under my shirt.

I needed some space to breathe.

But as I stepped back, the boat rocked hard and Haider lost his balance. He fell on top of me and knocked the air out of my lungs against the floorboards.

Grabbing onto the hammock, he sent its contents tumbling over us.

'Fuck.' Haider flinched as the boot hit his head, and he pushed against the floorboards, lifting his weight. 'Are you alright?'

I'd not been pinned under another man since Aland had last tackled me to the ground, returning from combat in pelting rain. I hadn't even noticed the hardness of the oak's protruding roots I'd landed on, though I would feel the soreness from the impact for weeks after. I'd welcomed the bruises though. Aland could've crushed all my ribs if it meant I could be sure he was still alive.

Are you hurt? He'd stroked my face with his muddy hand and kissed my cheek.

Wrapping my arms around him, I'd shaken my head, Relieved.

Holding onto his rain-soaked military tunic, I hadn't noticed my tears until I tasted them on Aland's lips. It had been a long day, and a bad one. Some of the blood hadn't yet dried on my jacket. I'd not had a break for sixteen hours, and I hadn't seen him for twenty-six. And not seeing a soldier inside the field hospital could only mean one of two things: they were either un-harmed or they weren't ever coming back—I would've rather stitched him up than waited to find out.

It made me sick I'd ever thought that.

Haider's hair fell into my face, hitting me with the scent of the sunny deck, sweat and fresh ocean breeze. The memories of mud, the smell of iron and gunpowder slipped from my grasp, like water through my fingers; faster the more I tried to hold on.

My muscles tensed. 'Get off–'

'Bear with me.' Haider pulled himself onto his knees, swaying as he held onto the now empty ham-mock.

Biting my tongue, I closed my eyes. I didn't want to be trapped beneath him for another moment. I didn't want the sea and the boat and this stranger. I only wanted what once was, what could've been. But the lon-ger he stayed close, the harder it was to hold onto that feeling, that nostalgia. I couldn't take it any longer. With a frustrated grunt, I shoved him off to the side.

'Life on a boat must be hard with two left feet,' I muttered. As a distraction. As a joke—but, too embarrassed of what I'd just done, I failed to bring light into my voice. My tone stayed flat.

Stunned silence stretched, long enough to force me to look at him.

Haider stared at me from underneath his hammock, mouth agape as if I had punched him.

Propping himself up, he scooted away from me.

'It's even harder without any,' he said dryly.

The words of apology dried up in my mouth, and my heart swapped places with my stomach.

My gaze fell onto his legs.

And the right half of the boots.

On his left, the hem of his trousers grazed the ground, revealing nothing as he struggled onto his feet; a movement marked with a hollow knock I hadn't noticed earlier—a piece of hardwood stomped against the floorboards.

It was my turn to lose all sense of balance.

'First time seeing a wooden leg?' Jamie asked, joining me at the side of the boat.

I cringed. So Haider had told her.

The bottle of rum she held towards me still bore the war-time label with the glorified sketch of an armed soldier in front of a royal airship.

Looking over the darkening waters, I accepted the drink and took a burning swig. 'Kind of.'

She raised an eyebrow. 'You aren't sure?'

'No.' I grimaced. 'Specifically? First time, yes.'

'And if you aren't being specific?'

'I spent the last two years on the frontline.' Scratching at the label on the bottle, I peeled the dishonest curve of the soldier's smile and tore through the airship that'd never come, letting the strips of paper drown in the sea below. 'You must have met some of the veterans.'

After all, they had traded a dream with one.

Jamie's eyes widened. 'Are you one of them too? A soldier?'

'Surgeon.' The word left a sour taste in my mouth. I washed it off with more rum. 'At least, I used to be.'

Now, I doubted I still had what it took to be a good one.

'A backstage hero.' Jamie nudged me with her elbow. 'I bet the Crown showed you some gratitude!'

'Bet again,' I said with a bitter smile, and continued picking at the label. 'Nobody got anything out of that ordeal…But it's not like I had to pay the price of serving the Crown in limbs.' Unlike the other civilians drafted into the army, I was lucky to be a doctor. They had made better use of me away from combat.

I wanted to say I had it easy, but it didn't feel like the truth.

Jamie adjusted her headband, tucking a loose strand of wheat-blond hair underneath it.

'But your partner did?'

I snapped my head towards her.

'I remember him, you know.' She slowed her words with caution. 'A happily ever after isn't something many people would trade. It stood out, like him, with the uniform and the bandages. I was wondering what went wrong.'

"I saved his life" wasn't a fitting answer, so I didn't

reply. And I didn't know anyway, whether it was myself or the war to blame.

Jamie glanced at me. 'He wouldn't have known he was trading you. None of us knew,' she added. 'Dreams are mysterious like that. They are usually more vague, more ambiguous when they reveal themselves—he must have really loved you.'

I bit my lip. Aland knew he wanted me gone. He knew when he refused to look at me, refused to speak. Whether he knew if I'd be given to someone else as a result didn't matter.

'I couldn't blame him either way.' Or, I shouldn't have. Aland had made the right choice by finding a way to forget. Taking a deep breath, I turned my face towards the waters. 'Can I trade a dream too?'

I stayed on the deck late into every evening, long after the last glimmer of sunlight disappeared over the horizon. Most of the crew retired below the deck, with a few finding their sleeping spots underneath the stars, wrapped in wool blankets. Haider secured the helm with rope and left the bridge, and though the cooling air raised goosebumps on my skin, I wasn't planning on joining him in his tight cabin. After the third night, he'd stopped asking me to.

With my back to the few settling on the deck, I leaned onto the railing, listening to the sea. In the vast blackness, the waves blinked back at the stars, taking the light of the galaxies stretched above for a ballroom dance on the water's surface. With the sky dark, and no light on deck, each and every star shined brilliant, and the galaxies painted iridescent arches across the sky. Looking all the way up, I tried to blink back the tears that blurred my vision and erased the guiding lights.

I had no dream to trade.

Not even a small one.

'Let's see if there's a dream to catch. Ready?' Jamie had asked with a copper dandelion clock in her hand.

I'd nodded.

'Blow.' She'd held it in front of my face.

Filling my lungs, I'd blown all the air out onto the head of the dandelion, my breath fogging its shiny little seed-umbrellas.

Nothing happened.

'These things can change, you know,' Jamie had consoled me. 'It's just right now, if you have something you dream of, well…you know it won't come true. It doesn't mean good things won't happen to you. Things you might not think of. And maybe one day, you will have a new dream, one that will come true. One that you could enjoy, or trade, if you still wished to.'

It was gone. My only dream, the one I once shared with Aland, was no more; and I had nothing else. I shouldn't have been surprised: I only wanted to get him back, or if that wasn't possible, trade a dream to help him.

There was nothing else I wished for.

The wind picked up and a cold drop of water landed on my face, then another and more as I stared into the starless night. The few sailors who had stayed on deck scrambled towards the hull in the heavy shower. They were all gone by the time the first lightning split the night.

I didn't move.

The rain drenched my clothes by the time the thunderclap caught up. I gripped the railing and leaned over, waiting for the next one. I was not concerned by the growing waves—all I wanted was to scream into the storm. Lightning struck, and I took a deep breath, filling that dreamless void with the salty air, before letting it all out, competing with but losing to the thunder.

When the peal of thunder died off and I ran out of air, somebody else's voice blended into the wind, making my pulse jump. 'Cillian!'

Before I could turn around, Haider grabbed my arm and pulled me from the railing. 'You need to get in!' he shouted over the howling wind, gripping my arm so hard it hurt. As if he was afraid I would lose my balance as easily as he had the day we'd met.

My heart skipped a beat.

Grabbing onto Haider, I nodded, and we made our way back towards the hull. We couldn't run, and I was suddenly aware of the boat's movements more than before. I never had to watch each step like I did then. I shouldn't have stayed on deck. If he got hurt, it would have been all my fault.

I needed to get him in.

A single lantern swinging from the ceiling illuminated the cabin, casting a yellow light onto my hammock, now made with a blanket and a pillow. Dry and tempting. Shivering in cold-saturated clothes sticking to me like a second skin, I gave Haider a sheepish look. 'Sorry for the trouble.'

He limped to the wooden chest, leaving small puddles in his trail, seeping into the cracks between the floorboards. Opening the chest, he pulled out two shirts in shades of faded blue and handed me one of them. 'Have this.'

I'd had a duffle bag before I ended up on this boat—it must have been lost on land, with all of my belongings, leaving me only what I wore.

I accepted the shirt. 'Thank you.'

'You have to be more careful.' He sat on the chest and pulled off his boot. 'The sea likes the taste of dreams.'

'It does?' I raised my eyes at him, casting them down as he peeled off his wet shirt.

'Trust me; I've learned the hard way.'

I looked at his legs, away from his dripping hair and the drops of water running down his rain-slick skin.

Haider sighed. 'I'm still getting used to it, you know.'

'Is it that recent?'

'The accident itself happened a few months ago. But I was on crutches until last week.'

Last week? Yet he had been wearing that leg all the time—way too often for somebody who just started using it.

Haider's brows furrowed as I stared at him.

I coughed. 'I'm sorry.'

He only shrugged. 'You should've seen the shark.'

My eyes flickered to his chest and the large shark tooth hanging from his neck.

Haider grinned when he caught me looking, but it struck me as a little forced, a bit more anxious than proud. 'Impressive, right?'

'Right.' I gave him a polite smile, turning my attention to getting out of my clothes. I knew better than to ask about his encounter with the shark and make him recall a time he might not wish to remember.

Not that I didn't want to ask him if he minded losing his leg or if he had rather died. If he was satisfied with his life. Happy, even. And if he'd forgiven the great fish. Things I couldn't ask a complete stranger.

But it didn't matter.

Because Haider wasn't Aland.

And the shark wasn't me.

I'd never had any difficulty falling asleep whilst working in camp. Unable to have a day off or take a break, I had often found myself waking on the ground in the flattened grass outside the field hospital or under the oaks behind our cabins. Sometimes, I would be underneath Aland's coat, which was always covered in dirt and carried the faint smell of sweat and blood—the scent of fear. Yet somehow, that's what I liked waking up to the most. Times like that, I'd hear him snore beside me, his back supported by an ancient oak, or feel his fingers in my hair and know we were alone and he was still in one piece.

It was only now when I had time to rest and the horrors of war were a thing of the past that I could no longer sleep in peace.

For the eighth night, I lay awake in my hammock, staring into the darkness of the cabin, a perfect canvas to screen the scenes haunting me. The sounds of the boat, the lapping of the waves and the muffled laughter of some of the crew conversing on the deck faded as I was transported back in time:

Another airship had been shot down. Another landmine blew up.

Hurrying to the freshly injured who were being thrown onto the beds, I'd held my hand towards the head nurse, Charlotte. 'Morphine!'

'We're out!' she yelled.

The soldier groaned.

I clenched my jaw, but I couldn't say anything. That sweating face, contorted in agony, had belonged to Aland. His right arm hung in crimson shreds, draining him into a dark puddle beneath the no longer white stretcher, pooling red on the ground. There was no trace of the fingers I kissed at dawn.

Still, Aland's eyes lit up with naive hope as they found me.

'Cil–'

I shook my head, unable to move closer.

'Dr Hale?' Charlotte's voice seemed distant. Unimportant.

'Get something.' My voice trembled. 'Alcohol.

Mushrooms. Anything!'

'Do you think I haven't tried already?' She snapped. With the airships getting shot down, we hadn't received any supplies for weeks. 'We have nothing. Let's not waste any time.'

Searching for the right words and finding none, I stood by as Charlotte fastened the leather straps around Aland's body and what had remained of his arm.

The hope flickered in Aland's eyes, and he gave me one of those weak smiles, filled only with nerves and anxiety, not joy. 'Please say you can fix it,' he begged, his eyes filling with tears as I picked up the scalpel.

In the distance, another explosion shook the ground. He wasn't the first and he would not be the last. The rules hadn't changed: save them. At any cost. We had to hurry, so we could take care of the next ones. We had to hurry, because a minute was long enough without medicine.

'I'll make it quick.' It was the only reassurance I could offer. Without thinking, I reached for his hand to squeeze, the way he'd always done when I needed him.

Shivers shocked me as I touched raw fringes of slick flesh and blood-soaked cloth. I shouldn't have let him see the horror on my face.

His breathing became shallow. Quick. 'You don't have to. Please. Cillian–'

'You can take it and so much more. You will liv–'

'But I don't want to!' Fear took the place of the dwindling hope in his eyes, consuming him until he stared at me like one looks at a monster.

'I do. And it is my duty to the Crown,' I mumbled my last excuse.

Anger flared in his voice. 'Fuck your duty. Where's your loyalty to me? Who are you doing this for?! Just let me–'

Charlotte shoved a wooden spoon between his teeth. 'Bite down hard, lad.'

Aland paled.

'I love you,' I mouthed, looking into his terrified eyes one last time, unsure whether I was doing the right thing.

Then I began to cut.

It was all so distant. The voices. The faces. The screams. As if I watched it all from above. I put down the scalpel, took the bone saw. My body was no longer mine as I sawed through the bone. It was methodical. Practised. The blade cut through Aland like any others—only this time some of that pain cut me too with every single slice severing the mangled mess. The ghost of its touches burned my skin; his palm rubbing my back when I had been sick behind the field hospital after the first day of fighting, the tracks of his gentle fingertips that over time had conquered my whole body, his arm across my chest, pulling me close last night, and his handprint over my heart.

When the limb fell onto the ground, it had shown no resemblance to the arm I used to know.

Burying my face into my wet pillow, I tried to muffle the sobs bubbling up my throat.

A soft whisper startled me. 'Are you alright?'

I froze and pressed my hands over my mouth, but couldn't calm my breathing, couldn't stop the shaking of my shoulders. Grief didn't care for my dignity.

'Cillian?' Haider stirred in his hammock, and I sank deeper into mine.

'Right.' He yawned. 'Stupid question.' The thump of his foot hit the floorboard and soon the lantern's light filtered through my blankets. 'I'll be on the bridge, if you need something. Here.' He placed something soft and light on the top of my head, but I waited until he hopped out the door to pull the blanket off my face and see what it was: a star-patterned handkerchief.

Haider stayed on deck, long enough for the handkerchief to soak through and my tears to dry up. I was not sure what I was hoping for, leaving the cabin and making my way upstairs, wearing only the shirt I'd gotten from Haider, his handkerchief still scrunched in my fist.

Without a lantern to cast a light or shoes to knock on the floor, I was sure Haider didn't notice me stepping into the night. He sat on the bridge in the small circle of his lantern's warm light, with a blanket over his shoulders and his maps laid out in front of him. Raising his compass, he looked at the stars before making a mark on the map. Spurred on by curiosity and not wanting to be by myself, I gathered my courage to edge closer; but my foot caught in a bundle of rope, tripping me. At the sound of my stumbling, Haider snapped his head towards me, eyes wide. Recognising me, he gave me a brief smile while pulling his blanket over his legs and the detached prosthetic by his side, covering it all up.

I took a step back.

'I don't mean to bother you. I just needed fresh air,' I said, though what I wanted was company.

Haider gazed at the stars. 'I'm not bothered.'

I found it hard to believe, after witnessing him covering up as soon as he'd seen me. It was a selfish thought to seek comfort from him. There had to be a better way of coping, a way to choose my own path and destination. 'I need to get off this boat,' I muttered, turning around but Haider's fingers locked around my wrist.

'Stay.' His voice was as warm and inviting as the glint of lantern's light in his eyes and his lambswool blanket.

I sighed. 'I didn't mean I was going to jump right now,' I said, still trying to resist. I didn't want to make him uncomfortable by staying, but he wouldn't let go.

Before, whenever things fell apart, Aland had always been there for me. Without him, I had nobody to lean on. I didn't know what to do.

And so, I stayed.

Haider's grip loosened, his touch lingering for a

moment as I sat next to him.

'I know this sucks. It's alright to feel like shit,' he said and pulled his hand back, removing the only touch of warmth against the chill night.

Glancing at his legs hidden underneath the blanket, I doubted he would say the same if he knew what had led me here.

I woke to a loud thud and Haider cursing like the sailor he was. Lifting my head I peered over the edge of my hammock, my eyes still tired from crying myself to sleep. Haider was on the floor in his nightshirt, his hand over the top of his peg leg.

I held my hand out for him, but he gave me a hard stare and pushed it away.

'I'm not some damsel in distress,' he growled. 'I've just got a stick for a leg. It only means I survived.'

I bit back the "I'm sorry," ready to slip out.

'Me offering help only means I would like to feel useful,' I said. It wasn't my job to help. He didn't want it. But it was a job I could take on for distraction—though just looking at him with his messy hair and bare thighs offered a distraction of a different kind.

Haider got himself up, wincing as he put his weight on his wooden leg. A stick, he called it, and I would've struggled to find a better word. It was a sad replacement when compared to the innovation of the new, mechanical limbs, all shining copper and brass with cogs, in the perfect shape of human arms and legs. They were expensive—but not too expensive to give them for free to the injured veterans, in case the Crown would call on them for another war. A copper finger can pull a trigger as well as flesh and bone. And it would feel no pain. Maybe it was better not to have one.

Pulling down my shirt, I got out of my hammock. 'What happened?'

'Fuck knows.' Haider sat on top of the wooden chest and leaned back against the wall, watching me as I stepped towards him, bare feet on the cold floor. 'I only know I can't stand.'

'Let me help.' I knelt in front of him, placing my hand above his knee, over the leather straps fastened around his thigh holding the prosthetic in place. He fixed his stormy dark eyes on me with a mixture of distrust and curiosity. 'May I?' I tapped one of the bronze buckles.

His muscles tensed under my fingers. 'You absolutely may not.'

I sat back onto my heels and lifted my hands. 'You take it off then.'

'What–'

'Did you sleep with that on?'

Haider stared at me, seemingly confused, and replied only after a long pause, 'Yeah..?'

I sighed. 'That can damage your leg. And you can't wear it if it's hurting you.'

He looked puzzled. 'What do you know? You nearly fainted when you first noticed it. I mean, look at you!' He thrust a hand towards me. 'You can hardly look at me now. I didn't want to take it off just to freak you out even more–'

'It's not that. It's… complicated. But it doesn't freak me out. I promise. It just reminded me of something I couldn't handle. Cannot handle. But I am a doctor. I can handle this.' As for not looking at him, I had to try not to stare, because Haider was stunning. I didn't want my eyes to wander, my thoughts to follow, and to be caught blushing.

'You're a doctor?' he asked, somehow seeming both more relaxed and disappointed at the same time. 'You should've led with that.'

'Fair.' I gave him a nervous smile. I'd only mentioned my past profession to Jamie—I didn't want to talk about what I'd been doing before my time on board. 'I guess nobody would want unqualified help.'

'Or'—He stared into my eyes— 'more likely, that's not what I'd first think of, when you throw yourself onto your knees in front of me.'

'Why, what were you..?'

Haider shifted and looked away, tugging the hem of his shirt downward, cheeks flushed.

My words evaporated under my heated skin.

I managed a nervous laugh. 'How optimistic of you!'

'How stupid,' he said through clenched teeth, eyes downcast. 'When I've only got half a leg…'

My heart dropped. As embarrassed as I was, I couldn't leave it at that.

'Hey. That shouldn't matter. It doesn't matter,' I said, unbuckling the straps over his thigh.

Haider drew in a sharp breath and reached for the straps.

"I've seen worse." I pushed his hand aside. Pulling off the wooden leg, set it on the floor. Haider's stump was a map of blues and reds and purples; all bruises and blisters caused by the prosthetic. "My partner—my ex,' I corrected myself, 'lost his arm. And I don't think of him any different. Any less…appealing.'

Haider leaned closer, a glint of dawn flickering in his eyes. 'Yes? That's all good, but weren't you already with him before it happened?' he asked, covering his stump with his hands while I checked the padding inside the peg leg's socket.

'I was,' I gave a short answer. 'Say, do you know where you have a medical kit and maybe a sewing kit on this boat?'

Haider shook his head, sticking with his topic of interest. 'So you don't know if you would've liked him, if that's how you met.'

'I do.' I sighed. 'Do you have any wound-healing creams?'

Another headshake, another dismissed question.

'How?'

'Well…' I put the leg in my lap, giving in. 'Firstly, I didn't fall in love with him because of how he looked. Secondly, I've not seen you before you lost your leg, but you–' Haider's eyes flicked to mine and I swallowed the rest of my words back down. I found him attractive, but something about him stopped me from saying it. Maybe because it would've led somewhere, down a path I was not ready to walk again. Not before knowing if there was such a thing as a second chance at happily ever afters. But how could there be? Even if I chose one for myself, I could be traded to become someone else's.

'But I..?' Haider tilted his head, a shadow of a playful smile lurking in the corner of his mouth.

I pressed my lips together. 'It slipped my mind,' I said, avoiding his gaze.

The wind changed over the next two weeks. Captain Blair ordered the crew to furl the sails and Haider to regain course. Humming a sea shanty, he unrolled his map and checked his compass before adjusting and securing the steering.

'It might take us a day or two longer to get to port,' Blair remarked, handing me a strip of torn flannel. I wrapped it around the makeshift bandage on the young deckhand's ankle. She'd fallen off the ratlines that morning, and since I had been helping Haider with his leg, he'd started bringing me the deckhands in need of medical attention. Soon, they'd come to me themselves with coughs and upset stomachs or sprained ankles, and I missed my medical bag for the first time in months. The boat was less than equipped for sickness and accidents.

Blair didn't notice when I handed her the excess fabric after securing the girl's foot: her eyes followed the cook wandering towards the hull. 'We should check on the food rations.'

'I'll go have a look with Cillian.' Jamie hooked her arm in mine when I stood. 'You don't mind, do you?' she asked, leading me.

'No.' I didn't mind having something to do, and somehow I didn't mind the delay. Not that I wanted to stay on the boat, but I didn't know what to expect when we got to shore. I glanced at Haider as we walked past the bridge and he flashed me a grin, looking up from the map. Suppressing a smile, I looked ahead.

Jamie elbowed me in the side. 'So, what have you done to that grumpy man?' She nodded in Haider's direction. 'I've not seen him in such a good mood since the shark took his leg.'

'Nothing.' I glanced back at him over my shoulder, away from Jamie's sceptical brow-wiggles. Haider was grinning all day and had a freshness about him which wasn't there when we first met—and it was because he understood what I didn't say. Him revelling in the knowledge I fancied him filled me with both worry and warmth, like a little bit of sunshine stayed with me as I followed Jamie into the hull. It was good to see him perk up like this—but I didn't want to be responsible for the eventual downfall.

'Say, Jamie, if one loses a happily ever after…will there be another one?' I asked as we entered the food store behind the kitchen.

She peered inside a crate of oranges. 'I'm a merchant, not a fortune teller.'

'Right. I was just wondering if it would be… worth pursuing one.'

Just like that, I had her full attention. 'Do you want to?' She squealed. 'I think you're a good match for our sailing master.'

'Don't jump to conc–'

'Look. You already know this: even when you have all the stars aligned for a dream to come true, it still won't if you abandon it. They are as much of our own making as they are fate: you need both. So if you want a chance, do your part. The road might be bumpy and uncertain, but you might just find yourself having fun along the way, regardless of where it leads.'

'But it matters where it leads.' With Aland, I didn't know if I'd done more harm than good. It was possible I ruined his entire life; he certainly believed so. 'I don't want to cause more pain.' Nor did I want to endure any of it.

Jamie put her hand on my arm. 'That man has a bulletproof heart, my dear. Don't worry about it.'

'I guess I should've expected that much from someone who fought off a shark.' I forced a smile.

'Is that how he tried to impress you?' Jamie laughed. 'Oh no, it was Captain Blair who saved him from the shark's jaws. And it was that heart of his that landed him in there—these waters could eat all the magic in the world if they flooded the land; it's dangerous to be swept overboard when you're carrying some.'

'Wait…' My brows knitted as I was trying to understand what she said. 'Haider said he wasn't a dream.'

'Oh no, he isn't. But he had bought an artefact we had—well, he is paying it off. It's not the kind of trade we'd normally do, but we needed a sailing master, so we agreed to give it to him if he signed on to work on the Gull for ten years.'

I swallowed. 'That's a steep price to pay.'

'He was young with a first-love heartbreak, you know.' Jamie shrugged. 'And who wouldn't want a magical armour around their heart to protect them from that pain? The shark must've smelled it. He's a lucky man to be alive—we could've used a surgeon on board that day.'

Haider never told me about his heart, and learning it from Jamie made me feel like I overstepped, stealing a secret that didn't belong to me. Yet, I couldn't pretend I didn't know.

It was high noon when the Gull pulled into the bustling harbour, docking between an old lugger and a navy steamship, unused and abandoned. We would only stay a couple days for the crew to restock the pantry and trade dreams with the locals: an exchange I might have to play a part of. Jamie organised the unloading of the cargo, and the deckhands carried all the goods down the gangplank, placing them on the pier by the side of the resting ship. I would have to join that line of dreams soon. The sight disappeared as a hat was put on my head, the brim obscuring my vision for a moment.

'You're catching sun, snowflower.'

Pushing up the front of the hat, I glanced at Haider observing the scene below with his arms crossed. 'I don't think this is right,' he said. 'That you might have to leave with any old stranger. What about your dreams? Or...'

'...Or what?'

He didn't reply. A small part of me wished he got me out of it somehow, claimed me for himself. But the trade would cost him one of his wishes, if he could afford it at all. And he wouldn't trust me with his heart, anyway. I couldn't ask him for that big of a favour. Not while, stupidly, I still hoped Aland would get me back. In my foolish daydreams, after forgetting me, he would find me here by chance and choose me again. We would start anew, build a future on the ruins of our past dream. Because we were meant to be. For that sliver of hope, I wouldn't protest; I'd risk being traded to be somebody's one-sided happily ever after, for that one chance in a million to meet him, even though it was wishful thinking. I couldn't picture Aland buying love in a fish market.

But it wasn't only the desperate who showed up. The townspeople who stopped by and browsed the dreams all did so for different reasons. An orphan wanted a dog, a widow needed wealth: both trying to fill a gap of a lost man who had not returned from the frontline. And a newly-wed couple, all smiles and laughter, wanted to trade dreams just for fun.

Once they'd chosen and paid the trading fee, Jamie had them blow the wishing flower and harvested their granted wish; the one they had given up in exchange for a new one. The pappi of the seed head spun with a quiet, metallic clacking, dandelion-fluff sparkling in the sunshine. One seed would lift, taking off on its umbrella when it filled with an abandoned dream. Jamie put it in a jar, sealing it with a cork. It would be traded again. The seed glowed and in a few hours, revealed the dream in some form. Some jars broke when the dream inside grew to have a larger physical form. Scratching my hand, I felt the scar of the now healed cut.

Customers came and went, but I didn't know any of them, so I stayed behind the lines of dreams, under the boat's shadow.

Not that I needed to worry about leaving with a

stranger. It's not that people weren't looking for lasting love—but they weren't looking for me. A few women and men wandered over, leaned in and took a closer look at me the same way they turned the jars in their hands, weighing the magic inside. But I wasn't like fairydust; I was, to them, ordinary. A bit too ginger, too sad-looking and sunburnt. My freckles were too many; my muscles, not enough. They pointed out the smallest undesirable features, the dull mud-brown of my eyes, the slight crookedness of my nose. Nobody wanted me.

By the time we started packing for the evening, I questioned how anyone could ever love me. Lifting a new jar of prosperity, I turned to help the crew take it down the hull, but Haider stepped in front of me, leaving the boat in a long, navy-blue travelling cloak, hiding his legs well from prying eyes. 'You're still with us.'

My face burned hotter under the late-afternoon sun.

'Yes—I have too many freckles.' The seagulls perched on the crosstrees squawked with mocking, cacophonous laughter. I tried to go around Haider, but he blocked my way.

'It's a feature. I could map out the night sky across your face.'

I frowned.

'Most people don't do that on the daily.'

'You don't want most people.' Haider took the jar out of my hands and gave it to one of the crew. 'Come. Let's have a look at the market while we're here.'

My departure from the military camp had not been a pleasant parting. Dr Hale? Dr Hale! I remembered Charlotte's voice calling my name somewhere in the distance, over and over again, when they'd let me go. My commanding officer's yell rang in my ears for minutes. Cillian! Drops of crimson pattered onto the back of my hand in my lap. It had taken a few moments to connect it with the stinging of my face and the blood-taste in my mouth.

'That was unnecessary,' Charlotte said with un-veiled disapproval. 'Uncivilised.'

I raised my eyes as she held a cloth to my mouth.

'Are you listening?' The commanding officer asked.

I didn't reply. Whatever he wanted from me, I had nothing left to give.

Since I had operated on Aland, I hadn't been able to stitch a single wound, let alone hold a scalpel. I didn't even have the will to eat or take a shower. Staring into nothing, I was waiting to wake up from that nightmare. For hours. For days? I wasn't keeping track.

The officer tossed a duffle bag into my lap and put an envelope in my hand. Charlotte tucked it inside my vest's pocket when I let it fall on the floor.

'You might need that to get yourself home,' the officer hissed. 'We thank you for your service.'

After I had gotten off the steam car, taking me from our camp to the closest town, I drifted from place to place without taking note of my surroundings, no more aware than a leaf riding the wind.

Now, as Haider took my arm and guided me away from the quayside, down cobbled streets and alleyways with stray cats, all the way to the market square in the heart of the town, it was a whole different, fresh feeling. I noticed the little things. How he slowed his stride around sweets stands and eyed the fudge, how the setting sun painted an amber glow into his brown hair. He squeezed my arm when he had found something to share with me: a building he liked the look of or his favourite parts of the market.

'You have to try this.' He pulled me over to a hat stand and put a straw hat on my head. 'I think you'll need one of these out at sea.'

His voice was hopeful but unsure, and I couldn't make promises. I wasn't even sure if I would've wanted to.

'Blair could still trade me tomorrow. I might have to stay in this town,' I said, putting the hat back onto the table. Haider's smile faded a little bit. 'I can always run back for it if it turns out I'm sailing with you for a while longer. But I don't want to spend on something I won't need.' I put my hand in my vest's pocket, feeling the envelope with the last bit of my wages. I no longer held a job, and also, I wanted to use the money to support Aland, if I ever found him.

'Right.' Haider followed me as I stepped away from the hats. 'But if it was your choice, would you stay on the Gull?' He reached for my hand. 'I wouldn't mind if you did.'

I was about to reply when a woman wearing a lavender-grey shawl over a moth-chewed corset bumped into me.

'Sorry,' I said, half to her and half to Haider.

She grinned and grabbed my vest. 'Oh, aren't you that dream for sale?!'

'Uhm.' I stepped back, but she was glued to me. 'Yeah?'

'Well! I might be interested.'

'Back off.' Haider put an arm between us, letting me step away. 'We are not here for business.'

The woman laughed and pulled the shawl closed over her chest. 'Are you jealous or is that how you speak to all of your customers? I'm just enquiring!'

'If you want anything, go back to the quay tomorrow,' Haider said, uninviting. 'But I doubt you can afford him.'

'Alright, sea-dog.' She lifted her hands in defence. 'Keep him, no need to bite.'

I breathed a sigh of relief when she turned around and left us. I didn't want to be tied to the Golden Gull, but I could also do without being tied to a stranger.

If it was my choice, I would be free.

'Thank you,' I said, sitting on empty crates in a quiet corner of the market. Haider bought elderflower cider from an old couple's stand and insisted I try it. Cool, floral and sweet with a lemon zing, I savoured the taste on my tongue. Haider's fingers brushed mine as I handed back the glass, and we paused there for a moment that had me feeling both brazen and baffled.

My eyes flicked to his and I drew in a shallow breath of summer-evening air. 'Why are we doing this?'

'I thought maybe you can get yourself a sunhat, and it's nice to walk on dry land–'

'I mean this.' I pulled my hand back, grazing his fingers with a slow, feather-light but most deliberate touch.

Haider's eyes, a brighter grey-blue in the sunshine, darkened as they flickered between our hands and my face.

'Show me again,' he asked.

I half-wanted to oblige. 'This is a dangerous game.'

'Some risks are worth taking.'

I curled my fingers into a fist, resisting him. 'Easy to be that brave when you've got an armoured heart.'

Haider stayed silent for a moment. I'd never told him I knew.

'Just because it can't break it doesn't mean it can't hurt,' he said at last, looking away from me. 'It just… takes the edge off.'

I remembered the time when I'd steeled my heart by the battlefield; acted as the doctor, not the lover. It might have been the right thing—but it was the end of us.

'You can't take the edge off of love. If you don't place your heart in the hands of another, despite knowing it might shatter, how could it be real?'

Haider leaned closer. 'Come on now, you are not telling me you want to break my heart, are you?' he asked in a hushed voice.

'No.' My face flushed. 'Of course not, I wouldn't want to. But…I need to be careful. Knowing this won't last–'

'So what? The cider was never going to last either, but you didn't turn that down. You could think of this the same way. As…something nice. A treat. Just some fun.' He kept his tone light, playful even, but there was weight—gravity—to his words. 'We're both here now.'

'That could change tomorrow.' Even to my ears, my words sounded like a weak excuse.

'It could. Or it could be weeks. Months. Even years. Why not enjoy the time we have? We both want it. Even though your heart belongs to someone else.'

'Belonged,' I whispered. My heart was stray, locked out from its home and scared to accept an invite to be fostered. But this might be the last invite I was getting—I didn't want to leave empty but for regrets. 'You're right.' I caved. 'Let's make the most of the time we have.' I stood and dusted my trousers. 'How is your leg?'

'I can walk a bit more,' Haider said, accepting my hand and letting me help him up, but didn't let go after. Nor did he move a step. 'I want you to relax and not think of this, but…' He took a deep breath. 'Could you help me out? Walking on cobbles is a pain with this leg.'

'You can just say you want to hold hands,' I joked, but took his arm. 'We can go back to the boat, if it's too much.'

'No, not yet. Most places here stay open late,' he said, taking the lead again, his lips stretching into a wide grin. 'And you've not even seen the fun parts of the town yet.'

The sunset made the sky blush and the clouds glow rosy gold as we walked arm in arm downtown, past jewellers and tailors and an apothecary I turned back to, pulling Haider inside. Colourful vials of medicinal herbs and bottles of remedies were stacked high on crowded shelves, and I filled a whole satchel with supplies for the boat: arnica balm to rub onto Haider's blisters, anise elixir to treat the cook's bad stomach. For accidents, I stocked up on gauze bandaging, opium and catgut for suturing.

By the time we exited the shop, the sun had dipped below the skyline of gable-roofed houses. A lamplighter was already climbing his ladder, lighting the streetlights, and fiddle tunes poured into the alleys from inside the inns and pubs.

On the wider streets, performers entertained the passers-by: magicians, jugglers and acrobats. One made a white dove disappear, one walked a tightrope, juggling blazing clubs. I stopped right in front, mesmerised by the flames flying and falling, illuminating a web of burn scars on the juggler's forearms. His legs quivered balancing on the rope, but his hands were steady and his eyes full of determination. As he got to the middle, a confident smile appeared in the corner of his mouth, as if to say, easy. He threw a club higher, sending the fire spiralling up above.

Then, he slipped.

My breath hitched, and I grabbed onto Haider, my muscles tense and ready for me to jump to the juggler's aid, but he pulled himself back up, two clubs still in hand, and catching the third one with ease as it came down. My jaw dropped. It was a trick, a success after hundreds of past failures. Glancing at Haider, I was met with him watching me, biting back a grin. His eyes flickered to my hands, squeezing his arm, practically hugging it, as I pressed myself against him in the gathering crowd, my heart racing. Remembering to breathe, I loosened my grip and a laugh of relief broke free from my lungs. Haider laughed with me, and for the first time in forever, the weight of my past lifted off my shoulders.

And there I had it, in the swirling flames mirrored in his storm eyes: happiness. Like the thrill of watching the clubs soar high and dip low, helped nudge my confused heart back in the right rhythm. Reaching for Haider's hand, I interlocked our fingers. The juggler didn't fear the fire—it was worth being brave.

We made our way back towards the harbour under the black-grey sky, our path lined by flickering streetlights and yellow light filtering onto the alleys through the windows.

Turning a corner, we found ourselves in front of

a bakery, still open. Fragrant, fresh bread and pastries adorned the display, their warm yeast and vanilla aroma wafting in the air. Behind the counter, a young woman with a shiny braid and a crisp apron was opening an oven; and a man stood by the till—a man I knew. Strong and rough, with a fresh haircut and, visible from under his rolled sleeves, a brand new mechanical arm. I felt my heart thud throughout my whole body. The sight of Aland, his charming, lopsided smile he gave the woman as she handed him a tray of fresh bread made me forget to breathe.

Aland glanced towards the door. Walking next to Haider, our hands touching, my face burned with shame and my feet rooted into the ground.

Haider stopped at the door next to me, sniffing the air and peering inside. 'Wow.' Eyes lit up, he stepped over the threshold. I shook the fog from my mind and grabbed his arm, yanking him back and dragging him around the corner where we couldn't be seen.

He tripped, squashing me against the wall. 'What the–'

'Sorry.' I locked my arms around him, holding tight while he found his lost footing.

'What are you doing?'

I didn't know. Loosening my arms around him, I let him turn towards me, but too weak in the knees, I kept my back to the wall. I didn't have the answer. What was I doing here with him, steps away from the person I was supposed to grow old with? I wished I could hide my heated face.

'Did you see his arm?' he asked, his face still lit up and eyes starry with the joy of discovery. 'Where do you even get something like that?'

'You don't want one.' My words came out sharper, more panicked than intended.

Haider took a step back and I dug my fingers into his arms again, not wanting to let go. His voice rang confused, and a little hurt. 'I do want one. I need to ask that guy–'

'It's from the military,' I blurted out. 'You get them if you were injured in combat. Otherwise you have to order one to be made for you from Steamworks—but the waiting lists are long for civilians. And they are expensive.'

'How do you know?' He asked while I was trying to catch my breath.

'It was part of my job to place the orders. We had

to keep a record. If you get one, it's almost guaranteed you will be drafted into the army if there's another war.' I'd erased Aland's order from the military records, but Steamworks kept their own list.

Haider opened his mouth like he had more questions, but I didn't wish to linger on the topic. 'Actually… could you buy me something from there?' I reached for the envelope in my waistcoat's pocket. 'Just don't ask about his arm—oh no.'

I searched deeper, turning my pocket inside out, then felt all my other pockets.

'What's wrong?'

'I swear I put the money back into my pocket…I had it earlier.' I scanned the ground but found only haydust between the cobblestones. Gasping for air, I patted my clothes again. 'It's gone.' That woman earlier was only after one thing: my pockets.

Haider's eyes narrowed. 'That thief…' He turned around, his eyes searching the crowd as he took a step in the direction we came from.

I caught his hand. 'Don't bother. She'll be long gone.'

'…Fine.' He sighed. 'What do you want? I'll get

it.'

'You don't need to. I can't pay you back.'

'I don't mind.'

'...I wanted you to buy me some bread from him and give him the envelope.'

'Bread isn't that expensive.'

'I know,' I said, looking into his eyes. I didn't want to explain myself—but I wished he could understand who the baker in question was: the man I still cried myself to sleep over every night. 'I...knew him.'

'What do you mean by knew? Him?' Haider rubbed his face, the corners of his mouth turning down. 'Cillian...'

'Something like, loved.' There was something wrong about this, asking the man I was trying to get with to help me support the one I wanted to get back to. 'I'm sorry. You don't have to–'

'I said I'd get it. You can choose anything.'

But I couldn't choose both of them.

'I should stay here.'

Haider took off his cloak and draped it over my

shoulders, enveloping me in his warmth and ocean-scent. 'In case you would change your mind,' he whispered, leaning in close as he pulled the hood into my face. Almost close enough to kiss me. My eyes fluttered closed—maybe it would clear my thoughts and all those tangled feelings. But he withdrew, clearing his throat and squeezing my shoulder.

'What would you like?'

I would've liked him to kiss me. I would've liked to cry and dig my nails in his back in the safety of our cabin.

And I would've liked to run straight back to Aland.

'Something sweet,' I said instead.

Haider entered the store, and I cooled my head against the flint wall by the doorway, stealing glimpses and listening for anything I might overhear. It wasn't much. The smile shared between Aland and a pretty woman, Haider complimenting the bakes and Aland's new arm, leaning in and taking a closer look. Haider putting his hand on the shiny brass of Aland's arm with a touch of longing both warmed and wrenched my heart. He kept positioning himself in a way to keep his peg leg where it'd be the least visible. I almost felt bad enough to go in and give back his cloak. I wanted to—but my legs wouldn't move. What would I say? I didn't even know how much Aland had forgotten of what happened, whether it was only the worst bits, or me over all. I feared I could ruin it all. And I would ruin it all, for at least one of the three of us.

So I stayed. Haider got to try a few tasters before he chose and Aland handed him a large bag with his order. Haider thanked him. 'I'm happy I found you,' he added. 'This is the best bakery in town.'

All I wanted was to wrap my arms around him when he stepped out of the shop.

Haider began limping more on the way back. Taking the warm paper bag from him, I draped his arm around my neck. 'Lean on me.'

He gave a reluctant huff of breath and I rubbed his arm in return.

'Sure?' He sighed, giving in.

All the way to the ship, his weight anchored me to the present.

Still draped in his cloak, warm and wrapped in his sea salt scent, I didn't mind his knee touching mine as we sat on the wooden chest in the small, intimate corner of our cabin and opened our bag of treats, unleashing the smell of baked goods. Aland had always wanted to show me his baking skills. I used to think we would be sharing a kitchen when it happened.

'I didn't have much on me…but I got what I could.'

And asked him to keep the change.

'It's a lot more than I could've asked for.'

'Don't worry about it,' he said, tearing an orange and pistachio loaf and handing me a small piece. In another life, I could have been sharing it with Aland, on land, in our home. Soured by my thoughts, the bite tasted more bitter than sweet in my mouth.

Haider must have noticed my fading smile.

'I'm sorry.'

'What for?'

'I wanted to cheer you up, going to the market. Today's been rough.'

Even like this, with Haider's face close to mine and our legs touching, the distance stretched too far between us. I missed Aland. I missed his endearing smile, I missed his arms around me and our late-night promises underneath the oak trees. One day, it will be quiet, I'd said, anxious to see the light of day creep over the horizon. There won't be gunfire in the morning, but a cockerel's crow.

And I'll be right beside you, Aland had replied, his hand in mine and his eyes fixed on the top of the hills to the east where the sky lightened, waiting for the sunrise.

He had meant it, back then.

After finding him, I mourned the loss of that future morning once more, but there was no Aland to tell me a better day would come and comfort me in his arms. And I needed nothing more.

Turning to Haider, I leaned in and closed my eyes, brushing my lips on his. He drew in a surprised gasp, and I waited for him to take the next step.

'Cillian…' My name was a soft whisper teasing my lips. His fingers raked through my hair, making my scalp tingle. Similar to how Aland used to. 'What do you want from me?'

Gazing into his eyes, looking for a feeling long lost, I found sparks.

My heart drummed against my chest as I reached for the buttons on his shirt in the pursuit of fire.

I didn't mind getting burnt.

The floorboards were cold under my bare feet when I slipped from Haider's hammock at the crack of dawn. He didn't stir. His face buried into his pillow and his wooden leg detached and placed underneath the hammock, he seemed comfortable. Satisfied. I adjusted his blanket, pulled it over his shoulders, and hoped my actions wouldn't change any of that.

I left while the whole boat was still asleep.

The town was only waking. The farmers were just arriving at the market, under the still grey sky, and the bakers had just begun baking fresh bread for the morning. I pulled the hood of Haider's cloak over my head as I stood across from the bakery where I found Aland.

He was kneading dough with that woman. I could see them through the window as they chatted and prepared for the day ahead.

Only the street separated us, a distance I could've crossed in a couple strides.

If it was fate or too late, I couldn't tell.

Unable to take my eyes off him but not daring to

move closer, I could only watch his every movement. Dawn turned to noon and, just as my stomach began to rumble, somebody touched my shoulder.

'We are about to leave,' Haider said.

He knew where to find me, and yet, he hadn't come sooner: he'd waited until I would no longer have to stand in line with the dreams for sale.

'Are you going to drag me back?' I asked, keeping my eyes on the little store.

'Was last night that bad?' Haider whispered. The sadness in his voice made my chest tighten. I didn't deserve him.

'It's not that. You are perfect.'

'Save that bullshit.' The pain in his voice had me turning to him.

'I mean it.' The diamond shine in his eyes told me he didn't believe a word I said. Nobody was "perfect." Taking off the cloak, I draped it around him and pulled the hood over his head, holding onto it either side as I looked up at him. 'I meant, good enough. Seriously.'

'So why do I need to drag you back? I couldn't do it. I don't want to. You should be choosing. And

I know I don't have a proper leg or skills like him to create that kind of stable life. And I know it's maddening to not be sure how long you would stay with the boat even if you choose to. I don't want to force it. But Cillian—I'm not sure what happens to stolen dreams.'

'Maybe nothing.'

Haider shook his head. 'I don't want to find out.'

I turned to the bakery again, just to catch Aland tip flour into a bowl and be engulfed in a white cloud. I'd never thought the sound of his laughter would hurt me once.

'Do you think he's happy?' Could we be that, without each other? With someone else?

'You don't owe him—'

'You don't know that. But…I might not have a second chance with him.' And the longer I watched him, the more I didn't want to find out. If he had forgotten me entirely, I would have to pretend we were strangers. If he remembered the good things, it'd either have to hide the truth or tell him the very thing he paid so much to forget. It could end in a heartbreak all over again. And I'd see no more of Haider Wright. I stepped closer to the store, watching Aland swipe flour onto the pretty woman's nose one last time.

I turned back towards Haider, my voice cracking. 'Could you get me that hat?'

If there was a second chance, I'd take it with someone else.

'Do you want me to try?' Haider asked me. We laid on the deck underneath the stars, talking about how I'd be traded, how some stranger could just blow on the dandelion clock, and, in an exchange for another dream, I'd be theirs. I wanted to avoid it—but not like that.

I shook my head. 'You said it should be my choice.'

Haider rolled onto his side, facing me. 'That's why I'm asking you first.'

'But I want it to be our choice, every day. Not because I'm already looking for a way out,' I added, turning towards him. 'It's more that, if we're bound by magic—I don't know if the commitment could be real.'

Haider reached for the chain in my neck and pulled out the locket from under my shirt. Opening it, he traced the engraved words before closing his hand around the pendant. 'I didn't think this was real—a happily ever after.'

'Is it?' I used to believe it was, but the dream I carried wasn't for me to live.

Love wasn't the fairytale it dressed as.

'I hope. But love is a storm that can wreck people. Why do you think I've got this?' He put his hand above his armoured heart.

'Because you're a coward?' I teased, suppressing a smile.

Haider snorted. 'Surely, if anyone, you understand.'

'Sure.' I rolled onto my back and stared at the stars, letting him have this one. But it wasn't love that had destroyed Aland and me—it was war.

And it was over, for now.

The sun wasn't up to see us. The porthole was black and the boat asleep while we tried to keep it quiet; all hushed whispers and muffled moans as we bathed in the lantern's modest glow for the opposite kind of acts. Regrets could wait. By the afternoon, we would be docked at a new harbour.

I no longer wanted to leave.

Curling up to the chest Haider sat on, I rested my head on his knee while he leaned back against the wall, his hand still in my hair, his taste inside my mouth.

I raised my eyes as he touched my face.

'To think someone traded a life with you,' he murmured, brushing his thumb over my lips.

Something cracked. The butterfly-tingles turned to barbed wire in my stomach.

'It was for a fair reason.'

'I don't get it—I'd give an arm to have you.'

I could imagine it too well, the crimson mess, the thud of his arm hitting the floorboards. The nausea and the dizziness was back like they never left, like I was still standing by Aland's bed, cut after cut after cut.

'Seriously.' Haider shook his head. 'He seemed like a nice enough guy, but what was he thinking? What's a good enough reason to give you up–what's wrong?'

His peg leg on the floor almost tripped me as I stood and grabbed my clothes.

'You had an armoured heart for so long you forget the rest of us don't.' I pulled on my trousers and turned my back on the cabin.

The sea was quiet, waves lapping against the hull in gentle licks as I leaned on the bow railings. Between the moonlit wings of the great gull, the obsidian waters melted into the dark.

Aland had done the right thing for himself. But a prickly feeling nagged me: he chose the easy way out, leaving me to deal with it all alone. I clenched my teeth. Clearly, I was not dealing with it so well.

I'd been outside long enough for the crisp air to penetrate my skin and make me yearn for the warmth under my duvet, but it was still dark when the sound of footsteps I came to know pulled me back from my thoughts. Thud. Knock.

I glanced behind my shoulder as Haider went to the bridge and, putting his lantern down, rolled one of his maps out. He looked up at the stars and checked his compass. Sighed. And turned towards me. 'Cillian–'

'Are we on the right track?' I cut him off, eager to avoid the conversation.

'You tell me.' He sank the compass inside of his pocket. 'I can read stars, not people.'

I turned back to observe the horizon, or where I imagined it would be, shrouded in the night. I had no sense of direction and no freedom to move.

'I don't even know where I would like to be.' Back in time? Maybe. If I could change the past. 'I still love him, you know.' I looked at Haider as I confessed. 'And it still hurts. And it's still a nightmare. I know you meant well, but–' With my back turned to the great gull, the thick fog we sailed into crept from behind my back, blurring out the boat.

'Don't move,' Haider said, his voice hard as the white mist filled the space between us, and he disappeared.

I froze in place. The creaking of the boat and the splashing waves were muted by whispers in the whiteness, by words I couldn't make out. Honeysuckle perfumed the fishy scent of the sea, filling my mouth with nectar, my chest with a new craving. My stomach churned as the fragrance changed from flowers to cassia to earth until I tasted mud, and the siren-talk of the hushed voices grew deafening. Sick and dizzy with feelings and desires not my own, I leaned over the railing, heart racing. Were they calling my name?

Haider pulled me back by my shirt and the noise

quieted. 'I hate this place,' he said, observing the misty waters over the rails.

'What is this?' I whispered.

'We got caught in a bad storm here once. Had to throw out the whole cargo to stay afloat—it was a fucking feast for the fish. I should've tied a rope around my waist.' He bit his thumb, his other hand gripping the railing. 'I thought I'd never breathe air again.'

'Is this where the shark got you..?'

Haider nodded. 'I didn't know if I would die drowning or getting ripped to pieces by that damned fish. It was after the armour—the mist over the water is the remnant of drowned dreams, the ones we threw overboard. It's like the ghosts of them still haunt here. Or they're still drowning. This is a dangerous vessel to sail, especially for ones like us. It takes one slip and you might come out a limb lighter, if you leave the water at all.'

Despite the immense guilt, I still asked the question lurking in a dark corner of my mind. 'Did you ever wish you never left the water?'

Haiders eyes flickered to mine, studied my face for a moment before he answered me. 'You don't have time for wishes when you're trying not to drown.'

'And when you were back on deck?' I pressed on, despite my increasing heart rate and the tightening knots in my stomach.

'Then I was sick. Either from the pain or the bottle of rum they forced down my throat, thinking it would numb it. Maybe it did. But I felt everything. Heard everything. It wasn't a clean-cut bite, someone had to fix–hey.' Haider's features softened, his eyes filled with worry as he reached for my shaking hands. 'I think that's enough. You should sit down.'

Looking at the thinning fog, sitting on top of the water, I told the practised lie. 'I'm fine.'

Without an answer, Haider wrapped his arms around my waist and sat, pulling me onto the deck.

'How about you tell me a story? I don't want to rip open wounds I don't even know exist. Help me out here.'

Closing my eyes, I considered how awful it'd be to relive the past, and how he might come to hate me by the end of it. How I might be gone tomorrow, without ever letting him know me. So I told everything. The war and how I found and lost true love. How when it came to the choice between having me but losing an arm and death, Aland would've picked the latter. And how I didn't let him choose it.

'It's no wonder he didn't want me after…' I trailed off and just listened. To the waves, to the drumming of my heartbeat, calming, as the first rays of dawn touched the sails.

Haider took a deep breath. 'Believe me, I was protesting too. When I saw Jamie with the butcher's knife, I would've rather they've thrown me after the shark.' He shuddered. 'But I'm glad they didn't. It's difficult at first—but I'm sure most people would feel the same.'

'He seemed to be doing well.' I looked away, trying to make sense of my feelings. Those thoughts I was ashamed of, the fact I couldn't be happy for him. Not yet, even though I should've been. But our parting had been so sudden, I couldn't keep up with it. A part of me went missing, but the ghost of it stayed with me. 'It was so strange to see him. I think a part of me stayed with him, a part I gave and he used to care for. Like my soul reaches, but can't touch his anymore.'

'I think I know what you mean. I still feel my leg, you know. Sometimes, there's an itch I just can't scratch, there's only air. It's…hard to put into words.'

That discrepancy was the cruellest: a constant, jarring reminder of our losses.

Noises below the hull signalled the waking of the crew. The moments we were sharing could have been our last moments together alone. I took in the morning sun sitting on top of his eyelashes, the ocean-depth of his eyes I had no time to explore.

Blair appeared on the deck with a stretch and yawn, and we exchanged a small smile, more regretful than happy as we got to our feet.

'If you change your mind—about wanting to be my dream—let me know,' Haider said before returning to the bridge and I looked over the bright waters, clear of the mist of broken dreams.

Stepping onto the gangplank after me, Haider caught my arm.

'I've not changed my mind,' I said before he could ask. 'But…if you could lay your heart bare and if it wasn't for a magically binding contract, I–' My throat tightened seeing a flicker of hope reignite in his eyes. I would've wanted it to be him, if it was my choice. I would've liked to give us a try. But as part of the cargo, it could never be my own choice to make. Not for the rest of our lives.

'You..?'

'Nevermind. Nobody will pick me, I'll probably end up stuck on the boat with you.' I smiled, wishing I could believe what I just said.

This time, Haider never strayed more than a few steps away from me as I sat on a stool among bottled dreams. That harbour was busier than the last, with people flocking to the Golden Gull and trading their dreams for a few coins. Jamie couldn't get a break between the demands for health and wealth, and the copper fluff of the dandelion spun, without a break into the sunset.

We were about to pack up when the fisherman came.

'Cap, have you sweet love for sale?'

'Aye.' Blair inhaled a lungful of smoke from her pipe. 'A happily ever after, no less.' She gestured to me.

'Great.' The man spared me a quick glance. 'It's for my poor sister.'

'Uhm.' I shifted. 'I'm sure she's more than deserving, but I don't know if I can–'

'You will do.' He gave a dismissive wave. 'How much?'

'An exchange dream and ten gold.'

Behind me, Haider whispered to Jamie, 'Can you get a dream for someone other than yourself?'

'You give it to whoever you want to. You just need to make sure to wish it,' she said, then put a hand on my shoulder. 'Are you good, Cillian?'

'I think I might have gotten sunstroke,' I replied, my stomach heaving. Someone was about to take the dream attached to me and drag me along with it.

'Ten? Everything else is five,' the fisherman grumbled.

'Fifteen. This price only goes up.'

'Fine. Ten.' The man reached into his pockets.

Closing my eyes, I braced myself for whatever was to come. A part of me wanted to say goodbye. And another, more desperate part never wanted to speak those words.

'That's enough,' Haider huffed behind me, and there was the twinkling sound again, pappi spinning on the wishing flower. But the sound didn't come from the fisherman's direction.

I opened my eyes.

Blair took another drag and waved at the man, refusing his money. 'I'm afraid it is gone.'

Gone? I didn't dare take a breath. I didn't dare hope.

'What?! He's right there!' The man snapped.

Blair signalled for the crew to start packing.

'That's ten gold off your wages,' Jamie scolded Haider as I turned around. In his hand spun the copper flower. A seed lifted.

My heart wanted to sink and leap at the same time.

Haider clutched his chest, gritting his teeth as he bent forwards. 'Damn it.'

It only hurt a little that he didn't listen to me. 'I asked you not to–'

'And I didn't. It wasn't for me,' he said, rubbing his chest. 'I got it for—ouch, Jamie! How long does this take?!'

'A minute or two.' She grinned, holding her open

palm underneath the twirling umbrella. Haider grabbed her shoulder.

Radiating a golden glow, the seed grew and morphed into something I knew of but had never seen: iron plates of armour, with its clasps now open, in the shape of a human heart.

Glow faded, it fell into Jamie's hand. 'Gross.' She tossed it into the crate with the rest of the artefacts. 'You still owe us two years.'

Haider nodded.

I sprung from the stool.

'Careful now…' He looked at me, raising his hand between us to stop me.

I wanted to cry. 'Who did you get it for..?'

'You.' He gave me a pained smile. 'It was the only right way.'

The chain warmed around my neck. Opening the locket, I watched the words melt away and the chain and locket sparkle into dandelion seeds, swept away by the wind.

I was free.

'I don't know how it works.' Haider straightened

up, one hand still on his heart. 'But I hope you'll find your happy ending. However long it takes, and wherever you decide to take it.'

Looking at him, risking his heart for my happiness and not asking for anything in return, I did not wish to take it too far.

For the first time in a while, I was deciding my fate.

I turned to Blair. 'Captain, I believe you could use a surgeon on board?'

Whether there were second servings of happily ever afters, I didn't know. But I wanted to give it my all, until we too were mist over the waters.

Until all our dreams found their place in the world.

In the profound silence of the caves, he'd observed the tapestry of a man's life unfurl and fray, and get sown back together. He understood all too well the depths of desperation one must reach to swap their love, their future joy, for an altered reality.

Yet amid the storm of emotions, Raama had felt a flicker of hope. Haider had found a loophole, a wish that had unchained Cillian. If Cillian could escape his bonds, maybe there was a chance for Aanee, a way to rewind time and right the wrongs that had been done.

"I will not forget you." His words had reverberated around the caves, fading as the orb drifted out of sight. Raama was alone once more.

As he cast off his sorrow, he searched for the next vision to study, but the cavern remained empty. He let out a sigh, stretching his weary bones, and set out on foot. There was no specific direction in mind, but walking allowed him the time to gather his thoughts. What had he truly learned? What did he need? Raama found himself no closer to unraveling this mystery than he was the day before. How long had he wandered through these caves? He couldn't even recall the last time he felt hungry.

Before long, another orb greeted him—in it a majestic black bird.

Part Four

Ravens Descent
By Beth Connor

As dawn broke, the first rays of the sun touched upon a solitary figure advancing towards the makeshift village. Lena had felt the absence of her beloved for an agonizing stretch of months, and now she could barely contain her excitment. Poised on the outskirts of the village, her heart pounded a relentless rhythm of anticipation. She was determined to be the first to greet Mira's long-awaited return.

Lena's eyes locked onto Mira's silhouette. The woman moved forward with purpose, a traveling cloak flowing around her. Her face, a map of hardships, peeked from beneath her hood, and a satchel, heavy with the fruits of her labor, swung at her side.

As Mira approached, Lena broke into a run, arms outstretched and they fell into a joyful hug. Soon the other villagers would come rushing to hear about Mira's scouting mission, but this moment was theirs alone.

"It feels like forever," Mira said softly.

"Six turns of the moon are forever when we are apart," Lena smiled. "I've missed you. How was the journey? Did you find anything useful?" She released her embrace, keenly aware of the prying eyes around them.

Mira nodded, looking at the damaged buildings. "It was tough, but I found fruit, medicinal herbs, and some other useful things." Her expression turned serious as she studied the weary faces that approached. "I worry about how much longer we can hold on. The storms are getting worse, and the land barely supports us."

Their eyes met. "We'll find a way. We always do." Lena smiled faintly. "So, I was thinking… tonight, let's meet at our spot. I've read the winds, and the weather should be okay. It'll be a refuge, if only for a while."

Mira's lips turned up into a small smile. "I'd love that, Lena. I'll leave after night falls."

A tall, older man with a weathered face and a

graying beard approached, giving Lena a slight nod. "Windreader," he greeted. Then, he turned to Mira, "Welcome back, Wanderer. I trust your journey was successful?"

"Yes, Elder Kashan. The population of many of our trading partners is dwindling, but I procured enough healing herbs for us. I did discover a new settlement in the northeast. They are healthy and robust, but their elder has not yet reached the age of nine and twenty. People are dying."

Elder Kashan frowned and shook his head, then gazed at the clouds. "Perhaps the air dwellers have had it right all the time. Maybe it's time to strike a bargain. I always believed we could heal our lands–"

"No! They exploit us." Mira replied. "They steal our resources so they can live in luxury. You give in to them, and we will become another slave city like the ones in the South."

"But, at least we will be alive," he replied, then turned to Lena. "What do the winds tell you, Windreader? Will we survive another season?"

Lena shifted uncomfortably under the Elder's stare. "Time grows short, but the winds still tell me we can heal."

"Then we hold on a little longer." Elder Kashan turned to Mira, "We will discuss the new settlement at the village meeting."

"Yes, Elder." Mira bowed as the elder turned and disappeared into the crowd.

"They have matched me," Lena whispered, her eyes turned down. "Haventown has a man who reads the winds, and their elder, along with Kashan, believe our children will inherit the gift."

"No." Mira whispered, then covered her mouth. "Why would Kashan get rid of our only Windreader. We can't survive without you. I can't survive without you, Lena."

"They have an engine. Elder Kashan thinks we can make an airship—"

A thin woman walking nearby turned her head toward them at the mention of an airship, and Lena quickly shut her mouth before continuing. "Later. I'll speak more of it later."

Mira just nodded and continued to stroll through the village silently, her hand so close but not touching. Before long, a young child dashed across the dirt road, eyes wide and excited. "Lena!" the child panted. "Will you tell my fortune, please?"

"Of course, little one." Lena smiled at the interruption. "Let's find a quiet place, and I'll read the winds for you."

Eyes twinkling, Mira mouthed, "I'll see you tonight." Lena nodded before attending to the eager child.

Under cover of dark, Lena slipped out of her family home, moving stealthily and mindful not to disturb the others. She moved with the grace of a seasoned cat, every step calculated to avoid the familiar groans and creaks of the old wooden floor.

Outside, clouds and smog shrouded the landscape in darkness, the desolate surroundings barely visible. Pockets of acidic soil lay exposed, stripped of vegetation, emitting a pungent odor that made her nose scrunch. She navigated around them and tried not to disturb the ground as her footsteps crunched in the eerie silence of the barren landscape.

Lena shuddered as she passed the skeletal remains of trees, feeling their dead eyes watch her every move. The twisted branches stood like sentinels, reaching to the dark sky like gnarled fingers, reminders of The Desolation's destruction.

As she continued, Mira emerged from the shadows, falling into step and walking next to Lena in perfect harmony. Once they had put enough distance between themselves and the settlement, Mira reached for Lena. Their fingers brushed before entwining in a tender embrace. Sharing a lingering kiss, love flared like a spark in the darkness. Hand in hand, they made their way to the secret hideaway.

Arriving at the sanctuary, Mira paused and her eyes darted around, taking in the familiar features and rocky outcroppings. Lena watched her, sensing the unease and stepping closer to Mira. The wind, which usually whispered through the branches, had fallen silent.

The silence held its secrets close, causing Lena's heart to drum a wild rhythm against her ribs as she followed Mira through the underbrush. When they finally pushed past the last barrier, the sight that met her eyes left her breathless.

There, cradled by the roughened embrace of the boulders, lay an enormous airship. It was a behemoth that seemed entirely alien against the backdrop of their scorched sanctuary. Its presence, a whispered apology, a silent plea for forgiveness to the earth it had marred.

The sight of the ship's great sails, fluttering like specters in the night, sent a shiver down Lena's spine. Their uncanny glow, an odd mixture of terror and beauty, cast a haunted aura over the disrupted glade, making her skin prickle.

Her gaze was drawn to the intricate apparatuses that decorated the sides. A dazzling array of brass and copper gears twinkled under the moonlight's soft orange glow. To Lena, they felt like stars fallen to the earth, embedded in the hull of this strange visitor.

An exquisite golden seagull perched at the bow, its sculpted wings forever frozen in mid-flight. Lena marveled at the artisan's skill. Every feather seemed alive, capturing the fluid grace of a bird in the air with stunning accuracy.

Standing before the ship, Lena couldn't help but feel a deep sense of loss for the world that once was. It was a world where birds soared through clear skies and nature thrived. The golden gull seemed to symbolize the vast divide between the wealthy and the struggling ground dwellers. It served as a poignant reminder of the beauty and diversity that had been all but wiped out in their existence.

Seagulls, as Lena had learned from her myriad of salvaged books, were once abundant creatures. Each description of their feathered forms, agile flight, and playful demeanor stirred a yearning within her. She imagined them as free spirits of the sky, with wings kissed by the salty sea breezes, and eyes reflecting the boundless blue expanse above. Yet, she had never seen one. The Desolation had swept them all away, along with so many other pieces of the world that used to be. The absence of these winged storytellers often haunted her dreams, their forms hovering just beyond reach. Her fascination with these long-gone birds filled her with a longing. It was an unfulfilled desire to witness the lively dance in the sky, a dance now resigned to the confines of her imagination and the faded words in her books.

Lena reached up to touch the owl feather she had worn since childhood, her fingers brushing against it, stirring the memory of her mother. The feather had been a gift when her family first discovered her ability to read the winds.

"I forgot!" Lena exclaimed. "I found this while you were gone." She reached into her satchel, retrieved a single black plume, and held it to Mira. "It's a raven's feather."

Mira's eyes widened with joy as she took the feather from Lena. "It's beautiful," she whispered, tracing the delicate barbs with her fingertips.

"Ravens symbolize transformation, intelligence, and mystery. They're also said to be messengers between the worlds."

A slow smile spread across Mira's face. Carefully, she tucked the raven's feather into her hair and brushed her lips against Lena's. At the tender contact, Lena felt a quick, breathless rush of exhilaration, then turned her attention back to the ship.

Despite her awe, she couldn't help but feel a sense of foreboding. She knew the potential such a vessel could hold for their community—it was large enough to house an entire village. However, she was also aware of the danger the previous owners could pose with their advanced weapons and disregard for the lives of those below.

They approached the ship, curiosity overcoming any initial apprehension. It loomed above them, the technology stark and foreign. Lena's eyes scanned every corner, trying to make sense of the unfamiliar design.

"I've seen the bottoms of airships sinking below the smog," Lena breathed. "But, this one feels different somehow."

Mira glanced at Lena, her eyes searching for reassurance. "What do the winds tell you? Is there any danger?"

Lena closed her eyes, reaching out with her senses to feel the subtle air currents around them. "The winds are quiet tonight," she replied, opening her eyes. "But we should still be cautious."

A plaintive howl abruptly shattered the night, leaving both women stunned and rooted to the spot. Time seemed to stand still as the cry reverberated through the desolate landscape.

"What was that?" Mira asked, her voice trembling.

"I don't know," Lena responded. "But we need to find out."

Driven by concern and curiosity, Lena followed the noise, her hand instinctively reaching for Mira's as they prepared to face the unknown.

As they neared the source, she came upon a sight that left her dumbfounded. A woman lay on the ground. Her porcelain-like skin and hair were as pale as the moonlight that bathed her. She appeared fragile and ethereal, as if she belonged to another world. Beside her, a tiny infant wailed, its cries echoing through the night.

The mother and child looked strikingly different from anyone they had ever encountered. In a world where dark skin and hair were the norm, this woman appeared almost otherworldly with her pale skin and hair.

"Is she… is she one of the air dwellers?" Mira whispered.

Lena nodded, her eyes locked on the woman's otherworldly features. "She must be."

"Do you think they all look like this?" Mira asked, unable to take her eyes off the woman. "She is beautiful."

"I don't know," Lena admitted. "But right now, we need to help her."

As Lena kneeled beside the dying woman, a whispering wind enveloped her. It carried a sense of intertwined destinies as if the stranger and her infant daughter were about to become inextricably linked with Lena's life. This unexpected encounter promised to alter their paths and shape their futures in ways that Lena couldn't have foreseen. And then, just as suddenly as it had arrived, the wind fell silent, leaving Lena to contemplate its message and wonder at the significance of what was to come.

The woman's ice-blue eyes flickered open, filled with fear and desperation.

"Please," her voice was weak and strained. "Help my daughter."

Lena picked up the wailing infant, cradling her in her arms, and the baby's cries softened.

"What's your name?" Mira asked the woman, her voice soothing.

But before the woman could respond, a shudder ran through her body. She was running out of time.

"Take her… home," she pleaded. "Promise me you'll take her back to her home, and her family."

"We will," Lena reassured her, feeling the weight of the promise settle. "We promise. But where is home?"

The woman attempted to speak, but her voice faltered and her eyes shut. With a final quivering breath, she lay motionless, her life snuffed out.

Lena hesitated for a moment, unsure of what to do next. She then cautiously reached out with her free hand, placing two fingers gently on the woman's neck, searching for a pulse. She could not detect even the faintest sign of a heartbeat. Lena leaned closer, placing her ear near the woman's mouth and nose to listen for breath sounds. Not a single hint of life remained. With a heavy heart, she accepted the grim reality—the woman was gone.

"I'm unfamiliar with the air dwellers' funeral customs," Lena remarked as she leaned over the body, cradling the baby with one arm. "May your spirit soar and find your way home in death."

"We can't bring her body with us," Mira stated, a hard edge to her voice. "The villagers care little for the air dwellers."

Lena nodded, understanding Mira's sentiment even if she didn't share it. Her gaze lingered on the deceased woman, a soft sadness filling her eyes. "She'll return to the earth, feed the life here, become part of the grand cycle," Lena murmured. "It's the most we can do, and hopefully, it will honor any deities she held dear."

Mira stayed silent at Lena's words, but her sharp nod conveyed her reluctant agreement. In this world, one couldn't afford to be picky about their allies, but Mira's disdain for the air dwellers was something Lena could never quite fathom.

As Lena cradled the sleeping infant, her mind was a whirlwind of questions. They found a few belongings -

an ornate comb, a tattered journal filled with an indecipherable script, and an unusual medallion. These things all seemed so personal, so tethered to a home, but where could that home be? The common lore suggested that air dwellers were nomadic, their ships serving as mobile abodes, never anchoring to one place for long.

"Could she have been referring to another airship?" Lena speculated, her gaze dropping to the tranquil face of the sleeping baby. "Where else would the air dwellers live?"

Mira could only respond with a shake of her head. "I'm not sure. Perhaps they have a land-based sanctuary we've never heard about?"

The mystery only deepened as they delved further into the ship. The lack of any other life was unnerving. Only the woman, the child, and their few belongings seemed to inhabit this large vessel. The strange silence and solitude were almost as if someone had tailored the ship for only the woman and her child. The thought struck Lena as odd. She clutched the baby closer, finding comfort in the child's rhythmic breathing amid the unsettling emptiness.

As they explored, Mira's brow furrowed. "How will we feed it? We have no nursing mothers at the moment.

We need to find something for her."

"When Aima was dry, we used the milk of a Saba nut," Lena suggested. "We'll figure it out, Mira. We always do."

Cradled in the strange stillness of the airship, the weight of their predicament pressed upon Lena. Bringing an infant, an air dweller's child, back to their community was a gamble. With resources already stretched thin, another mouth to feed was a burden they could ill afford. The resentment some of the ground dwellers held for the air dwellers could easily cause hostility towards the innocent babe.

"We can't let harm befall her, Mira," Lena declared a resolute glint in her eyes. "The villagers… they mustn't hurt her."

Mira, always pragmatic, suggested, "What if I claim her as my own? I was away long enough for a pregnancy to have been hidden. And since my return, no one has seen me without these loose robes."

Lena processed the idea. "It could work," she murmured. "But you'd risk Elder Kashan's wrath. Considering your beauty, he had high hopes of a beneficial match for you. Instead, you'd bring another mouth to feed. What if he banishes you?"

"He's family, Lena. He'll be angry, yes, but he'll come around eventually," Mira said with a shrug.

Lena bit her lip, her mind racing. "I can't let you bear all the consequences. We need a plan to make the villagers want to protect you and the baby, not bear grudges." She tightened her hold on the infant, the soft cooing noises from the child grounding her amidst her swirling thoughts.

An idea suddenly sparked in Lena's mind. "What if I claimed to have received a prophecy? I'll say that the wind whispered of the child's destiny, that she's our salvation, and the ship is a divine gift. I could even suggest she's destined to become a Windreader. It might even convince them to release me from my proposed match."

Mira nodded. "It just might work."

Lena looked at Mira. There was a certain comfort knowing that it had always been them against the world. A fleeting fantasy of taking the ship and escaping with Mira and the baby flashed through her mind, but reality soon intruded. The ship was far too massive for them to navigate alone. They would need a crew, and their village, their people, depended on them.

"But what about us?" Mira's voice wavered, her eyes filled with desperation. "I can't do this alone. I can't imagine life without you."

Lena reached out, her hand finding Mira's. "The prophecy will demand my presence to guide you and the child." she reassured. "Our hearts are bound, remember?"

Mira sighed, a hint of relief in her eyes. "You're right," she admitted. "If this plan works, we'll protect the child, and I won't lose you. We will find our moments, won't we?"

Lena squeezed Mira's hand. "We will do this together. Who knows, maybe after a time, we won't have to keep secrets anymore." She leaned in and kissed Mira gently. "You are my light. I love you."

"And you are the wind that keeps me afloat," Mira replied. "I love you too."

****

Standing at the edge of the village, Lena's heart pounded as they prepared to reveal their story to the gathered crowd. They approached the waiting ground dwellers.

Taking a deep breath, Lena stepped forward. "My people, the winds have guided us to a hidden treasure in the depths of the wastes - an airship, a vessel from the skies. It has been waiting, a beacon of hope for our people to take and change our fate." The villagers listened, faces unreadable. "The winds have gifted us something extraordinary that can improve our lives. This infant, born of one of our own, carries with her a prophecy of hope."

An elder of the village, his eyes wide and almost reverent, addressed Lena. "What words did the wind whisper to you?" he asked, his voice hushed as though he were in a sacred place.

Lena held his gaze, her voice steady as she recited the fabricated prophecy. "The Raven's offspring will bring about our renewal. Her plunge into the unknown will plant the seeds of our rebirth."

A young woman piped up, curiosity gleaming in her eyes, "What's a raven?"

Patiently, Lena explained, "A raven is a bird, a symbol of transformation and rebirth. Mira, who carried the child of prophecy, embodies the Raven, and the baby is her offspring."

Another villager chimed in, "If Mira is the Raven, then who are you, Lena?"

With a serene smile, Lena answered, "I am but a

humble messenger of the future, but if you wish for a title, consider me the Owl. Owls are known for their wisdom and vigilance. I will guide us on this journey, and we will salvage our world together."

When a woman with keen eyes challenged Mira's sudden motherhood, Lena felt her heart skip. Yet, Mira stood firm, weaving an intricate tale of magical conception that seemed to placate the gathering.

Lena then turned her attention to the villagers. "We have named her Skye, symbolizing the hope we've found in the limitless expanse above us. We believe embracing the skies can save our people and our dying world."

An older woman squinted at the baby. "Why is her skin so pale? Like the underbelly of the clouds before The Desolation?"

Lena swiftly interjected, "The pale color is a sign. She is of the sky, touched by the wind and kissed by the clouds. It's a blessing, a mark of her destiny."

As a low hum of conversation spread through the villagers, Lena held her breath, her heart pounding. She could see the skepticism, the curiosity, the fear, and the hope mingling in their expressions. Their acceptance was crucial, not only for Skye's safety but also for their village's survival.

Mira took a step forward, her voice steady despite the tension. "We need help, willing hands and hearts to join us on this journey."

A few villagers broke away from the crowd and stepped forward, their expressions varying from determined to apprehensive. Lena scanned their faces, a small measure of relief washing over her. Their first allies in this enormous endeavor.

She met Mira's eyes and gave a nod of approval. Mira returned it with a tight smile. Together, they turned their attention to their newly formed crew, a motley band of villagers bound by a shared prophecy and an uncertain future.

"Thank you," Lena addressed them, her voice firm but filled with gratitude. "Now, let's prepare ourselves. We have a long journey ahead."

The crew bustled around the ship, readying it for their journey, amazed at how effortlessly the vessel responded to their touch. It felt like the ship guided their hands, making the complex controls and mechanisms seem intuitive.

"I never thought it would be this easy," a large man said. "It's like it wants us to succeed."

"It must be a sign that the prophecy is true," another replied, conviction in his tone.

As they busied themselves with their tasks, a young boy, only ten years old, approached the ship with resolve in his eyes. "I want to join," he declared, his dark skin and hardened features telling the story of his life as a ground dweller. "I can help."

Mira paused in her work and looked at the boy. He seemed so young, but a fierceness in his eyes spoke of hardships beyond his years. "Where are your parents?" she asked.

The boy's eyes clouded, and he whispered, "They're dead."

Feeling a pang of sympathy, Mira continued, "What's your name?"

"Derick," he answered.

Lena stood near the infant in her arms, and couldn't help but feel pride in her friend's compassion. Mira softened her expression and said, "Alright, Derick.

You can be our cabin boy. I'll teach you everything you need to know."

As Mira reached out to take Derick's hand, Skye began to cry. Without hesitation, Derick reached out and gently stroked Skye's cheek. The baby's cries subsided almost immediately.

Surprised, Mira asked, "How did you know how to do that?"

Derick looked at her and said, "I had younger siblings, but they're all gone now, too."

As they readied for their voyage, Mira directed the crew with confidence. "We need to find space for everyone to take cover and sleep. Let's get to it!"

"Lena," she said, gesturing toward a private cabin nearby, "this will be your space for you and Skye."

With a nod, Lena accepted the responsibility of caring for the baby.

Working alongside the crew, Mira was a beacon of energy, her instructions ringing out clear and commanding. Lena was drawn to the rapidly darkening sky, her gaze fixed on the thickening layers of clouds. It was a sight she knew all too well, a herald of an impending storm.

"What's troubling you?" Mira asked, her voice cutting through Lena's thoughts.

"The clouds are gathering," Lena voiced concern, her eyes never leaving the ominous spectacle. "A storm is on its way, Mira, and it will be fierce."

Mira weighed their options. "Could we possibly take to the air to avoid it?"

Lena shook her head, a knot of worry tightening in her stomach. "The ship isn't flight-ready yet."

With their flight option out of the question, Mira swiftly shifted gears. "Alright, we'll have to weather it here on the ground. Everyone, secure everything you can and find cover!"

Lena watched as the crew sprung into action at Mira's directive, their movements a blur of quick and purposeful activity. Mira stood out as a natural leader, and the crew accepted her authority without question. Lena had easily slipped into the group's caretaker and advisor role. The prophecy that bound them may have been false, but the unity it created was real, and together, they braced for the storm.

As day transitioned into night, dark clouds grew on the horizon. The atmosphere was heavy with impending danger, and the crew knew how vicious the caustic rain could be.

Hushed voices murmured. "These ships were never meant to face the acid rain. They have always flown above the clouds."

"We're not ready to launch yet," Mira reminded them, standing tall. "If we launch early, and the engines fail, our fate will be darker than losing the ship. We will wait it out."

As the storm raged, each crew member retreated to refuge below deck. Meanwhile, shrouded in the cover of darkness, Lena, with baby Skye cradled carefully in her arms, ventured to Mira's cabin.

Once inside, Lena placed Skye in a small basket, her tiny body swaddled in a soft cloth. The infant's skin was as pale as her birth mother's, starkly contrasting the darkness outside. Her eyes were wide and innocent, shimmering like the surface of a moonlit lake.

Lena felt Mira's fingertips searching for hers, a touch as gentle as a feather's caress. Their hands wove together, fingers intertwined like vines climbing toward the sun. They found one another without ever having to look. And yet, when their eyes met, an invisible tether anchored them into a world only the other could encounter.

A kiss with any other would not suspend time or allow the world to melt away. As their connection deepened, Lena could feel their bodies merging into a dance of impassioned give-and-take. It was an exchange of exploring touches and vulnerable glances that stripped them down to their cores. Their bond was a haven of promise and hope in a world filled with darkness and despair. Two hearts beating in unison as they lay entwined in each other's arms, enjoying.

As they lay next to each other in the enormous bed, listening to the storm rage on, Lena's gaze wandered. Taking in the details of the cabin, she couldn't help but notice a small, inconspicuous compartment built into the wall. Intrigued, she carefully untangled herself from Mira's embrace and moved closer to inspect the hidden nook.

Mira joined her, curiosity piqued by the mysterious compartment. Lena opened it, revealing a dusty, antique-looking pendant. Someone had beautifully crafted it to feature three spirals interlocking in an elaborate design. Lena picked it up, marveling at its craftsmanship, then handed it to Mira.

As Mira scrutinized the pendant, Lena's gaze went to a well-worn logbook nestled within the compartment. She drew it out, flipping through the brittle pages lined with neat handwriting. Unlike the journal they had found on the strange woman, this script was legible. It was filled with echoing tales of forgotten voyages and hidden adventures.

Sitting shoulder to shoulder, Lena shared her discovery with Mira, her voice a soft whisper in the quiet cabin. "Look at this," she urged, pointing to the script. Mira's gaze shifted from the pendant to the logbook.

"It speaks of a land called Isdralan," Lena whispered. "The writer mentions an expedition, leaving this mysterious place to explore the unknown, and the ship is called The Golden Gull."

Mira leaned in, her fingers tracing the names of the crew and the ship's manifest listed in the journal. "These words, this language… It is foreign, and yet I understand it. What do you think it means?"

"Listen to this," Lena read aloud. "'To reach Isdralan, one must travel through the folds of reality itself, moving between worlds as effortlessly as a fish swims through water.' It's so strange."

Mira scanned the names of the crew. "Do you

think one of these people in the stories could have been Skye's mother?"

"It's possible," Lena mused.

"What if we could take our village to one of these places?" Mira wondered aloud, her gaze distant. "Places untouched by The Desolation, filled with the beauty these pages describe."

Lena paused, looking at Mira. "Mira, even if such a thing were possible," she began, her tone cautious, "I wouldn't even know where to start. This…this is beyond anything we've ever encountered. And even if we could, there's no way we could transport the entire world."

Mira's eyes met Lena's, a spark of defiance in her gaze. "We don't need to take the entire world, Lena," she countered. "Just our village, our people. Maybe, just maybe, there's hope in these stories. A chance for a new beginning."

Taking a moment to digest Mira's words, Lena breathed. The idea was enticing, yet it felt like a step to far, if it meant leaving the rest of the world to decay. She offered Mira a small, wistful smile. "That would be something, wouldn't it?" she said, her voice soft. "But for now, let's focus on understanding," she gestured towards the logbook and pendant, "before we start dreaming of transporting our village across time and space."

With a wistful breath, Mira pulled the pendant to her neck, but Lena stopped her. "We should give this to Skye when she's older. It might be important to her."

Mira reluctantly agreed, putting the jewel down with a tinge of resentment in her eyes.. The air between them changed, a faint ripple of discord marring their usually harmonious companionship. Lena, sensitive to this shift, felt a twinge of unease.

She couldn't forget their pledge - their vow to get baby Skye home. The pendant, laden with secrets and potential, ultimately belonged to Skye. It wasn't for them to use, regardless of the allure of the possibilities it presented. This unspoken divergence of their desires, the first of its kind, hung in the air like a ghost. It was subtle but potent, a small crack in their unified front.

Before either of them could address this new undercurrent, a knock echoed through the cabin, slicing through the silence. Their heads turned towards the noise. The women scrambled to dress and separate themselves within the room. Mira opened the door to find Derick standing in the doorway, his cheeks red with excitement.

"What is it, Derick?" Mira asked, face flushed as

she tried to maintain her composure.

Derick's eyes sparkled, and he bounced on the balls of his feet. "M'lady, the ship is unharmed! Not a scratch on it! It's as if magic! protected it." His eyes were worshipful as they darted between Mira and Lena, awed by the miracle he believed they had brought forth.

As the departure approached, the ground dwellers gathered around the airship, their faces a mixture of hope and apprehension.

"Do you think this will work?" Mira asked.

"I don't know," Lena admitted, her gaze drifting over the desolate landscape surrounding them. The once-fertile land was now barren, the soil tainted by an invisible force, and the ground dwellers' shelters crumbled. "But we have to try. For them, and we promised to get Skye home."

The crew members returned from their farewells, taking their positions onboard. Holding Skye in her arms, Lena watched as Mira gathered the crew.

"Listen up, everyone," Mira began, her voice strong.

"We are about to embark on an incredible journey, facing challenges and dangers we've never seen before. But we have a purpose; together, we will fulfill the prophecy and change the world. I trust all of you to give your best and stand united as a crew. Now, let's prepare the Golden Gull for lift-off!"

Spurred on by Mira's words, the crew members set to work, maneuvering an intricate network of levers and pulleys with determination. As they had toiled over the ship's repairs, there was an undeniable sense of synergy, as if the vessel wanted them there and willingly revealed its secrets. They had no manuals or instructions to guide their efforts, yet an inexplicable understanding dawned on them. It was as though the ship spoke to them, not in words but in feelings, in impulses that led them to the correct levers and guided their hands over the right gears.

Mechanisms clicked into place seemingly of their own accord, gears meshed as if under a guiding hand, and the entire ship responded as though recognizing its crew. It was an enchanting orchestration of man and machine, a harmonious dance between the crew and the ship, directed by some unseen maestro.

And so, as they set sail, Mira and her crew operated the ship like had been born to it, their movements smooth and coordinated. The ancient magic words Lena whispered seemed to stir energy within the ship, a hum vibrating under their feet. It was as though they had been sailing across the skies forever. The lines between the ship and the crew blurred, making them one on a shared journey.

They rose, great sails unfurling and catching the breeze. The ground dwellers looked on in awe, their hope blossoming as the golden gull figurehead sparkled, seeming to come alive as the ship took flight.

As it climbed higher, the ground dwellers' cheers filled the air, their voices carrying the names of their saviors: "The Owl and the Raven! The Owl and the Raven!"

Lena couldn't help but feel uneasy at the adoration, but she knew their journey had only just begun. They had a long road ahead of them, and the fate of their people rested on their shoulders.

"What's our next move?" Mira asked Lena, ensuring the rest of the crew wouldn't overhear their conversation.

"We need to find an air dweller ship," Lena suggested. "If we can convince them to help those living on the surface, maybe we all work together and heal our land."

Mira hesitated. "But will the air dwellers accept us?"

"I don't know," Lena sighed. "But I think it's our best chance."

They rose above the thick layer of clouds that separated the world of the ground dwellers from that of the air dwellers. The sky the clouds seemed more vibrant, an expanse of brilliant blue that stretched forever. Above, the air was clean, contrasting with the polluted atmosphere they had left behind.

The crew marveled at the world's beauty above the clouds, their eyes wide with wonder. Yet, amidst the awe, there was also a sense of guilt. They knew they had left their people to suffer in the desolation below, and the burden of responsibility weighed upon them.

After traveling for a few days, Mira spotted another ship in the distance. "Look over there!" she exclaimed, pointing towards the vessel.

"Another ship." Lena remarked.

Mira nodded. "Our first encounter with an air dweller."

To their relief, the other ship hailed them with a friendly tone, inviting them to come aboard. The two vessels neared each other, and the air dweller ship extended a series of mechanical clamps, which locked onto the Golden Gull with a satisfying clunk. With the ships tethered, a grand sky bridge extended between them, a marvel of engineering that defied the laws of gravity.

Lena turned to Derick. "Can you watch baby Skye while we go to the other ship?"

"Of course, Lena," Derick replied. "I've taken care of my younger siblings before. Skye will be safe with me."

With that assurance, Mira and Lena prepared to cross the sky bridge while the crew manned their posts. As they crossed, Mira said, "I never thought we'd encounter another ship so soon. Let's hope they're open to helping us."

Lena just nodded, her eyes filled with trepidation.

A bustling scene filled with life, and color greeted them. The captain, a robust man with curling dark mustaches, strode forward, arms spread in greeting. His eyes twinkled with a friendly, inviting warmth that seemed to defy his imposing stature.

The people aboard the ship resembled the ground dwellers, though their complexions were healthier. Lena and Mira exchanged glances, whispering in hushed tones, "Maybe Skye's people weren't air dwellers after all."

"Welcome aboard the Skyward Seraph, my dear guests," the captain announced, his voice booming with authority and charm. "I am Captain Barnabas Hawthorne, and it is an honor to have you join us."

Nearby, a group of women dressed in luxurious gowns tittered behind gloved hands, their eyes flicking over Lena and Mira's modest attire. Mira shifted uncomfortably under their judgmental gazes, her cheeks flushing with embarrassment.

Ignoring the women, Lena stepped forward to introduce herself and Mira. "Thank you for your kind welcome, Captain Hawthorne," Lena said, her voice steady and confident. "My name is Lena Davies, and this is my companion, Captain Mira Talbot."

Captain Hawthorne ran his eyes over them and extended a hand, his grip firm and warm. "A pleasure to meet you both, Lena and Mira. I trust you'll find our ship and crew most accommodating."

Mira nodded, her discomfort abating. "Thank you, Captain. We are grateful for your hospitality and hope our two crews can work together to better our world."

Captain Hawthorne furrowed his brow in confusion. "Better of our world?" he echoed, but then seemed to dismiss the thought, his gaze lingering on Mira with a hungry intensity. "Nevertheless, I would be delighted to invite you both to my quarters for a meal and to discuss potential alliances."

Lena noticed a slight change in Mira's stance, a subtle straightening of her back as if steeling herself against an unseen force. Lena followed Mira's gaze to find the Captain's intense stare fixed on her.

Mira drew a deep breath, the rise and fall of her chest barely visible. Lena could almost feel the weight of that gaze, a tangible pressure that Mira was clearly trying to bear with grace.

"We appreciate your invitation, Captain," Mira finally said, her voice steady despite the palpable tension. "We're eager to discuss how our people might work together." Lena admired Mira's composure, and her ability to articulate their intentions under such scrutiny.

As Captain Hawthorne gestured for them to follow him, Lena couldn't help but notice the jealous and angry glances from the nearby women. These finely dressed ladies, with their delicate features and upturned noses, seemed to resent the attention that the two newcomers were receiving from the Captain.

Leading the way through the ornate corridors of the Skyward Seraph, Captain Hawthorne guided Lena and Mira toward his quarters.

Stepping into the captain's quarters, Lena was immediately taken aback by the ostentatious display of wealth. Opulence poured from every corner, an overwhelming testament to the affluence of the air dwellers.

Rich tapestries, woven with a precision that made each scene palpably alive, adorned the walls. They told tales of air dweller history and mythology, a visual narrative threaded with golden hues. Lena found herself drawn to these intricate illustrations, her eyes following the rise and fall of the woven threads. Each tapestry depicted the air dwellers rising from the ashes of The Desolation. First the rebuilding, and then soaring above the earthbound citizens. The scenes culminated with the air dwellers, wreathed in clouds and sunbeams, looming like deities over the ground dwellers.

Sumptuous fabrics of velvet and silk, boasting intricate patterns, draped elegantly over the furniture. A massive table of polished wood, its surface reflecting the room like a mirror, commanded the room. Chairs surrounded it, carved from the same material.

As Lena took in the extravagant room with a mix of curiosity and distaste. Mira's eyes flicked over the tapestries, her face hardening at the arrogant depiction of air dwellers as gods over their ground-dwelling kin. The display clearly disgusted her, a sentiment Lena could understand. The imagery, though magnificent in craftsmanship, was a stark reminder of the divide between their two peoples.

Captain Hawthorne pulled out a chair for each of them, gesturing for them to be seated. As they settled into the plush cushions, he inquired about their ship. "Tell me about your vessel, ladies. It's not a design I've seen before."

The captain's sudden question seemed to catch Mira off-guard.

"We–" She stammered. Lena, sensing the precariousness of the situation, intervened.

"It has been handed down through the generations, from before The Desolation." Lena locked eyes with the captain, her gaze steady and unflinching. She could feel the weight of his scrutiny, yet she held his stare, her expression an inscrutable mask.

Her words hung in the air, a statement that brooked no argument, determination silently challenging him to question their claim. This was their ship, their heritage, and she would let no one cast doubt upon that truth. Mira blushed and looked away, embarrassed by her near slip. Lena could feel the danger that lurked beneath the surface of this unfamiliar world, and knew they would need to tread carefully.

Their conversation flowed on, meandering through various topics, from the mundane aspects of life to the depths of philosophy. Lena found herself captivated by the myriad curiosities that filled the captain's quarters.

Rising from her seat, she explored the room, drawn in by the wealth of knowledge and artistry displayed around her. The room seemed to be a microcosm of air dweller culture, each object a piece of a larger narrative. Her fingers traced the spines of the books neatly arranged on the shelves, their titles whispering tales of science, history, and literature.

Her gaze fell upon a particular tome, its worn cover suggesting a wealth of history within its pages. She picked it up, the weight of it reassuring in her hands.

"Mira, look at this!" Lena called out, her attention fascinated by tome in her hands.

Meanwhile, Captain Hawthorne had subtly closed the distance between himself and Mira. His hand came to rest on her thigh, a predatory glint in his eyes betraying his intentions. "Our ship is powerful, you know," he murmured, his voice low and insinuating. "You and your people would do well to have our protection."

Mira stiffened, her discomfort clear as she attempted to shift away from his touch. However, the captain's hand only slid further up her thigh in response, effectively trapping her in place.

"Captain Hawthorne," Lena interjected, her voice sharp enough to slice through the heavy tension in the room. "I think it's time for us to leave. We have much to discuss with our crew."

The captain smirked, a predatory gleam in his eyes as he shifted his gaze between Lena and Mira. "Oh, I think there's plenty we can discuss right here, my dear," he insinuated, his hand still resting on Mira's thigh.

With swift determination, Lena crossed the room, gripped Mira's arm, and pulled her away from the captain's grasp. "We appreciate your hospitality, Captain, but we must be going. Our people are counting on us."

Captain Hawthorne's face soured. He was clearly not accustomed to being denied. "Very well," he conceded, his voice edged with frost. "But remember, ladies, the world can be dangerous, and you may need my protection one day." His threat hung in the air, a lingering reminder of the power he wielded.

With Mira by her side, Lena led the way out of the captain's quarters, both women breathing a sigh of relief as they returned to their ship.

Lena, clutching baby Skye close, headed to the cabin where Mira was waiting. Her friend stood rigidly, her usually vibrant complexion washed out, and her eyes wide with a terror Lena had never seen before.

Mira's tremors, initially subtle, grew more pronounced, eventually evolving into a quaking rage. Her fists clenched tightly, the veins in her hand standing out in stark relief. "I won't seek the help of the air dwellers," she declared, her voice trembling with barely restrained fury. "I'll destroy them."

Lena watched in helpless silence, the sight of her friend's anguish clawing at her heart. But she knew she had to remain steady, for both their sakes. Her voice, soft yet firm, broke through Mira's seething anger. "Mira, not all of them are like Captain Hawthorne. We can't condemn them all because of one man's actions."

Before Mira could plan a response, a knock on the door interrupted them. Derick stepped into the room, a tray of food in his hands. "Here's your meal, Mira," he said, placing it on the table.

Mira's gaze, previously a storm of emotion, hardened. "I am the Raven, and you shall address me as such."

Derick recoiled, fear flickering in his eyes as he hastily retreated from the room. "Yes M– Raven"

Lena turned to Mira, her brow creased with worry. "Was that really necessary?"

The wrath on Mira's face evaporated, leaving her looking drained and vulnerable. She slumped onto the floor, a fresh wave of tears washing over her. Lena swiftly moved to her side, wrapping her arms around her love. "Mira," she murmured, her voice barely above a whisper, "I know you're angry, and you have every right to be. But we can't let one terrible encounter derail our entire mission."

Sniffing, Mira swiped at her tear-streaked cheeks. "I know, Lena. It's just… I didn't expect it to be like this."

Lena nodded, her hold on Mira tightening. "We knew there'd be challenges, Mira. But we can't let this change who we are or what we stand for."

Mira let out a weary sigh, her anger gradually giving way to resignation.

Lena paused, letting Mira compose herself, then spoke in a soft voice. "We can't let our mistrust of one person cloud our judgment of an entire group. There must be air dwellers who want to help, who share our vision."

"Maybe." Mira's expression hardened once again. "But we'll find them on our own terms, not through the likes of Captain Hawthorne."

Lena sighed, feeling the chasm widening between them. "We'll find another way. But need to remember we're in this together."

"Of course. You're right."

With tenderness, Lena leaned in, pressing her lips

to Mira's forehead in a soft kiss. Her voice was barely a whisper. "You are my light, Mira. I love you."

But the words echoed in the room, met only by silence.

The crew soon encountered another air-dwelling ship on the horizon as the Golden Gull continued its journey. The vessels approached each other, both crews unsure of what to expect.

A tall, imposing figure emerged on the deck of the other ship. His steel-blue eyes seemed to pierce through the air as he surveyed Mira and Lena. His neatly trimmed beard was flecked with gray, giving him an air of authority and experience.

"Welcome," he said flatly, his voice devoid of warmth. "I am Captain Eldridge. What brings you to our ship?" The captain's demeanor was as cold as his eyes.

Mira took a deep breath, steeling herself for the conversation. "I am Mira, and this is Lena. We come with the purpose of healing the world for the ground dwellers and everyone. We believe it is possible to restore the land and bring peace and prosperity to all."

Lena added, "And we were also wondering if you've ever heard of a place called Isdralan?"

Captain Eldridge's eyebrows rose, and a bitter smile spread across his face. "Heal the world? Amusing. But we have no resources to spare," he said, rubbing his gemstone rings. "The ground dwellers have their place, and we have ours. I have never heard of a land called Isdralan"

Lena's face flushed with frustration, but she tried to remain diplomatic. "We understand your skepticism, Captain, but we are certain others share our vision. Perhaps you could help us by pointing us in the right direction?"

Captain Eldridge scoffed, his icy gaze unwavering. "I have more important matters to attend to. I wish you the best of luck on your fanciful quest."

With a dismissive wave, Captain Eldridge turned and disappeared below deck. As the two ships unclamped and drifted apart, Lena looked at Mira, trying to gauge her reaction.

Mira's expression fell, and her voice trembled. "I'm not sure how many more rejections I can handle."

***

Lena stood at the door of Mira's cabin, the weight of their recent failures and the tension between them hanging in the air. She reached out, touching Mira's shoulder, trying to comfort her.

"Mira, I know things have been difficult, but we can't give up hope. We'll find a way," Lena murmured.

Mira's eyes remained fixed on the floor, her voice was distant. "Hope doesn't seem to get us very far, does it?"

The air grew heavy as Lena swallowed the bitter shards of Mira's words. "Mira," she said, her voice steady, "we've weathered storms far greater than this. These trials aren't roadblocks, but stepping stones. We just need to keep our vision steady. Remember when the crops first failed? It was you that discovered the root vegetables from the south were able to flourish still? We made it through that, didn't we? This is no different."

Mira turned to face Lena, her eyes smoldering with an anger that darkened their once shared dreams. "It's time we faced the storm, and use the Golden Gull to make the other ships quake in fear. They need to hear our voices, even if it's through battle cries."

The words crashed into Lena like a wave. "We are not raiders. We can't drench our hands in blood and expect to wash them clean. That path only leads to more devastation."

But Mira's resolve was a fortress, her voice a hailstorm, thrumming with a barely contained fury. "So what's your plan? Continue our pleas, let our voices fade into the wind while our people crumble? We need to act!"

Lena stood her ground, her voice a beacon amidst the growing storm. "We mustn't become what we fight against, Mira. There's always another path, a way that doesn't cost us our soul. We'll find it, together. But we can't lose who we are."

The silence that followed was a chasm, a void that seemed to yawn wider with every passing second. The once unbreakable bond between them was fraying, unraveling under the tension of their clashing views.

Mira stood at the helm of the Golden Gull, her eyes narrowing as she spotted another air dweller ship in the distance. Her grip tightened on the wheel, her knuckles turning white from the pressure.

"Lena, take Skye and go to your cabin. Now," She barked, not bothering to look at them. The coldness in her voice sent shivers down their spines. Lena hesitated, clenching her fists.

"Mira, I understand you're angry, but I can help. I'm a better negotiator than you are. Let me handle this," Lena implored, trying to reason with Mira.

Mira whipped around to face Lena, her eyes burning with fury. "I don't need your help. I can handle this on my own. Now, take Skye and go!" she snarled, her voice leaving no room for argument.

Lena clutched Skye close, trembling, and retreated to the stairs. From there, she observed with a lump forming in her throat. She hoped Mira's anger wouldn't consume her, that the storm of rage would pass without leaving irreversible damage in its wake.

As the two ships drew closer, it became apparent that the air-dweller ship had hostile intentions. Mira's anger boiled over, her eyes blazing with rage. "Prepare for battle!" she shouted to the crew. "We'll show them what we're made of!"

From her precarious perch on the stairs, Lena

watched as the crew engaged in fierce combat, their determination sparked by Mira's furious energy. Every clash of steel and grunt of exertion sent her heart hammering against her ribs, the taste of fear sharp on her tongue. Against all odds, they repelled the attack and emerged victorious. The captain of the attacking ship, finally acknowledging his disadvantage, raised the white flag in a gesture of surrender. As he requested a parley, Lena found herself pulling Skye close and clutching the railing tighter with her free hand, the cold bite of the wood grounding her.

Mira agreed to meet him on the sky bridge connecting the two ships, her every step fueled by seething fury. As the defeated captain approached Mira on the sky bridge, he extended a hand to negotiate.

Mira's expression was cold and unyielding, her voice dripping with venom. "You dare to attack us, and now you want to talk? You have no honor."

Before the captain could respond, Mira, full of rage, shoved him off the sky bridge. She watched silently as he plummeted through the clouds, his screams swallowed by the wind.

Turning back to the defeated ship, Mira ordered her crew to strip it of all its supplies and cast out its crew and their families. The Golden Gull had won the battle, but at what cost?

As the Gull sailed away, Lena confronted Mira. "What you did back there… it was too much, Mira. We can't let our anger control us."

But Mira's eyes were distant, her response cold. "They attacked us first. They deserved what they got."

The Golden Gull, like a bird returning to its nest, touched down on the familiar terrain of their settlement. Carefully stowed within its hold was the precious cargo, a wealth of supplies hard-won from their recent voyage. Crew members began to unload crates bursting with fresh foodstuffs, and rolls of vibrant cloth, their colors a feast to the weary eyes. As these treasures were brought to light, sparks of joy ignited in the eyes of their loved ones, the promise of comfort and sustenance rekindling hope in their hearts.

Lena positioned herself alongside Mira, their silhouettes blending in the fading daylight as they surveyed the unfolding scene. The relief and joy on their people's faces was indeed infectious, yet a gnawing unease simmered within Lena.

"This fleeting joy… it's a beautiful sight, Mira," Lena began, her voice low but intense. Her eyes remained fixed on the newly unloaded bounty, the vibrant cloth and the enticing aroma of fresh food doing little to mask the bitter taste of reality. "But we can't let it veil the truth."

She paused, a surge of frustration constricting her voice. "These supplies are a temporary relief. A soothing salve to wounds that run much deeper." Lena could feel her anger bubbling, not just at the immediate triumph but at the violent means employed to secure it. Her hand clenched involuntarily, nails biting into her palm as she grappled with her conflicted emotions.

Mira cast a sidelong glance at Lena, her face a mask devoid of emotion. "For today, it's enough. We'll do what it takes to keep them safe, to keep them provided for."

With a fervor that sent chills down Lena's spine, Mira rallied the villagers. They swarmed around the Golden Gull like a hive, transforming the once gentle ship into a formidable beast of war. The beautiful gold was replaced by a dark metal hull, shadowed by the inky void lurking in Mira's heart.

With each stroke of black paint on her eyes, Mira shed the last vestiges of her old self. She turned to the faces, now reflecting the same fierce resolve. "From this day on, I am the Raven. We will seize what we need from those in the skies and let them know we will not be silenced."

The villagers responded with a raucous cheer, rallying behind Mira, their spirits alight with the promise of a prosperous future.

Lena watched the transformation with a sinking heart. She moved towards Mira, her voice a whisper in the uproar. "Mira, are you certain this is the path we should tread? Isn't there a way less steeped in conflict, less drenched in blood?"

But Mira's eyes were icy mirrors, reflecting a resolve that seemed impervious to Lena's pleas. "The air dwellers have given us nothing but scorn. We will do whatever it takes."

Under the Raven's fierce command, their ship clashed and commandeered three more of the air dwellers' vessels. It looted their supplies and etched a notorious reputation in the lofty skyways. Now, docked at a different village of ground dwellers, the crew dispersed the spoils among the people who welcomed the bounty.

The villagers lavished praise on Mira and her crew. Chants of the Raven's prophecy echoed through the air, punctuated with the occasional mention of the Owl.

Standing tall amidst the sea of faces, the Raven, with her eyes painted a stark, defiant black, hoisted baby Skye up for all to witness. The crowd exploded into cheers, their roars rolling like thunder across the village. Raising her hand, she called for silence, and an expectant hush fell over the crowd, their eyes fixed on her with rapt attention.

"People of the land below," she proclaimed, her voice resonating with authority. "Today, we stand before you as evidence that the old tales and prophecies are more than mere folklore. We, the crew of The Raven, pledge ourselves to your cause—to fight for your right to a prosperous life, to a world where you are not forgotten."

She let her words hang in the air, permeating the silent crowd before continuing. "For far too long, the air dwellers have greedily hoarded their wealth, their resources, while you languish on this decaying land. They have dismissed your suffering, living their lives among the clouds, detached from your struggles. But this ends now!"

Mira's voice swelled, thrumming with fervor. "Together, we will rise against this injustice. We will reclaim what is rightfully yours, restoring balance to our world. The Raven will guide you to a future where the ground flourishes, the skies are free, and ground-dwellers prosper."

Lena, amidst the cheering crowd, felt a knot of unease tightening in her stomach. Yet, her love for Mira was undeniable, a pang in her heart formed as she watched the Raven's transformation. She was torn, caught between the urge to support her lover and the nagging doubts about their chosen path.

As the crowd's enthusiasm surged, Lena stood steadfastly by Mira's side. In that moment, she vowed to shield both Mira and the ground dwellers, willing to navigate the precarious path between love and duty.

The situation was spiraling out of control, and Lena felt a desperate need to intervene. Mira, or the Raven as she was now known, was slipping dangerously into the role of a ruthless marauder. Gathering her courage, Lena steeled herself for the confrontation to come. She held onto the belief that somewhere beneath the darkness, her beloved Mira still existed, and it was her duty to help her see the light.

As Lena neared Mira's cabin, she detected the sound of crying. Fear knotting her stomach, she knocked urgently, her voice filled with concern. "Mira? Are you okay?" Receiving no response, she hesitated, then slowly turned the knob and pushed the door open.

The sight that met Lena's eyes in the dim, flickering light of the cabin was as stunning as a blow to the gut. There, in the center of the room, Mira and a man from the village were entangled in an illicit embrace. His muscular arms wound around her waist, her fingers tracing the contour of his broad shoulders, their bodies intertwined. The man was handsome in a rugged sort of way, his sun-bronzed skin and chiseled features a stark contrast to Mira's soft curves.

Lena froze on the threshold, the shock rendering her mute. The picture before her clashed violently with the image of the woman she loved. The reality of Mira's transformation into the Raven, into someone capable of such actions, struck Lena with full force, leaving her reeling.

Mira, caught in the act, abruptly untangled herself from the man, pushing him away reluctantly. Her voice was as frosty as a winter's night, her words cutting through the tense silence of the cabin. "Leave us."

Her eyes, lined with the same black paint that marked her transformation into the Raven, glared at the man. The coldness in her gaze was a pronounced difference to the warmth that Lena had once known, a chilling testament to the depth of Mira's descent. Her voice, once soothing, now echoed with authority and an edge that made Lena shiver. The woman standing before her was a stranger, a ghost of the Mira she had once loved.

The man hastily collected his clothing and scurried out, his face a mask of shame. Mira crossed her arms covering her exposed breasts, her gaze evading Lena's stunned expression.

"Mira, what was that?" Lena stammered, her voice quivering.

Mira's reply was matter-of-fact. "It's a part of the village's tribute, Lena. They provide us with gifts as a token of gratitude for our support."

Lena's heart splintered, the weight of Mira's words

crushing her. The confrontation she had planned slipped away, drowned in the gulf between them. She studied Mira, her mind groping for the right words.

The love she harbored for Mira had irrevocably changed. Tears welled in her eyes, but she blinked them away, determined to hold herself together. As she watched Mira reapply the charcoal under her eyes, Lena was struck with a realization that things would not change. It would be up to her up to her to pick up the pieces when things came crashing down. And then there was Skye to consider.

A silent vow took root in Lena's heart, its echo filling the quiet cabin. She resolved to find Isdralan at any personal cost. She would guide Skye, an innocent soul ensnared in the tempest, towards her destined path.

Mira's descent into this form was irreversible, heralding a looming storm of transformation, promising chaos, but Lena would be there to pick up the pieces. For now, she would be a silent sentinel, her resolve a steady constant amidst the uncertainty. She understood that the intersection of love and duty was fast approaching a turning point.

Closing the cabin door behind her, a haunting cry pierced the quiet night, mirroring her inner turmoil. The sound was a spectral presence in the darkness, its sorrow echoing deep within her. Despite the imminent storm, Lena committed to confronting it head-on - for Skye, for Mira, and for the world that depended on them. In the face of the darkest nights, she believed in the certainty of dawn.

In the end, Lena held fast to her belief that the Owl, symbolizing wisdom, would ultimately triumph. Wisdom's light, love's strength, and the bravery of heart would dispel the enveloping darkness. Today might belong to the night, but tomorrow was a new day. Armed with this conviction, she stepped forward into the unknown, ready to face the future's challenges.

Raama watched as the world crumbled around these two women, so in love, trying to survive in a world split between sky and earth. What had seemed like a gift tore them apart. Who was he in this story? He would have liked to think he would see the good in everything, but he knew all too well how easy it was to sink into despair.

A plan had come to Raama. An experiment of sorts. Could he change things in these worlds? If so, all he needed was to find was the right orb!

It had been a practice run of sorts. Even though this bubble of time and space constrained him, he could sense the link. He had hoped to connect with the child through the Golden Gull. He focused, trying to leave a message in the very being of the ship, a small push, a soft whisper, hoping she would sense it as she grew up.

Sadly, Skye didn't hear his voice. The vision had faded, and it left Raama alone in the cave, keeping watch on the orbs, the ship, and the lingering memories of a love lost. He would keep trying, and all he could do was hope that one day, he would find his Aanee.

Part Five

Deep Breath
By Chris Morris

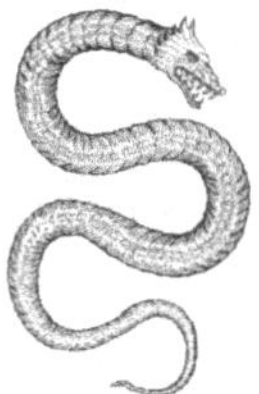

At the prow of the Golden Gull, the intricately fashioned feathers of the great seabird ruffled as the ship went. Catching the last of the disappearing light from the sun, each golden feather seemed to shake and dance, the huge wings appearing to flap in an effort to turn the ship in another direction. Any direction but the one it was now taking.

The gull's wings extended above its head, as though trying to cling to the chill above the choppy waters. The bird's eyes darkened as the light slowly vanished, the sun dulling and then disappearing above the great mass of the ocean. The gull's feathers flickered with the last dying specs of light, and then were swallowed by a black mass, lost in a dark oblivion.

A flash of blue and silver encircled the ship as it neared the bottom, and then was gone. With a hard thump that sent bubbles streaming upwards through the darkness and back towards the sun, it found the bottom. A place unseen by eyes that did not belong to unspeakable creatures. Even the shine of the figurehead was not enough to light the darkness that surrounded the ship as it lay there.

Upon the floor of the ocean, the Golden Gull wept.

Gilleon was surrounded by a freezing, biting darkness. Each pulse from within his head sent a sharp pain that shook his skull. Vibrant echoes of some distant memory sounded, joined by frantic, anxious splashes to his right.

'Hello? Is there anyone there?'

'Gilleon! Thank Seigorn!'

The voice of Naer. He sounded shaken.

'Where are we, Naer?'

'We're on the ship. Don't you remember, boy? The Gull.'

The Gull! Golden its feathers were, and –

'Come on, Gilleon. I think we'd better move.'

'Move? But why?'

'The water's coming in fast.'

Ah, the water! The splendid ocean! The sun shimmered off its waves, alighting the ship in –

'Come, boy, now! The water!'

'Yes… yes! I'm coming.'

'It's freezing! Enough to chill your bones so that even a skurg would take no interest.'

Frost. Snow. Much earlier than usual. Much too early. They say it's –

He felt it now. The water had trickled in past his legs and now Gilleon was waist-deep in icy, salty fluid. He could feel Naer, who had somehow found him in the darkness, tugging at his shirt sleeve. He was urged out of the water and into the man's arms.

'This way! Further into the ship!'

'I can't see a thing,' Gilleon said. 'Why is it so dark?'

Naer grasped hold of Gilleon's left hand and tugged him upwards. The sounds of rushing water became louder, but Gilleon could also hear parts of the ship's wood being bent, as though some great creature had a hold of it within its jaws and was pressing down.

Then, from somewhere outside the ship, he heard a roar. Naer's freezing hand seemed to become colder.

'What was that?' Gilleon asked. 'A whale?'

'No, boy,' Naer replied. 'That was no whale.'

'It can't sink the ship though, can it, Naer? Whatever that thing is. The Golden Gull is the hardiest ship on the sea.'

Gilleon could feel his shipmate glaring at him through the darkness. 'Gilleon, we're already sunk. Raidos is just playing with us.'

'Who goes there?'

Gilleon didn't recognise the gruff voice, but he was glad to hear it clearly; the sound of rushing water had considerably lessened in this part of the ship.

'It's me, Naer. And I have Gilleon here with me. Is

that you, Dathor?'

'Yes. And Paradin is here with me, though he's not talking much. I think the shock has gotten to him.'

'I think we're safer in here,' Naer said. 'The last place is flooded.'

'Where were you?' Dathor asked.

'I don't know,' Naer said. 'It's impossible to tell. I lost my way as we were sinking. I think the ship turned upside-down.'

'Yes,' Dathor agreed. 'The beast knocked the ship onto her side. Cursed thing.'

'Sorry,' Gilleon interjected. 'The beast? Are you really talking about… *Raidos?*'

Gilleon thought of the tales he had heard in his childhood. Raidos, the mighty sea-beast who had sunk every ship that had set sail from Mijira. A great serpent of the ocean who, it was said, was angered at the mere thought of men intruding on a part of the world that was not meant for them. Gilleon could see the shape of the beast now through the darkness that surrounded him. Huge, white eyes set upon a blue and silver head that roared with anticipation at the thought of swallowing a mouthful of men. But those stories were for children, who heard them from the safety of their beds, the wild ocean nothing but a mystical mass of intrigue beyond their windows.

But Raidos was just that. A story. A fairy tale.

Another roar shook the ship. Its shrill, high-pitched tone carried the wrath of the water with it. It buried its way into Gilleon's ears and spun around inside his head.

'Aye, it's really him,' Dathor said. 'Nothing else in all of Mhyrran could make a sound like that, make no mistake.'

'But it can't be!' Gilleon said. 'Raidos is just a story. A fable. Something to scare children with.'

'It's no story, boy,' came a quivering voice that Gilleon did not recognise. Paradin, the man that was with Dathor. His voice came in scratches, as though poking its head out of a dark hole to check it was safe. 'I saw the beast with my own eyes. It took gallons of water up with it as it rose its mighty head out of the ocean. Its body was longer than any of the towers of the castle in Mijira, mark my words. And the *force* he hit us with…'

'He hit us?' Gilleon asked.

'Don't you remember?' Naer said. 'Of course he did.

That's what sunk us.'

Yes! A sudden clash and clatter and the ship reeled. The oil lamp beside the bed fell and shattered. Fire! But the ocean would have taken care of that. Other problems to focus on now...

'If we're at the bottom of the ocean, how have we not drowned?' Gilleon asked.

'We're in an air pocket,' Dathor said. 'Ever put a bowl upside-down into some water?'

'Yes.' Naer agreed. 'But Seigorn knows how long the water can stay out of it. Especially if the ship is rocking.'

'And the air won't last forever,' Paradin's cracked voice said.

'What are we going to do?' Gilleon said. His voice wobbled more than he wanted it to. There was a thick hush for a moment, and then Dathor spoke.

'There are only two choices. Either we stay here and wait to drown, or starve, or suffocate. Or we swim.'

The hush thickened. Among the gentle sounds of trickling water and the creaking wood of the Gull, Gilleon could hear his own heart beat as it too realised that it was trapped here. Neither option was even thinkable. To sit in the cold and the darkness and wait for death, or to rush out of the ship and into the bottom of the ocean where, if the water did not kill them, then Raidos certainly would. Each hammer of Gilleon's heart brought about the thought of another possible future. And every one of them ended with death.

Not to mention…

'Well,' Naer said. 'Let's think about it. How far down do you suppose we are?'

'Impossible to say,' Dathor said. 'None have ever explored the depths of the sea, for Seigorn made us not with gills.'

'They say the depth of the ocean is greater than height of Mount Efhrio, or Jadir,' Paradin said. 'I've even heard it told that the ocean may be bottomless.'

Gilleon heard Dathor scoff. 'A fantasy. A child's tale.'

'Aye?' Paradin said. 'That's what Gilleon said of Raidos.'

'It matters not,' Naer said. 'I felt the ship hit the ocean floor. There *is* a bottom. But how much water is above us? That's what we need to know.'

'I think I hit my head shortly after the attack,' Gilleon said. 'When I awoke, we were already under the water. I don't know how long we were descending for.'

'Difficult to say,' Paradin said. 'In the chaos and confusion I did not think to count. Two minutes, perhaps? Three? How far do you think a ship can sink in such a time?'

'I suppose the question is: can we swim upwards faster than it takes a ship to sink downwards?' Dathor said. 'If we can, we may have a chance. If we can bear the awful chill of that water.'

'So we're really considering this, then?' Gilleon said, voice wobbling once more. 'You really think we should attempt to swim to the surface?'

'What other choice do we have, Gilleon?' Naer said. His voice was not unkind. He placed a frigid hand upon Gilleon's shoulder.

'We must first find a way out of the ship,' Dathor said.

'That will be difficult in this darkness,' Naer said. 'If only we had the power of the fire master. Then we could conjure some light.'

'And some warmth,' Paradin agreed.

'We must begin our search,' Dathor said. 'We'll need to feel our way around. Try to find an opening of some sort. But you'll need to be sure it's a way out of here. A porthole perhaps. You know the shape of them. Or the hole that Raidos made. That will be more obvious. Don't stray too far.'

'I don't think there's much chance of that,' Naer said, and the slow sloshing sounds that Gilleon heard confirmed that he had begun his search around the freezing water.

Gilleon did not know where to begin. He had fled the crews quarters when the water had rushed in and found Naer. But then the two of them had scrambled… where? With his feet on the ceiling, it would most likely be difficult to recognise where he was even if the Gull was suddenly enveloped in light from some ancient Gilhalian magic. He splashed through the icy water and shuddered. Reaching out in front of him, he found a wall and began shifting his hands down it.

No. Nothing here. Just wall and floor. Or wall and ceiling, rather. I must get deeper into that biting water.

He kept his hand pressed against the wall as he first let his knees, then waist, then most of his upper body sink into the freezing water. His breaths came in painful gasps and his hand continued to feel around for any sign of a porthole. He had very little idea of how much space was in front of him, and he knew this was as far as he would be able to go. The only thing to do now was to check under the water to see if he could find a hole of any sort.

Yes, one that you can fall out of, and find yourself alone at the bottom of the ocean, with no idea where the ship has gone, or how to get back into it.

He tapped his foot along the wall he had discovered. Each kick sent a hard smacking sound upwards and echoed in whatever part of the ship the men were in. But one kick missed.

By Seigorn, I've found one!

'Naer! Naer, are you close by? I think I've found a porthole!'

Gilleon heard sloshing water approach him. 'Where?' Naer sounded eager.

'Here, at my foot.'

Naer took a breath and Gilleon heard him disappear under the water. In a moment he was back, a hand once again at Gilleon's shoulder. 'Yes, Gilleon! You've found a porthole. Though, I wonder if it leads outside. I can't see a thing when I poke my head out of it. Come, let's get out of this freezing water for a while.'

They scrambled out of the water and back towards the area where they had spoken to the others. Naer held Gilleon's sleeve in his hand as they walked. Gilleon could feel the deep chill exuding from Naer's own body as his continued to tighten and shake. The two men shivered as they made their way forwards in the darkness.

'Dathor! Paradin! Gilleon may have found us a way out!'

No response.

'Perhaps they're in another part of the ship?' Gilleon suggested. 'They might have swum into another air pocket.'

Or out of another porthole.

'Perhaps,' Naer agreed. 'But I hope they can find their way back here. Dathor! Paradin!'

A splash of water announced their arrival, followed by Paradin's animated voice.

'There! I knew I'd find one. That is where they are kept.'

'How many did you find?' Dathor asked. 'Just the one?'

'One is all we'll need if we strike the beast in the heart.'

'But what are the rest of us supposed to fight with?'

'Dathor!' Naer called into the darkness. 'Paradin. You've found a weapon?'

'Yes,' Dathor replied. 'Paradin has one of our harpoons. But it's too difficult to find anything more in this darkness.'

'Gilleon found something,' Naer said.

'Another harpoon?' Dathor asked with hope in his voice.

'Something even more important,' Naer said. 'A porthole.'

'Where?' Dathor asked. Gilleon could hear him sloshing through the water he must have been standing in.

'Over here,' Gilleon said. 'Follow my voice, I can take you to it.'

Yes, a porthole. And even a weapon to help should Raidos come for us. But there's a bigger problem than that...

Gilleon could hear the other three men splashing around behind him now. Naer took Dathor and Paradin to the porthole.

So… we're to dive under the water, go through the porthole, get out into the open ocean, and then what? Drown, most likey.

He heard splashes of water and gasps as the others re-emerged from inspecting the porthole.

'Aye, I think I know where we are,' Dathor said. 'This porthole should lead us outside. But I can't see anything at all out there.'

'No,' Paradin agreed. 'We're so far down, there's no light.'

'How can that even be possible?' Dathor said.

'Too much water for the light to pass through,' Naer said. It sounded like a guess.

'That's a lot of water,' Dathor said. 'We may drown on the way up.'

Say it Gilleon. You need to tell them. Tell them now!

'It's our only chance,' Naer said. 'Either wait here and die, or try to escape.'

'Yes,' Paradin agreed. 'We just need to go as swiftly

as we can.'

Say it!

'How will we know which way is up?'

'What of Raidos?'

'If we don't drown, the beast will surely catch us.'

'One harpoon might not be enough.'

'How far did we sail from those islands?'

Gilleon drew a breath. 'I have something to tell you. Something you all need to know.'

The chatter stopped. The sound of creaking wood and dripping water was all that was left for a few moments.

'Yes? Gilleon?' Dathor said. 'What is it, lad?'

'I…' Gilleon started. 'I can't swim.'

Naer sat with Gilleon in the glum darkness and eerie quiet. Dathor and Paradin were deep in conversation across from them, though Gilleon could not hear what was being said. His revelation was not met with any amount of enthusiasm from the others, and now they were all presumably trying to work out what was to be done with him.

'You never went into the water as a young boy?' Naer said.

Gilleon shook his head before remembering that Naer would not see it. 'No. I was afraid.'

'Afraid of the water?'

'Afraid of Raidos.'

'I thought you said you didn't believe in the beast?'

'Every child believes in such tales.'

And now, it seemed, every fully grown man. Raidos was always real. What else was? All the tales Gilleon had grown up with, the wizards of Gilhala, Praeya and Mytham, skurgs and morters… which of those were also real?

'A brave decision to board a ship, when you can't swim,' Naer said.

Gilleon scoffed. 'Brave? Foolish, mayhap. I just wanted to be of some use.'

'That's noble,' Naer said. 'You wanted our people to be safe.'

It was true. Mijira, and every town and city beyond had not known such a freeze before. Searching the mysterious lands to the south seemed the best course of action. Find out, once and for all if there were safer lands that their people could move to. Away from whatever madness had caused this great chill.

'Have you much family back home?' Naer asked.

'None,' Gilleon replied. 'At least, none that I know of. I was raised with the other orphans in the lower half of the city.'

The *lower half.* Such an excruciatingly plain and somehow false way to describe the poor part of Mijira. But Gilleon realised now that he hadn't ever asked Naer anything about his own family. Many on board the ship had come because they were leaving very little behind. But what of Naer? Was he the same?

'Do you think there's anyone else alive down here?' Gilleon asked. 'Besides the four of us?'

Gilleon heard Naer sigh. 'Could be. Mayhap there are other pockets of air, with people inside them. But we mustn't dwell on that, Gilleon. There's nothing we can do for them.'

What would they do? Were they planning the

same thing as this group of survivors? Perhaps they had already attempted to surface. Perhaps they had already found themselves inside the great mouth of Raidos.

'Did *you* see it?' Gilleon asked. 'The sea monster, I mean.'

'Raidos?' Naer said. 'No, no. Not I. But I believe Paradin when he says he did.'

'Why?'

'Because I think I saw Raidos before. Many years ago now. When I was about your age, I would say. My father and I were out fishing. A pleasant day, it was. But the sky turned. The clouds seemed to darken suddenly. And I heard a rumble.'

'Thunder?'

'Thunder, aye. But something else, too. There was a roar from deep beneath the sea. I said the same thing as you did - thought it was a whale. But my father's face went pale, and that's when I knew. The water around our little rowboat trembled, as though the ocean it- self was afraid of what was coming. And then, a flash. Lightning in the sky, at the same moment as a flash of something else entirely in the water. Blue and silver.'

'That's what I heard of Raidos too,' Gilleon said.

'A great blue and silver serpent. Teeth as sharp as great daggers and huge, white eyes. Fifteen times the size of any man.'

'Fifteen?' Naer said. 'In every tale I've heard, he's talked of as being larger than fifteen men. It's what I thought when I saw him, too.'

'Are you sure it was him? You're sure you saw Raidos?'

'Either it was Raidos, or we should be afraid of all the other things that dwell in these waters.'

Gilleon thought that if they had been trapped somewhere warm, even the great desert of the Forsaken Lands, he would still have felt the same shiver creeping around his body as he felt now. And as though to reaffirm his existence and presence, another loud roar shook the sunken Gull.

'Alright,' a voice from the other end of the pocket sounded. Dathor. 'We must make a move. What shall we do?'

'The lad can't swim, Dathor,' Paradin said. 'What *can* we do? We can't leave him here.'

'We won't have to,' Naer said. 'Gilleon will come with us.'

Gilleon was so shocked by this, he clutched in the darkness at Naer's shirt. 'What? But I can't, Naer! *I can't!*'

'You can. With my help.'

'What do you mean?'

'I'm a strong swimmer,' Naer said. 'Always have been. Wrap your arms around my neck and I'll take us to the surface.'

'That's madness!' Dathor cried. 'You'll drown!'

'What other option do we have?' Naer said. 'I will not leave him down here. Do either of you wish to carry him?'

Silence met Naer's question.

'I will not drown,' Naer continued. 'And nor will Gilleon. We'll make it to the surface, and we shall see the great walls of Mijira once more.'

'Do you agree, Gilleon?' Dathor asked. 'Will you come with us?'

Gilleon thought he might not be able to speak properly, for his heart beat with every ounce of panic and anxiety at the thought of attempting to make the surface upon the back of Naer. But the words came, slowly, and with more tremour than he'd wished for.

'Y-yes. Yes, thank you, Naer.'

'Just remember to kick your legs,' Naer said. 'It will aid us.'

'Well then,' Paradin said. 'That's it settled. I suppose we ought to get going.'

More silence. Gilleon felt like asking the men for a moment to prepare himself; the rest of them had no doubt been thinking about the swim to the surface for a long while now, but Gilleon had only just begun to think about how it might actually be. But he couldn't. If they were ready to go, then they'd best go now, or risk losing the courage to.

'Alright,' Dathor said. 'Take in all the breath you can. You'll need it. When we get out of the porthole, we swim *straight* upwards. With all the strength and agility we can muster. We should make it far enough to see the light, at the very least. Then, perhaps we'll see how far there is to go.'

'Mayhap it would be better not to look,' Paradin said. 'Seeing the distance may not be very encouraging. Depending on how far it really is, of course.'

'Let's get into position,' Dathor said. 'When we

feel ready, we'll go one at a time. I'll go first.'

'I'll follow you,' Paradin said. 'I have the harpoon, after all. It will make for difficult swimming, but it may be necessary. I think I should be in the middle of us all. Better chance for me to pierce that beast.'

'That leaves us for last,' Naer said. 'Very well. Dathor, go to the porthole.'

All at once, every possible end to this mad situation flashed through Gilleon's mind. He dared not even think about the possibility of actually making it to the surface, for fear that such thoughts might have brought a false hope to him. He decided it was better to try and keep his mind in the moment.

Just think about the present. Focus on what you need to do now.

The first step was getting back into the freezing water, and waiting for his turn. He grasped hold of Naer's arm, and together, they waded waist-deep towards the porthole. He stood, heart racing, and waiting to hear Dathor's voice.

It came far too quickly.

'Alright, everyone. I'm going. And Paradin, if you see that dreadful thing, do not hesitate. Put that harpoon through his head. Good luck.'

A few large gasps of air, a splash of water, and Dathor was gone.

Paradin took some huge breaths of his own. 'Naer. Gilleon. Good luck. See you at the top.'

Another splash of water.

'Are you ready?' Naer asked.

'Yes,' Gilleon said, but in the darkness, he shook his head.

'The porthole is too small to fit both of us at once. I'm going to put you through it first. When I'm on the other side, put your arms around my neck and kick your legs. Hard. Do not stop until we get to the top.'

'Okay,' Gilleon said.

'After three,' Naer said. 'Take some quick breaths, and then a deep breath. The deepest of your life.'

Gilleon began taking in as much air as he could.

'One… two… *three!*'

The deepest breath of his life, then he closed his eyes and ducked under the water. He felt Naer guide him through the porthole, being careful not to let go of the fistful of Gilleon's shirt that he had clenched on to. And then Naer was in front of him, and he took Gilleon's arms, guiding them around his neck.

Gilleon kicked.

Gilleon's eyes remained squeezed firmly shut. He felt Naer turn his body upwards, and then his legs kicked as hard and as fast as they could through the hard water. The water around him felt like nothing he had experienced before; the black liquid was felt so terribly heavy that Gilleon thought he might be crushed by it. It clenched at his lungs as though trying to squeeze the air out of them. His heart slammed so harshly inside his chest that he feared it might make him want to inhale deeply, but even a small inclination to do so would surely result in his death. Perhaps Naer's too. He felt Naer's arms reach upwards and then fly down at their sides, spilling bubbles around Gilleon's ears. The frantic sloshing sounds of the water were all the indication Gilleon had of what was going on. He thought he could even hear either Paradin or Dathor to one side as he swam upwards.

Perhaps I should open my eyes? I might get a better

idea of the situation.

No, Gilleon! For one sight of Raidos and your lungs will fill with the ocean quicker than the Gull was sunk.

He could only cling on, and hope the surface was near.

Your legs, Gilleon! Remember what Naer said!

He kicked as swiftly and furiously as his heart would allow. This seemed to encourage Naer, who increased the vigour with which his own arms and legs moved. The sounds of water rushing past Gilleon's ears became shriller. His lungs continued to tighten.

Don't breathe. Don't breathe!

He wrapped his arms more closely around Naer's neck, and then quickly loosened them, fearing that he might have been making it more difficult for the man. He wondered how far below them the Golden Gull now sat, its lonely figurehead watching as the men made their escape. Perhaps it lay only a few feet downwards, or perhaps they weren't swimming upwards at all. How could they know which direction to swim in? Even if Naer's eyes were open, he'd see nothing more than Gilleon could with his eyes closed.

The strain on the lungs was becoming more than uncomfortable now. Gilleon's mind, against all reason and logic, begged for him to breathe. Every kick of his leg and every slam of his heart was beyond painful. He could not let his thoughts drift to what might happen if he lost the ability to hold his breath any longer; he could only stay focused on keeping his eyes closed, his legs kicking, and his breath held.

Naer began tapping him on the arm as he swam.

Did he want Gilleon to open his eyes? He must have spotted something.

Raidos, perhaps!?

Or maybe the surface.

Gilleon's eyes slowly opened.

The first and only thing he noticed was the pain. The salt stung his eyes like staring straight into the sun. He let out the smallest cry of pain and remembered he needed to keep his lungs full of all the air he could, and he stopped himself. After five or six blinks, he looked around him. He looked downwards. Upwards.

Blackness.

Horrified, Gilleon's lungs seemed to lose more air.

He kicked harder but began to lose hope.

I am nearly out of breath and I can't yet see the sun! This is how I die!

But as his head snapped to and fro, from the corner of one stinging eye, he caught a glimpse of something. The first sign of anything but darkness since the Gull had first sunk.

Light! Over there! We're swimming towards it!

But it's so far away.

He tried to kick his legs faster but they were nearly spent. His lungs now felt like two iron weights in his chest that both weighed him down and sent horrible pain streaming across his body. They demanded air, and Gilleon could give them none. And now more parts of his body began to ache too; his shoulders, elbows, knees and ankles suddenly flared with a pain so great he thought he might have to stop assisting Naer in pushing upwards. Looking towards the tiny sliver of light once more, he began to realise with terror that they likely would not reach it. But Naer continued to force the pair of them upwards, and so Gilleon would continue too. Continue until they reached the fresh, wonderful air above them, or until the ocean claimed them.

Now Gilleon could see Naer in front of him. His hair swam behind him as he forced his body up through the water. His open eyes fixed towards the direction of the light but they seemed tired. Exhausted. His face was etched with all the signs of weariness, pain and fear. For a brief moment, Gilleon's heart found a small but important piece of hope at the sight of another's face, for he had guessed his eyes might have given up hope of seeing anything more than the blackness ever again. But the light above them was still so far away, and Gilleon's body now screamed in pain and his lungs begged him to give up.

At his side, and a little above him, Gilleon now spotted Dathor and Paradin. Each man looked as exhausted as Naer, even without someone clinging to them while they went. Their movements were slower than Gilleon had expected, as though the water itself was made of some thick soup. And their faces were filled with the same pain and fear as Gilleon felt deep within himself.

I need to breathe. I must breathe!

He almost wished he had counted how long he'd been in the water. Would this have helped? How long had it been? A minute? Two?

And the light was no closer.

Every kick of his leg now took an excruciating and overwhelming amount of effort. Naer's own legs and arms had slowed considerably. He was fading. Perhaps, if Gilleon had learned to swim, or stayed behind to allow Naer a chance, or had never boarded that cursed Golden Gull in the first place, the man might have survived. But because of Gilleon – stupid, worthless, miserable Gilleon – Naer was to die.

He wouldn't allow it.

He let out a sliver of breath. Bubbles rushed past his ears, darted past Naer, Dathor and Paradin, and made their way to the target above them. His lungs thanked him for the effort; releasing a little air seemed to help.

It gave him enough courage to let go of Naer.

Naer's head spun around. His horror-struck face glared at Gilleon. Gilleon did not know what expression his face told Naer, but he nodded confidently to him and flashed a single, upwards turned thumb before reaching his arms up – *oh! How they ache!* – and beginning the first of his own strokes towards the surface.

He dared not look at the face of Naer. He had no

idea how the man would react to this; he might have been glad to be rid of Gilleon, or he may have tried to snatch him back. Either way, Gilleon did not want to see it. His own fate was now firmly in his own painful hands. As he pulled his arms downwards and kicked his weary legs as hard as they could manage, he found that he could do it. He could swim. Perhaps not as well as any of the others, but well enough that he might dare to imagine that he could make it now. He could reach the top of the ocean and see the beautiful, wondrous world once more. He looked upwards. The surface was closer. Just a few seconds now. His lungs burned. He let out a little more air. Once more, it helped, but he was nearing the bottom of his breath now, and soon there would be no space left.

Just keep going, Gilleon. Keep it up. You can… you will make it!

Before he knew what was happening, he struck something. Something that had apparently floated into his path to freedom. Fearing at first that it was some deathly creature of the sea, a little more of Gilleon's breath escaped in fright. But when he managed to twist his body around it and look at what it was he had hit, he realised it was much worse.

Dathor. Lifeless. Pale face still twisted with the

pain that had clearly been suffered as he had neared the surface. His blank eyes stared into Gilleon's as he floated away.

And Gilleon's hope, it seemed, went with him.

If Dathor couldn't make it, how could I?

His lungs no longer ached. Instead, they now started to give up. The urge to breathe turned to an urge to fill his lungs with salty water and rejoin the Golden Gull at the bottom of the ocean. He could not see where Paradin was now, but doubtless he too had succumbed to the same fate as Dathor, But Gilleon's heart sunk deeper than the Gull when he caught a glimpse once more of Naer.

Below Gilleon, Naer was nearly motionless. His eyes fixed to Gilleon's. His legs still gently flapped but his energy was nearly gone. And Gilleon's heart lifted once more.

Giving little thought, Gilleon swam downwards. Naer was but four or five strokes away, and when Gilleon reached him, he wrapped both of his stiff, painful arms around his body and then kicked his legs as hard as he could. Looking upwards, he could see the surface. Just a few strokes away. But his lungs had no time for *a few strokes.*

And as though he had needed any more reason to lose hope, Gilleon now caught sight of a magnificent blue and silver streak as it zoomed past.

Raidos! No!

The creature's great body seemed endless. It snaked and spiralled around the water to the side of Gilleon and Naer. But just as Gilleon could see its massive head, Raidos darted downwards and opened a gargantuan mouth. Dathor's body was gone in a moment, and Raidos disappeared with it.

It will be back in no time. Must escape!

Gilleon could no longer find the courage or the energy to lift his head to see how near to the surface he was. In front of him, Naer did not move. Gilleon could feel no heartbeat. His own began to slow. His kicks became so feeble they might have done nothing to the smallest of the crustaceans that swam in the ocean.

This is it… fading… won't see the surface…

As he closed his eyes, he let the last of his breath rush out of his body, the accompanying bubbles popping close to his ears. Everything, all sound, all sight, all feeling began to fade.

And then his head rushed out of the water.

The sudden rush of air to Gilleon's lungs was almost more painful than anything he had experienced on the way up. He drew in breath until there was room for no more, and panicked at the thought of letting more out, for even the huge intake of air seemed insufficient.

I'm out of the water, but still drowning!

Once more he filled his lungs, and the pain in his head seemed to dull. This time, when his breath came out of him, it came with a scream somewhere between agony and relief. A glint of light came into his eyes and he realised that he'd been temporarily blinded. His vision was coming back slowly. He took some more steady breaths, and gradually, he felt some sort of normality return to his body.

When his eyes regained their vision, he suddenly remembered about Naer. He still clutched the man tightly in front of him, but he wasn't moving.

'Naer! Naer! O, you must wake, *you must!*'

He tried shaking him, but found himself ducking back under the water. Then he used one had to tread the water while the other struck Naer's face again and again.

The man showed no sign of life. His eyes remained closed and his head drooped to one side.

'Naer! *Naer!*'

'I think he's gone, lad.'

Gilleon turned his head. Paradin was beside him, face as pale as Naer's, the expression upon it filled with the same fear that Gilleon had felt on every inch of the journey from the bottom of the ocean. In his right hand, he still gripped on to the harpoon he had carried from the ship.

'No!' Gilleon cried. 'No, he can't be!'

Gilleon continued shaking and striking Naer, but none of it made any difference.

'Come on, boy,' Paradin said. 'We'd best make a move. Raidos has had a taste for blood. You can be sure he's not yet satisfied.'

But Gilleon couldn't leave Naer. Not when this was the man responsible for rescuing him from the depths of the sea. Naer had saved Gilleon's life, but in doing so, Gilleon had taken his, for Naer would surely have made it if it wasn't for having to carry someone else with him. It wasn't right.

'Naer! Naer! Please wake! Please!'

'Gilleon, you'll bring the beast to us with your shouting. Come on, we must go!'

Gilleon's balled fist now struck the chest of Naer. Perhaps he could beat his heart back into life.

'Naer!'

A coughing and spluttering announced Naer's return to the world. He eyes and mouth opened, water spilling from the latter. Then the same gasping for air that Gilleon had experienced upon his return to the outside world. Gilleon felt a large and relieved smile spread across his aching face. Even Paradin now looked both shocked and glad to see their comrade return to life.

'Gilleon!' Naer said when he could. 'And Paradin! We made it? We reached the surface?'

'Yes!' Gilleon cried with enthusiasm. 'Yes we did, my friend. And I'm only here because of you.'

'That's not what I saw,' Paradin said. 'Gilleon turned from the surface to go back for you. It seems you owe each other your lives.'

Naer had only a moment to look at Gilleon with

surprise and delight before a low, rumbling sound made Gilleon feel a lot colder. The noise seemed to shake the very water they were in, and Gilleon's spirit dropped as low as the Golden Gull.

'Surely that can't be what I think it is,' Naer said.

'I'm afraid it is,' Paradin said. 'I fear that every drop of water in the entirety of Mhyrran would not be enough to conceal the roar of that beast. We must move.'

'But where?' Gilleon asked. 'We have no idea where we are.'

'North,' Naer said. 'We must swim north. Back the way we came.'

'Yes,' Paradin agreed.

'But which way is that?' Gilleon said.

'That way,' Naer nodded in the direction to Gilleon's right.

'How do you know?' Gilleon said. 'The position of the sun?'

'No, Gilleon.' Naer said. 'Look closer.'

Narrowing his eyes, Gilleon could see it. Just barely. A large but very distant mass of green. Land.

'An island!' Gilleon said. 'Either Mira or Jira. It must be!'

'Yes,' Paradin agreed. 'Let's make for it. And pray to Seigorn we reach it before Raidos finds us.'

They set forth. Gilleon's arms and legs still ached but he swam as strongly as he could manage. Paradin went with one arm, the other clutching hold of the harpoon at his side. Naer let out a painful breath with every other stroke, but Gilleon was only glad to hear more life coming out of the man. The sea was fairly calm, with only the occasional wave slapping Gilleon in the face as he went. Often, he would look down into the water below him and wonder if he might catch a frightening glimpse of blue and silver, but no sign of Raidos could be seen – or heard – for several minutes now.

The island didn't seem to be getting much closer. Gilleon wondered how much the vast, open sea could have an effect on his perception of the distance. Perhaps a distance that looked to be a mile would be more like five, or ten. But it was useless to think of for now; he simply needed to keep swimming. Eventually, the island did indeed begin to look closer, and Gilleon allowed himself to feel just a little glad, for his arms now felt as though they would at any moment seize up, and he might find himself once more at the bottom of the ocean. His mind was filled with every dark thought of the things that might lurk underneath the waves. If Raidos was real, and dwelled in the very waters that Gilleon had dreamed of exploring as a young boy, what else might exist? The great sea monster surely could not be the only beast that called the ocean home.

The water began to feel a little different. There seemed to be a different current now; water rushing beneath them and towards the island. Gilleon's first thought was a hopeful one; perhaps the current was some ancient magic left from Gilhala that would help stranded seamen reach the islands much quicker. But when he looked down, he saw what it was.

A flash of blue and silver.

'No! Naer! Paradin! It's the beast!'

Neither man slowed their swimming. Each of them remained focused on propelling themselves forwards as swiftly as their no doubt exhausted and aching limbs could go. But the space between where they were now and the island was suddenly filled with a nightmarish image.

The water in front of them seemed to burst up-wards, like a mighty waterfall that flowed backwards. The sound of vast amounts of rushing water was painful to Gilleon's ears. Much of it splashed him in the face and he had to look away for a moment before rubbing his eyes and turning back to the spot where the water had suddenly appeared. Now, in place of it, Raidos' great body stood tall and slender. His face was consumed with a terrible fury, and his white eyes stared downwards at the three men who had halted in the water and could only look on with fear and awe. A massive mouth opened to reveal several long, white teeth, some still stained with the blood of his last victim.

'*Raidos!*' Paradin screamed at the beast. He held the harpoon high in his right hand, and without pause, he pointed it towards Raidos and hurled it. The pointed end struck one of Raidos' scales, but did not pierce it. The weapon bounced off and splashed into the water in front of Raidos. For a moment, Gilleon was afraid the harpoon was lost to the ocean, but it bobbed back up again and lay atop the water, drifting slowly back towards them.

Raidos roared.

The water around them trembled. Gilleon could feel the wind coming from the mouth of the beast. He wanted to cover both of his ears but he might have fallen once more into the ocean, and it would be difficult to find the strength or the courage to pull himself back out of it once more.

'It needs a harder strike!' Naer cried. 'Throwing will not be enough!'

But Raidos moved first. He lunged his great head downwards, toward Paradin, his mouth widely open.

'Paradin!' Gilleon screamed. 'Move!'

Paradin took a breath and dived under the water. Raidos followed him. The wave that came afterwards was so great that Gilleon was swept underneath it. The sounds of rushing water filled his ears and he suddenly didn't know which way was up. He forced himself to open his eyes and he saw Raidos' great mass swirling in the water. No sign of Paradin or Naer. But he could see the light from the sun and he followed it until he broke through the surface of the ocean once more.

He was breathless as he emerged. This was almost as awful as the first time he had found the surface. If he was swept underneath again, he might really drown this time.

'Naer! Paradin!'

It was difficult to see much through the choppy waves that Raidos had created. Gilleon could see no sign of the two men until a splash of water at his left side announced the emergence of one of them.

'Naer! Thank goodness. Did you see Paradin?'

'No. Let us hope Raidos' teeth did not meet their mark.'

As though in answer to Gilleon's darkest questions, Paradin's head popped up out of the water now too. He was unharmed.

'The harpoon!' he cried. 'Where is the harpoon?'

Gilleon searched the waves around them. Could Raidos have sunk it?

'There!' Naer said, pointing forwards. Gilleon saw it, floating a few strokes ahead of them. Without any hesitation, Paradin swam towards it and gripped it firmly in his hands, just as Raidos' head and long body emerged from the water once more. Close enough for Paradin to strike.

'Hit it, Paradin!' Naer cried. 'Now! With all the strength you have!'

But Paradin only had time to raise the weapon above his head before Raidos lunged again. This time the mouth fell straight around the area of water that Paradin had been occupying. The harpoon rushed out of the way as the huge mass of the sea monster took Paradin down into the ocean with it.

'*No!*' Gilleon screamed. '*Paradin!*'

He was swept under the water again. This time he managed to emerge much more swiftly, and he found Naer a few feet to his left.

'Take the harpoon,' Naer called. 'Take it, Gilleon! There's nothing we can do for Paradin now.'

Dathor. Paradin. If they could not survive this, what chance do I have?

He took the harpoon in his hand. Of course, Naer meant for him to pass it over. Gilleon could no more slay a pig than a great sea monster like Raidos. If this world was meant for warriors, Gilleon had no place in it. He urged his tired arms to take him towards Naer with all the speed he could muster.

But once more, Raidos appeared, sending water out of the ocean, flying in all directions. This time his long teeth were stained with a deeper scarlet than before, but his great white eyes told Gilleon that he was hungry still, for what kind of meal is a simple man or two for a giant like Raidos? Gilleon's body froze in the water. His hand, unmoving, clenched the harpoon at his side.

Raidos roared, louder than before, his eyes now fixed on Naer.

'Strike him, Gilleon! Bring him down!'

Bring him down?

Even if Gilleon could find the nerve, he might not find the strength. If he could find the strength, he would not have the precision. Or speed enough to ensure he struck the monster before he descended upon Gilleon's final comrade. If he could somehow find *all* of that, what damage would a single harpoon do to the great and mighty Raidos? What damage could a toothpick do to a fully grown adult?

'Now, Gilleon! Strike him now!'

He had perhaps one single second. A single second to decide his next move. Attempt the impossible, avenge the deaths of Dathor and Paradin, and every other sailor on board the doomed ship, and do the unthinkable: bring down the legendary Raidos. More than this; save Naer. Save the man who risked his own life – very nearly sacrificed it – so that Gilleon could live.

Or tread water and watch Raidos take him. It was no decision at all.

He closed his eyes and forced the harpoon forwards with every ounce of strength he could muster, keeping his fingers firmly clasped around the body of the weapon. Without the aid of his vision, he was making the best guess possible. Raidos had been right in front of him, his great slender body sticking out of the water. He couldn't miss. He *couldn't*. But he couldn't look either. He had found the courage to fight Raidos, but some deeper kind of bravery was needed to be able to watch.

Before he knew it, he felt and heard the harpoon connect. At first, he thought he'd hit something else entirely. The figurehead from a magically resurrected Golden Gull would have made more sense than Raidos. What he had hit felt impossibly hard. And the metal head of the harpoon clashed against it with a sound more like steel than the scale of a sea monster.

He opened his eyes.

The harpoon remained in his hand, stained with a single drop of blood from Gilleon's own palm. The force he had struck with had been just about the most power that he could have managed. And his target in front of him remained completely unchanged. The blue and silver scales reflected the sunlight that the crew of the Golden Gull had chased so fervently. Now that crew was about to be reduced to a single person. A boy from

Mijira who had no business being the last one alive.

'Dive, Naer! Lose him in the waves!'

But Raidos was too swift. In the blink of an eye, he lunged downwards, and dragged Naer into the ocean.

'No! Naer! Please, no!'

Gilleon was once more caught in the frenzy of waves from Raidos' mighty sweep. Underneath the water, he kept his eyes closed for fear of catching a glimpse of the dreadful creature, or of Naer, his companion, his *friend*, as he was torn to pieces.

What if I just stay here this time? Stay under the water. Drown myself or wait for Raidos to do his horrid work. There's nothing I can do now, anyway.

It would be easy. Simple enough to just give up. Lie there and close his eyes. Await death in whatever form it chose to come for him in.

But no.

He had not come this far for it to end this way. He had survived a brutal ship sinking. Swam from the very bottom of the ocean. Faced off against the famous Raidos. The island – Mira or Jira – was only a short swim away now. He had struck Raidos once, he could do it again. With more force than before. His eyes were surely not as strong as his scales. He did not need to kill the beast, only teach him. Teach him that the might of Mijira will come down hard upon those that harm the men, women or children of the city. Yes, he might well die in the process. But he would die fighting.

He swam upwards. And emerged with fire in his soul.

'Raidos! Where are you, you wretched beast? Show yourself! Come and face me!'

Now the water around Gilleon seemed to be swirling. Underneath him, the familiar flashes of blue and silver began dancing around in a circle. It moved Gilleon so that at one moment he was facing the island, and the next he was facing away from it.

He's creating a whirlpool! Trying to drown me? No. Trying to confuse me.

The harpoon was now welded to Gilleon's right hand. When the beast emerged, he would be ready. He would not hesitate. He would drive the harpoon forwards with all the might of every man on board the Gull, and every person in the great city of Mijira.

A drop of Gilleon's blood fell from his hand to the

water. It was caught in the swirl and sunk down towards Raidos.

'Yes, have a taste, Raidos! A drop. A morsel. Enjoy it. It's all you shall have. Now come and face me, you coward!'

Raidos appeared to hear Gilleon's call. His great head appeared on the surface, bringing the usual rush of water with it. Gilleon's stinging eyes did not blink when the salt hit them; he kept them focused on the large white eyes of Raidos. He raised Paradin's harpoon to his shoulder, and pointed it towards the beast's belly.

'Raidos! You have claimed many innocent lives today. My friends. Men who had hopes and dreams. In the name of Seigorn, I *will* destroy you. For Dathor! And Paradin! And Naer!'

Then Raidos did something unexpected. His great mouth opened, just a little. And a deep, foreboding tone escaped it:

'You shall not defy the will of the ocean.'

Gilleon's heart froze. For when Raidos opened his mouth to speak, an arm dropped out of it. Naer's still body lay against the huge red tongue of Raidos, a single tooth piercing through a leg. His head moved towards

Gilleon.

He's alive!

But now Raidos lunged for Gilleon, and his thought once more turned to what he needed to do next. Raidos came for him at a tremendous speed and Gilleon's harpoon matched it. This time, he kept his eyes open. This time, the force was greater. This time, the harpoon sailed into the middle of Raidos' left eye.

The beast roared with pain and rage. Naer's body tumbled out of his furious mouth and splashed into the water beside Gilleon. Raidos' body raised out of the water, his head extending towards the clouds above, and Gilleon acted once more.

'Leave us, Raidos! Go back to whatever dark dwelling you came from!'

The harpoon raced forwards again and connected with one of the blue and silver scales. This time it felt like breaking through rock. The pain in Gilleon's hand was so great that he had to let go of the harpoon. But something in front of him joined the harpoon in the water.

One of Raidos' scales!

Another roar from the beast, and he lunged.

But not for Gilleon or Naer. His great head disappeared into the water, the injured body following, and Gilleon saw the legendary sea monster's flash of blue and silver as he dashed away from them.

When he hit the sandy shores of the island, Gilleon barely had the strength to pull himself or Naer out of the water. Naer hadn't said a word during the swim from the ocean to the beach. Gilleon had had to drag his body through the water the entire time, using what felt like the very last of his energy. Naer was bleeding from several deep cuts and bites scattered around his broken body. He left Naer on the sand, his legs still washed by the gentle waves from the sea.

'Naer, can you hear me? Naer?'

Gilleon sat beside him, and placed a single hand upon his heaving chest. Naer's eyes were shut, and his face looked as exhausted as Gilleon felt.

'We made it, Naer. We're here. On the island. We made it!'

Naer managed a small nod. He opened his eyes and looked at Gilleon.

'No, Gilleon. I think *you* made it.'

'No! Don't say that. You're wounded, but I can help. There are people on this island. Give me a moment, I'll find somebody that can help.'

Gilleon made to move, but Naer shot a surprisingly strong hand up and grabbed at his shirt.

'Stay with me, Gilleon. I doubt the islanders can do anything much. My wounds are too grave. You should have left me in the ocean.'

'Don't talk like that,' Gilleon said. 'I wouldn't have made it to the surface without you. I couldn't leave you for Raidos.'

Naer managed a weak chuckle. 'I think you have a strength in you that you don't yet realise, my boy. You might have gotten out of that ship and escaped Raidos had you been alone. My time is passing. Mhyrran must now look to the likes of you.'

Gilleon did not know what to say. He pressed his tired face into his trembling hands. No sound but the waves and the wind and Naer's laboured breathing was made. He peered out into the ocean. The sun would soon disappear behind it. The air grew colder still. He should have been thankful to have survived. But he was not.

'Gilleon…' Naer said. His voice was almost drowned out by the water splashing to the sand. 'You, my friend, are destined for greatness.'

Gilleon faced him again, and now he took his hand in his. Naer's eyes were closing. His pale face was still. And then he stopped breathing.

'Go to Seigorn, Naer,' Gilleon whispered. 'And be at peace. I will always act in the knowledge that you are watching me. And Mijira shall not forget you.'

He kissed his friend's hand, then laid it gently to the side. He thought he should be weeping, but no tears came, for he had not the vigour for them. Instead, he lay down in the sand beside Naer, and looked up at the grey clouds above. The last of the sun's light reflected from them, and they looked to Gilleon like rain clouds. He turned his head from them towards a rock to his right. A bird had perched there, and was looking at him quizzically.

A gull. Of course it is.

And then something white fell from the sky and onto the beak of the gull. A single white snowflake. It melted upon the bird's beak before it stretched its wings, catching the last golden light from the sinking sun, and solemnly flew away.

Gilleon was cold, but he did not have the will to move. When his eyes closed, he did not have the fortitude to reopen them. A rest. A long rest was what he needed, and then he would move. For now, sleep was all he wanted.

Raama had awoken with a start, the orb upon him, and the vision drawing him in with no time to prepare. Chaos engulfed him—the sea and storm swirling around him, all too familiar. Yet, this vision felt different; he sensed the great beast wrapping around him, pulling him down to the ocean's depths.

Amid this turmoil, he felt the boy's fear, and he whispered words of faith and encouragement, urging him on. When the vision finally released him, Raama pondered the lessons from this tale. Victory often came at a price, a truth Raama knew all too well; Gilleon had lost his friends in his battle with the sea monster, a sorrow Raama shared.

However, it was Gilleon's transformation after the ordeal that resonated with Raama. It reminded him that every experience, no matter how painful, held the potential for growth.

He realized that his quest to bring back Aanee might not solely be about reversing a tragic event. It was also about understanding the intricate tapestry of life's experiences. As the next orb floated into view, Raama felt ready, his heart beating in sync with the glow. The tale's aura of the Golden Gull carried the brave passengers in an endless river and through different worlds.

Part Six

The Red Diamond
By Redd Herring

The Journey Begins

King Armon sat astride his horse on the black sand, waiting for the ship and growing restless. He scanned the beach where the crew was assembled with their gear. Armon turned to the wizard, who had become his personal advisor as of late, "Ubel?"

"It will come," the wizard assured him. "My sources are never wrong." The king did not seem to share Ubel's confidence, but the wizard knew he could count on the seers' information.

Smoke rose from the surface of the dark lake. A faint light appeared, and the cloud swirled around it, growing thicker with each rotation. The light intensified and flickered from red to blue to green. Most of the crew took a few steps back. They did not trust magic or those who dealt in it. The light grew so bright that they shielded their eyes or turned away altogether. There was a flash, like lightning, and then the smoke was gone. A longship bobbed calmly on the water where nothing had been only a few moments before.

Ubel smiled at the king, "The Golden Gull, Sire."

After much persuasion, the Golden Gull was loaded and ready, crew uneasy as they gripped the oars. Ubel stepped into the water and turned back. The king gave a slight nod. Ubel returned the gesture, pulling his hood back to reveal a face that was more bone than flesh. The visage was ripped and torn as if from the claws of some otherworldly beast. Most of the crew turned their gazes from the sight, but not Delo. He had seen things in battle that would drop a man in pure terror. He stared straight at the face, not showing any intimidation. He despised magic, and that feeling went double for this sorcerer. Delo did not trust him at all, and the fact that the king let the wizard into his inner circle in such a short time made Delo even more suspicious. Ubel raised his arms high and let out a hiss. The water around the Gull began to churn and steam rose, almost enveloping the crew. Some stood as if preparing to jump overboard.

"Hold fast!" Konrad ordered. They calmed somewhat at the voice of their captain and slowly returned to their posts. He shouted to the king, "Armon, remind them of their duty!"

The king rode across the black beach, "The wizard will transport you. Travel upriver and meet the seers. They will take you the rest of the way." He dismounted and walked into the lake to stand next to Ubel. "Only you can find the Red Diamond. This is the key to peace in the kingdom and the end of the warring." He raised his fist in the air, and the crew did the same. "Go with the gods. Travel swiftly, and if it is your fate to die today, die with the fury your house deserves." He pulled his fist down to his heart and dropped to one knee in the black water, "You honor us all!"

The crew dropped fists to their hearts and rattled the oars three times. "For kingdom, for honor, for glory!"

The wizard let out another hiss and pointed to the figurehead at the front of the Golden Gull. The gemstone eyes glowed bright red, cutting through the steam that surrounded the longboat. The crew gasped as the outstretched wings began to tuck in tightly and feathers seemed to ripple against the side of the bird's carved body. Throwing back his gruesome head, Ubel let out a scream that filled the mouth of the golden seabird mounted on the bow. More steam rose, obscuring the view from shore. There was another scream, and the Golden Gull vanished.

The Seers

"We have passed that same tree four times now, Erik," Delo said, gripping the figurehead on the bow. There was no reply. "Erik?" He turned and walked the length of the low-slung craft, "Erik!" Still no reply. Each crew member followed him with their eyes. These confrontations were becoming more frequent as the journey wore on.

Delo stopped a few feet from the pilot. He crouched down and waited for Erik to raise his head. Their eyes met. He could see that the pilot was looking for any excuse. Delo decided not to stoke the fire this time. "Erik," he spoke in a soft, even tone. "Can we discuss our route? I think we may be lost."

"No discussion needed," Erik replied. "Captain said to head upstream," he pointed and spat over the side, "that's upstream."

"Konrad!" Delo yelled.

"Captain," the man growled at Delo between clenched teeth. The crew rested their oars as they watched the scene. "Who said stop?" Konrad roared. They all turned to avoid his wrath and continued rowing.

Delo rolled his eyes and took a deep breath, "Captain," he sneered and pointed to the shoreline. "We have passed that tree four times today."

The captain stood and took a long, studied look. "I see a lot of trees, Delo." He sat again.

"Konrad!" Delo started. The captain stood up with surprising speed. Delo held his hands up and took a step back, "Captain." He motioned for Konrad to follow as he pointed, "The tree with the double trunk, see? That's the fourth time we have passed it. We are going in circles."

"It's a river," the captain grinned, "there's only one way to go!" A ripple of laughter swept through the crew.

Delo shook his head and returned to the bow, "There is never only one way, Captain. When you know that, you are able to continue when others falter." He used his hand to shield his eyes from the sun and continued his watch. A few crew members mumbled and nodded in agreement.

"Row!" Konrad blasted. The crew put their heads down and looked at the ship's floorboards. Konrad sat again and leaned toward the pilot, "Keep an eye out for that double trunk tree." Erik nodded, squinting at the shoreline.

They had been navigating the river for too long, and Konrad was concerned. The king told them the mission was simple, and when it was done, Konrad and the crew of the Golden Gull would be showered with glory and riches. But from the moment the Golden Gull appeared on the river, all he had was an overcrowded ship, short supplies, and a bickering crew. Konrad sighed. Nothing was ever simple.

"Captain!" Delo shouted.

Konrad did not need to look. He knew they had passed the tree again. He stood, shaking his head. "Hold!" he thundered. The crew sat up straight and squared their oars in the water, slowing the Gull. They made slight adjustments to hold the craft steady in the current. "Make for shore! Port side!" The crew turned the longboat and rowed while Erik handled the steerboard.

As they neared the shore, Delo jumped out with the mooring line and pulled the Gull snug, tying off to a tree. He quickly repeated this at the stern so that the boat was parallel with the shoreline. The crew disembarked, stretching and groaning after hours at the oars.

"Camp here for the night," Konrad handed gear over. They laid items out to dry and began setting up camp, while Delo and Erik gathered wood. There was no chatter. Every man knew his job and worked to get it done before anyone rested. After five years, and more quests than most could remember, the crew worked as one. However, this was the first time they had sailed the Golden Gull, and the few who had heard of the ship were leery of it. The stories varied wildly, but most ended in disaster. "Rumors," the wizard assured them. "Nothing but silly tales told by tavern rats seeking attention." Despite this, most of the crew remained uneasy about being on the infamous craft.

They finished setting up and drifted in small clusters toward the cookfire. Smells of rabbit and potatoes drew them in. They had eaten mostly dried fish for a week, and anything fresh was a welcome relief.

"Smells wonderful!" came an unfamiliar voice from the shadows on the edge of camp. Everyone was instantly at the ready, weapons drawn and on high alert.

A young man stepped into the firelight, hands held up to show he had no ill intentions. He was slight, with an almost child-like face. He looked as if he might blow away in a strong wind, but the crew knew not to judge on appearances. "Apologies," he took a few more steps, causing the men to tighten grips on their weapons. "It smells so good," he reached the fire and took a seat, picked up a bowl, and held it out. "Is there enough for a weary man to have a few bites?"

"I am Delo," The warrior filled the bowl as the small man sat.

"Syx. Thank you, friend." The young man smiled and began eating. "This is delicious! Compliments to you, Gavin! You are a fine cook." He waved at a man on the far side of the camp. Everyone stopped and stared. "Did I say something wrong?" He flashed a smile.

"I think maybe you did!" Gavin stormed toward the small man, drawing a knife. Delo jumped to his feet and stood between the two. "How do you know my name? We have never met!" He pushed toward the stranger. "Delo, this is some sort of sorcery!"

Delo held his ground with considerable effort. He looked over his shoulder and managed to say, "Friend, now is a very good time to put some distance between yourself and us. I can't hold him off much longer." Gavin continued to inch forward.

Syx calmly put the bowl down and stood. "Let him go." The rest of the camp began to gather around the commotion. Delo grunted, giving Syx a questioning look. Syx took a few steps away and nodded, "It's fine. Let him go."

Delo stepped aside, and Gavin almost bowled him over as he charged. The small man stood his ground. Gavin screamed in rage, his knife raised high. As he brought the blade down, Syx calmly dropped to the ground and rolled between Gavin's legs. He stood and kicked the big man square in the seat of his pants. The camp exploded with laughter. Syx smiled and took a bow for the crowd.

Gavin turned, his face red with rage. "You just sealed your fate, little one!"

"SEAL?" Syx grinned. He stretched his arms out and clapped his hands together, barking like a seal. Everyone almost doubled over at this. Syx went to the supplies in a little hopping motion and bent at the waist as he shoved his head into a box. He stood back up with a dried fish hanging from his mouth. Hopping around in a circle and clapping his hands, he continued making barking sounds around the fish. The crew was in tears at this point.

Gavin could stand no more. He charged again, lowering his head to ram his opponent. Syx pirouetted away and smacked Gavin on the cheek as the charging giant fell face first into the dirt. Gavin spun, searching for his knife. He turned from side to side clawing at the ground trying to find it.

Syx twirled the knife. "This could be dangerous." Gavin stood and readied himself to attack again. Syx moved, almost faster than the eye could see. In an instant, he had the tip of the blade at Gavin's back. "Friend, I do not want this to end badly for either of us. You are too valuable, and I do not fancy dying today." He slid a few steps back, allowing Gavin to turn and face him. "Please, sir. Accept my sincerest apologies. One of my many faults is letting levity get the better of me and making a serious situation turn foolish. I truly meant no disrespect to you at all." He turned the knife to hold it out by the blade. Gavin reached tentatively. Syx nodded, and Gavin took the weapon.

"I think I still owe you a beating," Gavin growled.

"On the contrary, friend," Syx held out a closed fist. "It is I who owe you." He opened his hand and revealed a gold coin. "I humbly ask for your forgiveness."

Gavin took the coin and turned it over to examine it. He nodded, "This will do little one, but let us not have to revisit this matter."

"Done and done!" Syx grinned and started to walk away.

"How did you know my name, and that I was the one that cooked the stew?"

"Oh that," Syx spun around. "I am a seer, along with my brother and sister." He pointed to the trees as two figures stepped out, "Gavin, I am sure they would love some of your fine stew."

Again and Again

Syx stood at the bow with Delo. "How long have you been on the river?"

"This is the seventh day," Delo answered.

"Has the scenery always been so…" he tilted his head as if listening to someone, "consistent?"

"You noticed it too?" Delo pointed to the shore. "I seem to see the same trees again and again."

Syx looked back at his siblings in the middle of the boat. They were talking in low voices and pointing out certain trees and rocks. "She noticed," he motioned to Tynn. "She wondered what you had seen so far."

Delo turned to look at Tynn. She doesn't look like a witch, he thought. Delo knew she was not, but to him and the crew a seer was just another one who dealt in magic, like that loathsome wizard the king so blindly trusted. The girl turned toward him, staring with eyes that had the slightest hint of red at the edges. He froze and wondered if she could read his mind. The corners of her mouth crept into a slight smile and she gave him a wink. Delo quickly spun around and went back to surveying the shoreline. He tried thinking of nothing, which was impossible when you tell yourself to think of nothing.

Delo recalled their discussion with the seers the night before. Syx said that they were part of a family that had been given the gift of sight, some with stronger skills than others. Each child was named for the order in which they appeared. His brother, Sevyn, told them that appeared was the most appropriate way to describe it as they were not actually born in the normal sense of the word.

"Who raised you?" Gavin had asked.

"No one," Sevyn replied. "We just appeared, and the others filled us." That comment drew curious looks. He explained that each successive member of the family was more skilled, because they received the collective knowledge and abilities from all the others before them, so they were filled by their siblings.

"We protect our newest from harm, keeping them free to focus on their talents," Syx added.

The crew kept looking at Tynn and waiting for her to tell them more. She sat in silence, almost in a trance. It made the men uneasy.

Delo looked at all three, "I will ask the obvious question. If you are Syx, Sevyn, and Tynn, where are the others? Are there not five before you and also numbers eight and nine?"

Syx nodded. "Yes. The five before me have all moved on." He stared at the fire. "They are not dead, but they do not live in this existence that we do. When we have fulfilled our purpose, we move on."

"Move to where?" Delo asked, leaning in to focus on the answer.

Syx shrugged, "I do not know. I have not moved on yet." He stood and stretched. "We are all very tired. Could we continue this another time?" He turned to Gavin, "Sir, you are a master with the cookpot. We have not eaten so well in many a moon." Gavin smiled slightly at the compliment.

Delo held up a hand. "Syx, could we impose just two more questions before you all retire for the night?"

Syx sat down once more. "What happened to eight and nine?"

Syx sat for a while in silence. The mood became dark. Finally he spoke, "They fell victim to him." He pointed to his brother, who looked at the ground.

Everyone turned to look at Sevyn. "Victim?" Delo finally asked.

"Yes," Syx replied. "Sevyn ate Nyne." He hung his head and shuddered.

"Is he… crying?" Gavin asked as he came closer. "Syx, are you OK?" He turned to Sevyn. "How could you do such a horrible thing?"

Sevyn leaned forward, falling to his knees. Syx put his arm around his brother. Both were shaking. Sevyn fell forward, then turned over on his back and let out a howl. Syx did the same.

Delo turned it over in his mind. "Seven….. Eight….. Nine." A wide grin spread across his face and he bent over. "Seven ate Nine!" It spread across the camp like a fire. Soon everyone was laughing.

"What's so funny? Gavin stood, looking around the camp. A silence fell over the group and all eyes were on him. After a few seconds, they all burst out into even louder laughter.

"Apologies, my friend," Syx patted Gavin on the shoulder. "We heard that one from a sweet lass in another time and place, and I could not resist." Gavin still looked confused. "No worries. I will explain it to you later."

Syx spoke to Delo, "Actually, Ayte and Nyne have taken an unfortunate path. Sometimes, a jest helps us forget for a moment." Sevyn let out a sigh, and Tynn pulled the hood of her cloak tight about her. "What was your last question, my friend?"

"How did you get here?" He asked. "I mean here, at the river's edge tonight."

The three stood, and Tynn spoke for the first time. "We were told to come here to wait for you." Her voice was almost a whisper, yet every man in the camp could hear her words as if she spoke only to him.

"Who told you? The king?" Delo asked as they walked into the shadows on the edge of camp. He thought for a while then sneered, "Was it that abomination of a wizard? Was it Ubel?"

Tynn started to answer him, then turned. "No more questions tonight. You may not like the answers, and

I surely won't like trying to explain them to you." The three disappeared into the darkness.

"There!" Syx yelled, pulling Delo back to the present. Syx pointed, almost jumping with excitement. "Right there, Delo! I have seen the same rock formation before!" Syx ran to his siblings, pointing. They looked across the water and nodded.

Delo joined them and said, "So, we are going in circles!" He looked directly at the captain and grinned.

"Not exactly," Sevyn told them. "It's more like we are traveling a stretch of road from beginning to end, then starting over and doing it once again."

"Hold!" The crew steadied the boat. Everyone looked to the captain for instructions. Konrad stood and addressed the seers, "How do we fix this?"

Syx approached the captain. "We need to get a look at the river from a different perspective."

Bird's Eye View

"You want to see the river from above?" the captain asked. Syx nodded. "Very well. Make for shore!" Konrad shouted.

"Hold!" The crew turned in confusion. The new order was not the problem, the one giving the command was. "Apologies, Captain," Sevyn looked up at the big man. "No disrespect intended, but we do not need to go ashore."

Konrad gave Sevyn a long stare. "You do not need to climb the trees?" Sevyn shook his head. The captain let out a sigh. "How do you propose we get your view from above?" The seer pointed to his sister.

Tynn began to walk the boat. Her hands were held out, brushing against the men as she moved. Each shivered and closed his eyes when she made contact.

She reached the bow, turned, and retraced her steps. At almost midship, Tynn stopped. A young man with ice-blue eyes looked up. She placed her hand on his shoulder and nodded.

Sevyn approached him. "You are the eagle?"

The young man replied, "I… I am Adlar." He gave the captain a questioning look.

"Yes," Sevyn smiled. "The one who flies."

Tynn nodded again and motioned for Adlar to stand and follow her. When they reached the stern, she pointed to the pilot. Erik stood, almost in a trance, and stepped aside. Adlar took the seat as if he knew what she wanted without her saying it. Tynn gave her brothers a glance and moved to the bow once again. Syx took position amidship, and Sevyn remained aft with Konrad. "Captain," Syx said, "have the men raise the sail." The crew balked at this.

"We can't, little one." Gavin spoke up. "We are running upriver against the wind. If we raise sail, the wind could turn us broadside, then the current may capsize us." The men murmured their agreement.

"He is right, Syx." Konrad said. "That is a dangerous thing to do in the current."

"In most circumstances we would agree, Captain." Sevyn remarked. "But as you can see," he leaned out over the side, "we are no longer in the current."

The crew looked over the edge and saw that the Golden Gull was floating above the water. The boat lurched to one side, almost dumping half of them overboard. In an instant the ship righted and, once again, floated calmly above the water.

"Sorry," Adlar said sheepishly as he gripped the steerboard tighter. "I am still figuring this out."

"Sir," Syx called to the captain, "could we try again, please?"

Konrad walked to stand beside the seer. "Men, give him your best." They gripped the oars and awaited instructions. Konrad slid into the spot previously occupied by Adlar and took up the oar.

"Wonderful." Syx looked at Gavin. "I need you to hoist the sail and hold it steady. It will be difficult." Gavin took the rope and pulled. Syx seemed to stretch himself just a tiny bit taller, "Everyone extend the oars, pull, and hold that position." The crew did as instructed. The oars moved back along the sides of the ship, seeming to form two huge wings. Syx looked to his sister, "Ready."

She placed her hands on the bow. The figurehead's eyes glowed, this time deep blue, and the wings of the carved bird spread wide. The boat jumped forward a little. The sail filled, and Gavin leaned back on the rope with everything he had, but he was dragged forward. Syx moved to his side to help. The wind picked up. The Gull lurched again. The crew was anxious and looked out over the sides.

"Hold the oars, men!" Syx yelled above the wind. He looked back to his brother, "Now!"

Sevyn put his hand on Adlar's shoulder. He leaned close to the young man's ear, "Let the wind guide you. It will tell you what to do." Adlar nodded and tightened his grip. The bow lifted, and the boat inched forward.

"Hold fast!" Syx reminded the crew. They leaned back, holding the oars in place. The Gull continued to rise. Soon, they broke above the treeline. The craft rocked from side to side as Adlar struggled to keep them steady without the trees to shield them from the wind. Tynn left her position and walked down the aisle, giving each man a light, calming touch. After a few moments, the crew started to make adjustments with the oars. This worked in conjunction with Adlar at the stern. Once they got the feel of being in the air, the Gull rode the wind more easily.

"Captain!" Delo stood beside Konrad. "I think you may want to get a better look. I will take your place." Delo sat and took the oar.

Konrad walked to the bow and looked out. He saw mountains that seemed to go on forever. He turned full circle. It was as if they were trapped in a bowl. There was a ribbon of water below. Following with his eyes, he saw a huge waterfall feeding the river. The falls looked as if they poured straight from the rock. He could see no source above it. What had Sevyn told them earlier? It's more like we are traveling a stretch of road from beginning to end, then starting over and doing it once again. He ran between the men back to the stern. Shading his eyes from the sun, he peered behind them. Almost at the edge of his vision, he saw another waterfall like the one in front of them. "That's it, Sevyn!" Konrad smiled. He went to the middle and turned his head from front to back. "We are on a road, or a river in this case, going from beginning to end and then doing it once again!" He pointed one arm in each direction. "Do you see it? Waterfalls on each end and we are forever between them on this stretch of water only a few leagues long." He leaned over the side and pointed down at the river. The boat lurched to the left, almost spilling the crew, and Adlar had to quickly recover. Konrad was too excited to notice. "We need to fly forward to the river's source."

"Captain," Sevyn called out, "I see no source, only rock."

"Just because we cannot see it does not mean it is not there."

Tynn placed her hands on the bow again. The Golden Gull moved faster, headed for the river's source. The crew kept the oars in tight formation. As they neared the waterfall, the ship jerked to a stop and turned broadside to the falls. The wind quickly changed direction, causing the sail to billow out backwards and dump Gavin on the boards. He scrambled for the ropes. Just as he got hold of them, the wind stopped altogether and the sail fell limp. The ship floated in the air, not moving in any direction. The only sound was falling water.

Everyone was still. The longer they floated in place, the more the falls seemed to fade into the background. In a short while, there was practically no noise at all. A feeling crept over Delo. He looked at his arm. All the hairs stood on end. He closed his eyes and tilted his head to the side, straining to catch any sound. He heard a faint creak from the boards of the ship.

Delo opened his eyes to see Gavin staring and

leaning out to reach toward the falls. There was the slightest hint of a shadow behind the rushing water. Then, a faint sound, almost whisper-like, tickled Delo's ear. He closed his eyes trying to block out everything. The tickle turned to a high-pitched whistle, then there was a gasp.

"He's hit!" Konrad shouted. The ship rocked violently. Gavin was on his back in a pool of blood, an arrow in his shoulder. The crew scrambled for their weapons, trying to find the source of the attack. Syx and Sevyn crouched in the front and shielded their sister. The chaos on the small craft grew quickly. Delo leapt up, knife in hand, looking for the enemy. Konrad spun with his sword to face the falls. He saw no attackers.

They all seemed to realize at the same time that the scene was now almost as still and quiet as before. Only one arrow had been fired. The boat steadied, the crew relaxed somewhat, and calm was slowly returning. Syx moved to help Gavin with his wound.

Delo caught movement from the corner of his eye and looked up toward the top of the falls. Standing there on the rocks was a tall woman with fiery red hair, her bow trained on him.

"Apologies," she yelled down. "One of mine was a

bit anxious when your man leaned in a little too close. You know how young warriors can be. I hope your man is not badly hurt." She flashed a smile and lowered her weapon. "Permission to come aboard?"

Warrior

The woman disappeared back over the rocks. After a short time, a wooden plank extended from behind the falls until it rested on the edge of the boat. A man walked through the falling water with a cover made from animal skins held above him. It stretched behind him and past the falls creating a sheltered walkway. He reached the Gull, stopped, and waited until Konrad nodded. The man stepped into the boat, still holding the cover above him. The woman emerged and crossed the walkway. Konrad extended his hand as she stepped in.

"Thank you," she took his hand and smiled. "Are you the captain of this vessel?"

"I am," he answered. "Konrad is my name."

"I am Scarlet. I wish I could say 'well met', captain, but I am afraid you might take issue with that." She moved to Gavin. "My deepest apologies. My man was worried you were about to step through the water and attack."

Gavin gave a weak smile. "Just a scratch. Think nothing of it."

"I am sure it is more than a scratch. The poison from the arrow tip must be causing you much pain by now." Scarlet stood and waved back toward the waterfall. A man trotted across the plank with a small leather bag. She knelt next to Gavin and examined the wound. "Whomever removed this did a fine job. Our arrows have small notches in them that tear flesh when pulled back out instead of pushed through." She reached into the bag and came out with a bundle of green leaves pinched between her fingers. She pressed them into the entry point. Gavin winced, but said nothing. She lifted his shoulder and gently turned him on his side. "Yes, the exit wound is worse. The purple lines here show the poison is at work." She took a much larger amount from the bag and began stuffing the leaves deep into the hole." Gavin could not contain himself this time and let loose a string of curses that would embarrass a sailor.

"Apologies, my lady." He was gasping to get his breath.

"None needed," she patted his shoulder. "We

caused this, remember? It is I who owe you the apologies." She stood and turned to Konrad, "Captain, he should be fine in a few days. You will need to clean his wound and apply more tomorrow." She handed over the bag.

Konrad nodded. "Thank you, my lady."

"Scarlet," she interjected, "and no title is necessary. I am just a warrior."

"I doubt that you are just anything. You seem to have an air of leadership about you, but if you insist I will oblige. Thank you for your assistance, Scarlet." He stared at the waterfall. "Where are you from? Is this your home?"

She shook her head, red locks catching the sunlight. "You might say that this is our home, for the moment, but we are not from here. We are Stone Clan," she pointed up, revealing intricate tattoos on her arm, "from the other side of those mountains, but we have not been able to return since we crossed here to hunt. All roads are blocked with some sort of magic. Now it seems we are stuck here."

"As are we," Erik said from the stern, "ever since we got to this point. We are dead in the water." He looked out at the river below. "Well, dead above the water."

Scarlet looked down, "I would not be in a hurry to return to the river. It is usually not what it seems."

"I agree," said Konrad. "From what we have gathered, it looks to be like a long road with waterfalls on both ends. We keep traveling it only to repeat the journey."

Scarlet nodded, "I have heard stories since I was small about this river and how it confounds travelers."

"What is it called?" Konrad asked.

"It has many names." Scarlet replied. " I know of a few, but I am sure there are countless more. Some call it The Enigma. Others have named it Long Water. My father speaks of ancient songs about the River of Deceit that are told by a great, but tormented, storyteller named Alice. I have even heard it called Tam, named supposedly for a great warrior that is yet to come."

"I know it does not seem ideal," Konrad looked down. "But, how do we get back down to the water?"

Scarlet shrugged, "I was wondering how you got up here to begin with."

The Golden Gull floated in the air for hours. Konrad tried to find a way for them to get back to the river. They unfurled the sail and turned it in different directions, but there was no wind to find. Syx worked with the crew to move the oars, hoping this would propel them. It had no effect at all. Delo suggested they add weight to the ship in order to sink it. Scarlet's men brought rocks across the wooden bridge. At one point there were more stones than crew members, but still the Gull did not move. The men now had to unload the rocks, but they did not mind. They had been on the boat too long and needed to move.

Erik sat beside Adlar. "Go and stretch your legs a bit. I will handle this." Adlar thanked him and walked toward the front. Erik laid his hand on the steerboard, and suddenly the Gull fell. Men dropped to the deck in fear. Erik frantically tried to steer the vessel, but they kept falling.

Tynn grabbed Adlar, spinning him to face her. "Go to your post!" He scrambled over the crewmen and lunged for the steerboard, knocking the pilot over. As soon as he laid hands on it, the Gull slammed to a stop and once again floated in place.

Adlar turned to Erik with a puzzled look. They seemed to be thinking the same thing. Adlar gave a shaky nod and tightened his grip. Erik slowly reached out, hesitated for a moment, and took a deep breath. He shut his eyes as his hands closed around the handle. Nothing happened. They heard the crew let out a sigh of relief. Adlar laughed and clapped his hands together. Screams rang out as the ship fell again. He quickly grabbed the handle, but they did not slow. Tynn sprinted to the men and ripped Erik's hands free. They jerked to a stop. Half the crew looked seasick.

"It is who touches it and when." Tynn told them. "Adlar, let go." He hesitated. "It's all right," she assured him. He released his grip. They floated gently in place. Tynn looked at the crew. "Everyone, back to your places." After some shuffling, they were all ready. She looked to Adlar. "No one is touching the steerboard, but you had it last. You should be able to make us fly again. Concentrate on what you want the ship to do."

Adlar closed his eyes, took in a breath, and gripped the handle. Syx unfurled the sail, and the ship rode the wind up to the top of the falls. Tynn smiled. "Adlar, keep your hands there. Erik, grab it as well." Everyone braced for the fall. Erik grabbed the handle, but nothing changed. "Yes," Tynn nodded. "Adlar is in control, so Erik does not affect anything. Now Adlar, release your grip." He did so, and the Gull plummeted down. Adlar grabbed the board, but still they fell. Erik let loose, and they came to a stop. Now, the entire crew looked ill.

The Lo Road

Delo suggested that Scarlet's group join them. He mentioned being safer in large numbers and possibly finding a way home for them. She agreed. By the time they loaded all of Scarlet's men on board, it was dark. They decided to sleep with the ship floating where it was. It seemed safer than going to the river's edge again. At dawn they discovered another quirk about this place. There were currents in the air similar to the river, and they woke floating in midair next to the waterfall at the opposite end of the river. The crew voted to return to the water. Flying did not agree with most of them. Now, they were rowing steadily upstream again, Erik at the helm.

"I am curious," Scarlet told Delo, "how we can all fit in this ship. It does not seem to be nearly large enough."

Delo ran a hand through his curly, black hair. "I

agree. Nothing about this ship, or this journey, seems to make sense. Most think the Golden Gull is witched."

"The Golden Gull." She ran a hand over the gunwale. "I have heard stories, but this cannot be the same. The stories told to me were of a great three-masted sailing ship that met a fiery end."

"I have heard a similar tale, and more than a dozen others, about a ship that is not bound by time and travels between worlds." He stared out at the river and shook his head. "I never believed any of it, yet here we are on a river with no end in a ship that flies."

"There are other worlds," Sevyn told them. "My siblings and I have visited several."

"How?" Scarlet asked.

"There are paths that cross on occasion, letting one slip between the cracks." Sevyn leaned out and scooped a handful of water. He ran it over his head. "Most are found near water or in moonlight. Some folk are more tuned to magic than others; merfolk, elves, pixies and the like."

"Is that what Adlar is? Magic?" Delo asked, looking back at the stern.

"Him? No," Sevyn let out a chuckle, "He is just

tuned to air. Certain folk are more connected to the natural elements - fire, air, earth, water - than the rest of us. Those who are can cooperate with that element in a way. Tynn saw it when she touched him. It is one of her gifts."

"How did you find these paths to cross worlds?" Scarlet asked.

"We first heard of them from a lovely young selkie named Muireen," Syx joined them. "She was like moonlight in a bottle."

The water around the Golden Gull started to stir. The crew saw a tail crest, then disappear again beneath the surface. A sound, like a mix between a whisper and a whistle, floated in the air. It was almost musical. The men dropped the oars and sat, listening. The music morphed into a word, half spoken and half sung.

Muireen

A small seal broke the surface, its black eyes locking on to Delo. Muireen… He shook his head, trying to clear his thoughts. He heard it again. Was the seal talking to him? They locked eyes again, and he felt himself drifting away. He could hear more voices, all repeating the name.

Muireen Muireen Muireen Muireen Muireen

"Enough!" A voice smashed through the haunting song. Delo turned toward the sound. He saw a small girl in the water. Her dark hair fanned out on the surface like a lion's mane. It was pulled back to reveal pointed ears. She had a slightly crooked grin that gave her a mischievous look.

Sevyn came to get a closer look. "Are you merfolk or elf?" he asked.

"I am Lo," she replied with a smile as she spun full circle with her hands held high. "I am just me." She dove under, revealing a tail that produced a huge splash. Sevyn had no time to react and was doused from head to toe. The seals all barked little laughs. Lo resurfaced on the other side of the ship. "Do you know Muireen?" she asked, swimming in a circle.

"We do," Syx answered. "We met her one night on a little beach. Are you a friend?"

"I am Lo," she said as she dove under again and popped up near Scarlet. "Oh, you are like fire!" she smiled and held out her hand. Scarlet bent and touched Lo's fingers. "You are strong like a stone! You must be a fierce warrior." She swam over to Syx. "Does Muireen call you friend?"

"I would like to think so," he answered. "Are you part of her family?"

"We are the same clan," she swam back and forth in front of them. The small seals stayed further away and mimicked mer motions. "But, we are different." Lo brought her tail to the surface and spun. The moonlight played with the colors, creating a rainbow around her in the water.

"You are merfolk and she is selkie?" Sevyn said. "Are you part elf as well?"

"I am Lo," she dove under and splashed him again. She swam a complete turn around the Gull, stopping to admire the figurehead. "Pretty," she stared at the carved bird, then touched the front of the ship, "this bird can fly and swim." She came to the side and asked Sevyn, "Why are you here?"

"We are searching for the Red Diamond."

"I think you have found it," she told him. Most everyone on board spun to face the girl.

Konrad ran along the boat and leaned out, "What have we found?"

"The red stone." Lo swam under the boat and surfaced on the other side. "Take it under the falling water. That is where diamonds belong." She spun in a tight circle. "Follow. We will show you the way." She dove, slapping her tail on the water. The seals swam alongside the boat.

Follow Follow Follow

Lo led the way as the Golden Gull followed. The seals played, swimming back and forth under them as they made their way upriver. After an hour of rowing, they reached the falls.

"Travel through the tunnel." Lo told them. Her voice danced on the wind above the noise of the falls, reaching every ear.

"Where is the tunnel?" Konrad shouted.

"Under the falling water." Lo swam to the edge of

the waterfall. "Here."

Konrad motioned for the crew to row closer. He squinted. "There is nothing behind the water but solid rock. We cannot go through here."

"Not through, under." She spun several times, then swam to the front of the ship. "The river flows down." The seals splashed around her.

Down Down Down

She ran her hand over the carved feathers that extended down to the keel. "The seagull, she can swim." Lo dove and reappeared on the starboard side. She looked up at Tynn. "Find the fish. He can take you."

Tynn began walking the length of the ship as before. She stopped beside a very young man, practically a boy. "What is your name?"

"Fiske," the boy replied in a whisper.

The seals began to yap and bark. They swam excitedly around the Gull.

Fiske Fiske Fishke Fish Fish

Tynn led the young man to the stern. Erik stood and released the steerboard. Fiske reluctantly took the handle. The Gull began to sink. The crew yelled and prepared to throw items overboard to keep her afloat. Fiske let go. The Gull stopped, water almost to the gunwale. They were no longer sinking, but they were very close to it.

"Adlar." Sevyn called out. "We need Adlar to raise it back up."

Adlar got up and moved to the back. He gripped the wood. The crew let out a sigh as the ship started to rise. Adlar whooped and held a fist in the air.

"Adlar!" the captain yelled. "I think that will be enough, thank you." Adlar looked over the side. They were several feet above the water and still climbing. He let go and motioned to Erik. The pilot laughed and took the handle. The Gull dropped immediately, splashing down hard, throwing people and gear all about.

"Sorry, Captain." Erik said as he rubbed his sore back.

"Use the fish. Go under," Lo said.

"Lo," Konrad looked over the edge at her, "we cannot sink our ship. We would all drown."

"Use the fish. Go under," Lo repeated. "The red stone keeps you dry." Everyone looked more confused after her statement. Lo rolled her eyes and dove. She came up near Scarlet, with a small stone in her hand, and held it a few inches below the surface. "Take it." she said.

Scarlet reached for the stone. Steam formed around her hand, and the water parted. She was able to take it without getting her hand wet. "See? You are like fire!" Lo exclaimed. "Now, a sword." Scarlet looked at Delo. He handed her his weapon. Lo laughed and spun around. "In the water." Scarlet knelt to reach over the edge. She eased the sword into the river, and the same thing happened. The water parted, and the blade remained dry. "Yes, yes!" Lo clapped and swam to the front of the boat. "Like fire! You are the shield when the pretty bird swims," she laughed as she pointed to the gull on the bow.

After some time, and direction from Lo, the crew stored the gear and was ready. They formed a sort of roof from their shields. Scarlet stood amidship with her hands above her head, touching the shields. Fiske waited at the stern, while the rest of them manned the oars. Lo circled the ship twice, then stationed herself in front of it.

"Yes," she smiled, "follow!" She turned and dove. The seals splashed and barked at them.

Follow Follow Follow

Konrad glanced at Scarlet. She nodded and spread her feet, trying to brace herself. "Now, Fiske." The captain gave the order. Fiske took the handle in his hand. Now, the figurehead's eyes glowed green and the wings tucked in tight at its sides. The Gull began to sink. When the water reached the gunwales, the crew looked nervous. "Steady," Konrad assured them. "All is well." As the ship sank further, they took on water. It ran over the sides and covered the boards. Fiske let loose of the steerboard, and the Gull stopped moving.

"No!" Scarlet shouted. "Keep going. It will work!" She closed her eyes and mumbled, "It has to work."

Fiske started again. They continued to sink. The crew took a collective breath and, in a few seconds, they were fully submerged. All around them, the seals swam and played. Scarlet wondered if they had been tricked. Had Lo just led them all to their deaths?

Lo swam to Scarlet and touched her shoulder. Be

like fire! The words formed in Scarlet's mind. She closed her eyes and thought of how the water parted before. The ship was suddenly surrounded by thick fog. Scarlet could not even see if Lo was still next to her. After a few moments, the fog dissipated, and the ship was dry under the shield roof. They were surrounded by water, but they were dry inside a sort of bubble.

Delo let out his breath and tested the air. He could breathe! He reached out and touched the water at the edge of the boat. When he pulled his hand back, it was dry again. Delo stared at the water intently. Was there something out there? He moved closer to get a better look. Lo's face burst through the wall of water, sending him backwards head over heels onto the floor.

"Follow!" She disappeared back into the river.

"You heard her," Konrad shouted, "follow!" Delo scrambled back to his place as the crew began rowing. Syx and Sevyn stood at the bow, each leaning to one side and watching Lo in the murky water ahead. They pointed, helping Fiske stay the course. He had discovered that, while they were submerged, he was able to steer as well as tilt the board up and down to control their depth. The Gull was moving smoothly, and actually picking up speed now. Then, the ship jerked to one side.

"What did we hit?" Konrad yelled, looking around wildly.

"Something hit us!" Fiske pointed in the direction of the port bow. A huge shadow passed in front of them, and they lurched again. A second later, they took a hit from above. One of the shields fell, and water poured in.

"Help with the shields!" Scarlet shouted. She dare not take her hands away for fear of the entire roof collapsing. Delo sprang into action, grabbing the shield and throwing it to Gavin, who worked furiously to put it back in place. They took another hit, and the structure started to buckle. Delo moved next to Gavin to help hold the shields up. Water was up to their knees now.

"Down!" yelled Syx, "Lo is diving! Take us down, Fiske!"

The Gull was heavy with the weight of the water still flooding in. He fought the board, leaning his entire body against it to get it to respond. Another blow hit the ship, and tore a hole in the side. Water rushed in, causing the Gull to list.

"There!" Sevyn pointed forward in the direction they were leaning, "Lo is swimming for the tunnel! Follow her!" He ran and took a seat at the oar near the hole. "Row with all you have!"

The crew leaned on the oars and picked up their pace. The ship was moving faster, but was also at a precarious angle as she leaned to one side. Delo was sure they would roll at any second.

Fiske threw all of his weight against the handle, straining to keep the ship on course. There was a thunderous crack as the steerboard snapped. The Gull entered the tunnel at full speed and struck the ceiling, tearing the shields away. Fiske stared down at the red water around him. He felt a calm come over him as he closed his eyes and fell.

Cavern

Fiske opened his eyes, trying to focus on the chaotic scene around him. He was lying in the mud at the edge of a lake. He tried to sit up, but the pain in his side was too much to bear. Gasping, he lay on his back. High above was solid rock, possibly the ceiling of a cave. It was hard to tell in the dim light. His vision blurred. Fiske closed his eyes and tried to piece together what happened when they hit the tunnel. There had been a horrible noise as they crashed into the rock, screams everywhere, and water rushing in from all sides.

"Fiske!" The noise jolted him back to reality. Delo was pulling him further up the shore. The pain almost caused him to black out. "Stay awake!" Delo shook him. "Hold this here until I come back." Fiske looked down at the bloody cloth. His hand slid off to the side. "No! You have to hold this here!" Delo moved his hand back to the cloth and pressed down hard. Fiske groaned. Delo held Fiske's head so that their eyes met. "Keep it right there. I'll be back soon." He watched Delo run toward the screams.

Delo ran as fast as he could across the slick shore. Up ahead were Scarlet's men with swords drawn, frantically trying to get everyone off the Gull. A huge creature with crablike claws at the end of tentacles longer than five men was tearing at the hull. Syx and Sevyn managed to get to shore and were carrying their sister as far from the action as they could. She lay limp in their arms. Gavin was waist deep in water at the stern, pulling crew members out as fast as he could, while Konrad faced the beast head on with a sword in each hand.

Delo reached Scarlet. "How many are still on board?" he shouted. There was a crack, followed by horrible shrieks, as the monster tore into the hull. Some of the crew fell to the mud, cut in half by giant claws, still alive and screaming in agony.

"Not sure," Scarlet drew her bow and shot at the creature. The arrow fell to the ground without inflicting any damage. She shook her head, "We have not been able to slow it down with anything."

A group of about a dozen men charged the beast with their blades. With the swing of a tentacle, they were thrown into the underground lake. As they hit the water, a huge fish broke the surface and swallowed at least half of them. The remaining men splashed and tried to swim for shore, only to be plucked under one by one.

Gavin ran to Delo, "Distract it! I need you to get its attention!" He spun and sprinted down the shoreline. Turning his head he yelled back, "Hurry!"

Delo headed toward the giant, waving for Scarlet to follow. They ran in the opposite direction from Gavin. Delo banged his sword against his shield. Scarlet yelled and continued to fire arrows as fast as she could at the monster's eyes. A few found their mark, not penetrating, but doing enough to irritate the creature. It turned to them, swinging three tentacles along the ground. Delo was just out of reach, but Scarlet could not avoid the attack. She flew high in the air, landing hard where the muddy sand met rock. Delo ran to her.

"Go back," she managed, breathing hard. "Gavin needs you." She sat up a little, "I will be fine. Go!"

Delo nodded, and ran back, banging the sword. The huge eyes were focused on him, and claws swept the sand, searching. He glanced back toward the ship. Gavin was with Erik and Adlar, cautiously climbing into the back of the Gull. Just as they cleared the water, a gaping mouth latched on to Adlar's leg. He let out a scream as he was pulled down. Gavin dropped down inside the ship and popped back up with the anchor in hand. He leapt over the side and brought the anchor down, burying one of the flukes deep in the fish's head. Adlar pulled free, and they climbed aboard and scrambled for the stern. Gavin saw that the handle was gone.

"Broken off," Adlar told him, "it ran Fiske clean through." He pointed to Fiske lying on the beach in a pool of blood, the fight over for him.

"Grab hold here!" Gavin pointed to a small piece of the handle that was still attached.

Adlar wrapped his hand around the broken piece. The Gull lurched and tried to rise. The stern was a few feet above water, but a tentacle lay across the bow. Gavin pushed Adlar's hand away and motioned for Erik to take the handle. The ship dropped hard back down. Gavin nodded to them both. Adlar grabbed the wood again and the boat rose up, then Erik took the board and the ship dropped. The men repeated this over and over. The monster was busy dealing with the attack from Delo, and could not turn its attention to them.

The Gull finally broke free. The ship was torn and

mangled with the bow hanging lower than the stern, but it was still in one piece. It rose until Adlar let go and held the ship in place. Gavin looked over the side. "Push the beast back!" he yelled out to Delo.

Delo charged, but he was of no concern. An arrow whistled overhead and hit the monster's eye, then another. They came in a furious volley. He looked back and saw Scarlet sitting up, her back against a rock, firing as fast as she could. The creature let out a roar and slid back away from the attack. Gavin cheered from above and urged Scarlet on. After another round of arrows, the creature moved away from her again. The Golden Gull floated above the beast. It turned and reached out its claws, intent on finishing the ship for good.

Then, the monster howled, slashing at something in the water. Erik saw Lo swimming just out of range of the deadly claws. She was screaming with an intensity that shook the whole cave. All of the beast's attention was focused on her, and it followed as she moved away from the shore. She lured it directly under the Golden Gull.

Erik grabbed the broken handle and the ship slammed down. The carved bird's beak dug into the monster's eye. It thrashed and threw the Gull about, then let out a long sigh and fell still.

The Diamond

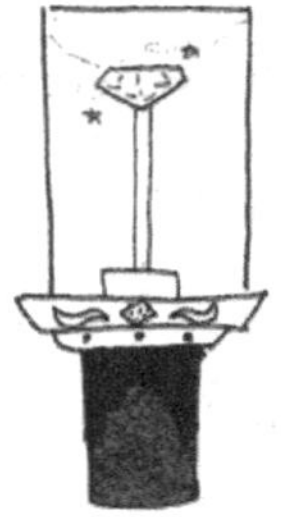

Delo spent the next few hours trying to account for everyone. Almost all of the crew were gone. The seers were safe, but no one could find the captain. Erik and Adlar buried the bodies they did find.

The Golden Gull was battered beyond repair. Gavin pointed out that they did not even know where the tunnel was, nor did they have a plan to get back, so it really did not matter. He tried to salvage what he could in case they were stranded in the cavern for a while. Being underground, they could not tell the time of day. At some point everyone just knew that they were too tired to continue. Gavin managed to start a fire using some of the wooden gear boxes. They found dry sand further from the water and sat in a circle close to the flames. Supper was a small amount of dried fish that had survived in one of the crewman's bags. Most fell asleep quickly or were nodding off.

Delo heard a faint rustling noise. As his vision adjusted to the low light, a figure emerged on the other side of the fire. He scrambled back when he recognized the face, reaching for his sword. He stood and shouted, but no one woke.

"Well warrior, we finally have a chance to talk."

"Talk about what?" Delo moved to his friends and tried to wake them but got no response.

"The diamond, of course."

"How did you get here, Ubel?" Delo glared at the intruder's twisted face. It looked like a skull in some places. In other spots the flesh seemed to crawl and move.

"Why are you surprised?" the figure replied, "After all, I am a wizard." He stood and took a step forward.

"You are a lot of things," Delo sneered, keeping distance between them. "Why are you here?"

"For the same reason as you, to find the Red Diamond." Ubel pointed at the Golden Gull, " It looks as if you've had a bit of trouble." He crossed the mud to where the ship lay, still on top of the tentacled giant. He sighed, bending to give the monster a gentle pat, "You did your best."

Delo gripped his sword tight and charged the wizard. "You sent that beast to kill us?" He stopped suddenly, dropping the blade and clawing at invisible hands around his throat. As his face began to turn blue, Delo dropped to his knees.

"Let's not end things this way." Ubel waved his hand. Delo gasped as air returned to his body. "I did not send anything to kill you. I just needed it to make sure you would be unable to return."

"If you knew where to go, then why send us?" The warrior reached for his sword. It slid across the sand and into the water.

"You are persistent." Ubel laughed. "I did not know you would be in this place, warrior, until you got here. The only certainty was that I needed to put you on the river. After that, I knew only what little my loyal companions could see through their sister." Two small men stepped into the firelight. Delo knew immediately who they were. Ayte and Nyne have taken an unfortunate path.

"You would betray your own blood to follow this serpent?" Delo growled at them. They said nothing.

"Did the king know about this?" He struggled to his feet.

"That fool?" the wizard's bony face broke into something resembling a grin. "I needed him to assemble a crew after these two located the Golden Gull. He played his part."

"The warring clans, and bringing peace, that was all a lie?"

"The fighting is true. Only I am not interested in peace." He turned boxes over, spilling the contents on the sand. "Once I have the diamond, I can conquer that tiny kingdom and so much more." He kicked through the pile, then stared at the water. He walked toward the dead beast.

"We never found a diamond!" Delo spat the reply. "Your plan is finished." He stumbled back to the fire and tried desperately to wake the rest. They were all breathing, but no one stirred. It was as if they were under a spell.

"I am just beginning, warrior." Ubel saw a small splash and reached across a tentacle. "What have we here?" He stood up holding a seagull. He carried the bird back to the fire. "Where is the diamond, little one?"

The gull's eyes shined bright red. It spread its wings, hopping from Ubel's lap and flying in a low circle around the cave. The bird finally landed next to Scarlet. Delo watched in amazement as the tattoos on her arms began to glow fiery red. She rose in the air, spinning furiously, red hair flying out around her. When she finally stopped, she floated above the fire. Her arms were covered in red diamond patterns.

When Ubel reached out and touched one of the diamonds, it left her arm and drifted toward him, growing bigger. It surrounded him in its red glow. After a few seconds, the diamond disappeared. Ubel held his hands out. They were shaking. Taking a deep breath, Ubel turned toward the broken ship. He held his hands out and clapped them together. The sound was like thunder in the cave.

Delo watched as the Golden Gull was crushed like a small toy. With a wave, Ubel sent the pile of rubble flying across the cave and into the lake. He touched another diamond on Scarlet's arm. This time, what enveloped the wizard was even bigger. When it finally faded, Ubel stood almost twice as tall as before, his eyes burning red like the ones in the figurehead of the Golden Gull.

Suddenly, a scream shook the cave so hard that Ubel almost lost his balance. He spun around to see Lo at the lake's edge. As the wizard raised his hands to conjure a spell, Delo advanced, gripping the hilt of the sword he took from Gavin when he tried to wake him. He plunged the blade into Ubel with all his might. Delo stared in horror as two arms grew from the wizard's back. They pulled the sword out, and Ubel turned to face him.

"If I were you," he said with a wicked smile across his skull-like face, "I would run."

Delo reached for the knife in his boot and sighed. Nothing was ever simple.

The wizard Ubel had captured Raama's attention, reminding him of the Citadel mages who twisted truths to serve their own agendas. Like those mages, Ubel sought to control the power of the Red Diamond, seeking dominance.

In Delo and the other's collective strength, Raama found inspiration. Maybe facing this challenge alone was not the answer. But where should he seek help?

The realization that each tale held a fragment of the solution he sought struck him. All he needed was to piece them together. Yet, he suspected that the answer he sought might not be the one he had hoped for.

Part Eight

Trading on Vanir
By J.C. Lovero

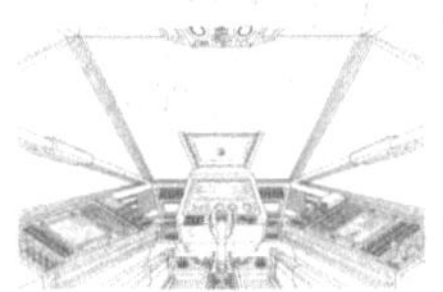

Impact

A brilliant splash of bright light washed over the display. Vraxed vessels appeared on every side of the Golden Gull, materializing out of thin air where the ship's instruments had only detected open space.

"Why are they attacking us?"

Silgryn Eridanus hunched over the readout, trying to activate the ship's nano shield, but before he could, an enormous crash rocked him out of his chair.

He pushed himself off the floor, breaths laden with the lingering weight of the impact. "EDIS, status update."

The holographic image of the ship's artificial intelligence flashed in front of him. "Hull integrity remains stable. Seven guns warped in the explosion."

"Seven?!"

"Affirmative," EDIS said, her voice diagnostic.

Silgryn pulled up a cylindrical display of readouts and instrument controls at his station. He was down to one gun, and through the glowing monitor, a large force of over one hundred vessels breached the perimeter.

The ship trembled with another crash.

"Two hundred additional vessels incoming," EDIS said.

Silgryn's chest tightened. It was a foolish notion to think he could escape without being detected. He should have known better than to accept the job with the Vraxed, but he was down to the last scraps of rations. To cover the cost of his mother's medpacs and polybiotics, he sold scrap parts from his ship, but it wasn't enough to last the entire month.

The Golden Gull was a mid-size survey ship, ideal for stealth jobs along the perimeter of the Argus system. It could handle one-on-one skirmishes here and there, but not a full-blown assault. He wouldn't stand a chance with one gun against three hundred vessels, but he had to do something.

Silgryn slammed his fist onto the control console. The cylindrical display around him shimmered as the ship's defense bubble activated. He adjusted his grip on the helm as the Golden Gull staggered from another explosion.

"EDIS, activate the jump drive." He traced his finger along a lighted projection display, ending on the surface of an unknown, nearby planet.

"Calculations are not complete. The current path has a thirty-seven percent chance of success."

"We can't fight them, EDIS. Not an entire fleet. It's better than zero."

"Inquiry: are you certain? Your heart rate has increased by forty-two percent."

The display flickered off when a massive explosion pierced through the force field, hitting the bridge. The roof of the Golden Gull ruptured in a shower of sparks and debris.

Silgryn dodged a chunk of metal rubble as the smoke billowed around him.

"EDIS, now!"

Echoing screams ripped through the ship. Silgryn slammed into the wall behind him before a deluge of bright white light washed over him. His eyes strained to focus on the display as the holographic shape of EDIS melted into a blurry haze.

\#

Judgment

Silgryn winced as his eyes squinted against a vibrant periwinkle sky, splashed with hues of pumpkin and magenta from the rising dawn. He wasn't in the Golden Gull anymore, but a jail cell. His memory was fuzzy, but he could recall being captured and falling in and out of consciousness after the crash. How long he had been imprisoned—or the fate of his ship—he could not say.

The cell door scraped against the stone floor. He squinted to adjust his vision amidst the shadows.

"Get up." A man stood in front of him, wearing a tunic spun of indigo silk embroidered with silver trimmings. Raven black hair was tucked behind his ears, which extended away from his face into points that matched the spears of his crown. He stood expectantly—stoic—as if this was a practiced ritual from years of training. If he wasn't so serious from all the frowning, he'd look… pleasant.

Handsome, even.

"What's going on?" Silgryn asked.

"Follow me."

Guards stood on both sides of Silgryn as they marched out of the dungeon and into a cavern. The only sounds were his shallow breathing, paired with the throbbing on his head, along with the clanking of metal armor against the stone floor. Torches lined the walls, lighting their way in an otherwise dark corridor. After what felt like an eternity, a sliver of orange light at the end of the path greeted them.

And then came the voices. Sounds of a teeming crowd echoed in the passageway. The armed escorts tugged him forward into a cacophony of laughter, shouting, and whistling. The end of the cavern opened up into a massive arena with a rioting crowd.

Silgryn couldn't make out what they were shouting, but he had a good enough idea. The stone floor of the cavern was replaced with slick mud, and he struggled to keep his footing as he walked.

The guards stopped him in front of a floating platform erected above the crowd. An older man wearing a jewel-encrusted crown sat on a throne, who raised a hand to silence the roaring stadium.

"I am King Malec. What is your name?"

"Silgryn. Where's my ship?"

"You stand accused in the high court of planet Vanir."

"Wait, what for?" Silgryn's muscles tensed.

"For conspiring with the Vraxed, sworn enemy of the Argus galaxy," the King said.

No, he couldn't get caught. Not like this. His parents still needed him. Alive. He'd been in worse situations before: the slave pens of Eleteirys or stranded in the mountains of the Titan Nebula during winter without food or shelter. Growing up in the slums of Earth taught him a thing or two about survival. "I'm not a... spy. I stole cargo from one of their battleships."

"So you're a smuggler?" The King frowned. "You're far from home, human."

A sinking feeling settled in his stomach. According to the intergalactic treaty between the Milky Way and

Argus, some crimes were punishable by death on certain planets. He knew nothing of Vaniren laws. If only he had EDIS with him, he might talk his way out of this.

The handsome one nudged him with an elbow. "Just answer the question." His eyes held an intensity within them. Some stares were curious. Others, judgmental. But this was more… reassuring.

Silgryn sighed. "Yes. I'm just a smuggler, trying to make ends meet."

The collective gasps of the crowd whooshed across the arena like a tidal wave. Not good.

"Some stars in the Argus system would execute you without question," the King said. "Luckily, for you, Vaniren law is more… forgiving."

The crowd chanted in unison. "Dar Mataan. Dar Mataan. Dar Mataan."

The guards stepped off the platform and moved to a portcullis on the far end of the arena.

The crowd continued their chant. Silgryn turned to the man beside him. "What does that mean?" he asked.

"It's an ancient Vaniren tradition." He took Silgryn's hand, setting three vials in his palm. Dar Mataan proves one's honor in battle. If you emerge victorious, the King is bound by the Goddess to grant you whatever you request."

Silgryn's chest tightened. "But I'm not a warrior."

"These will help." He pointed to the vials. "Orange is a speed stim. Red is a strength stim. Blue is a healing stim. Use them wisely."

"Who are you?"

"My name is Prince Kalec Morrowith." He held out a crystalline sword. "We found this amidst the remains of your crashed ship. You will need it."

The ornate blade was unlike the plasma blasters he was accustomed to. The sword was embedded with jewels and filigree, more decorative than practical.

The guards raised the portcullis, yet there was no enemy to be seen. The crowd quieted to a murmur, and the ground rumbled below him. When he turned back, Kalec was no longer beside him, instead seated beside his father on the floating platform above.

Silgryn gripped the sword hilt as he walked into the slick mud. Something rushed toward him, but from where, he could not say. And then it appeared. A giant worm, its mouth filled with razor-sharp teeth, barreling towards him.

The crowd erupted, cheering the worm towards its next meal.

Silgryn ran.

\#

Dar Mataan

Silgryn had heard of the magic on Vanir. How the Vaniren could harness the power of the elementals and bend nature to their will. Intergalactic history spoke of shamans and ritualists who could manipulate the ambient air and water to extract its healing properties and cure illness. Vanirens were often hired by larger transport ships to serve as onboard medics.

What people spoke less about was the other side of their magic. The destructive side, harnessing fire and earth, and the creatures within.

Silgryn slid and slipped on the mud, which transformed into trenches as he ran, providing another barrier for him to overcome. A maze. One wrong turn could lead to a dead end, where he would surely meet his demise.

The crowd roared, drowning out the chomping

and crashing sounds of the gigantic worm. The growing stench told him it was gaining on him, closing the distance between them. He found a fork in the muddy maze and veered right.

When Silgryn was a child, he used to steal food from the Sector Seven vendors when they weren't looking. Whenever law enforcement chased after him, he hid in the nooks and crannies in alleyways and sewers, waiting them out until nightfall, when he could sneak in the shadows. And although he couldn't wait out a hungry worm, he needed to find a safe spot where he could come up with a plan.

He turned right at another fork. He had lost count of how many turns he had made. Although he had no proper training on how to wield a sword, it was his only weapon. Perhaps he should turn around and fight.

Silgryn dared a look over his shoulder, and heat surged through him as the worm thrashed. He slipped and slid into a muddy wall, losing his momentum and any distance he had gained. Two rows of sharp teeth gnashed as the creature screamed, and the crowd roared in excitement as the gap between them closed.

Silgryn pushed himself up and veered another right. The crash behind him was enough to send a rush of adrenaline through him. The crowd's collective gasp sucked the air out of the musky arena. Above him, the King and Prince watched, both with frowns on their faces. And although the King's scowl seeped of disappointment, the Prince's was softer, almost like… concern.

Silgryn nearly missed a slender opening because of that look, but he skidded to a halt to squeeze himself through the gap. It was too small for the worm, and if it couldn't break through the mud, it would buy him some time. As he pulled himself through the gap, the mud shifted once again, and he'd gotten stuck. He pushed and pulled, but the mud was too slick, and held fast like transformed stone.

The trench trembled from the worm's movements. The chomping noise grew louder. No, not like this. It couldn't end like this.

Silgryn raised the sword and stabbed, hoping to use it as leverage to push himself out of the trap. The ground below him rumbled, and the stench intensified around him. He carved into the wall, and another shriek sounded off. Teeth clicked together, the sound growing.

A clinking sound in his pocket caught his attention. The stims. He reached for the red vial and gulped it. The concoction burned down his throat, then through his veins as if he had ingested a bowl of spicy ravasaur soup. With newfound strength, he stabbed into the wall once again, adrenaline coursing through him. There was a squelch, then a sudden release of pressure, as if the mud reacted to him, and he fell through the crack before it closed up. A crash reverberated around him, and the crowd sighed as the worm launched itself over and above him.

Curious—why would it do that? It would have seen him struggling with the wall, and if it could jump like that, it could have just sprung upon him and ended it there.

The faces of the crowd were fixed with disappointment, their eyes focused at the other end of the muddy arena, following the trail of the worm. And that's when it dawned on him.

The worm was blind.

The walls of mud shifted, and an enormous pit opened up before Silgryn. The crowd leaned over to peer inside, reaching the same conclusion: there was no way out. Silgryn was trapped. The walls were too steep to climb, and the mud much too slick.

He had one advantage over the worm.

Silgryn rolled in the reeking mud, covering every inch of his body. Face, hair, armpits, everything. The crowd hissed as he coated himself in it, completely masking his human smell from the gigantic worm on the other side of the arena. If the creature truly was blind, then it would rely on its other senses to find its prey. In order to get out of this alive, he needed to be invisible.

Back on the planet Pangaea, Silgryn was hungry for food after a bounty mission. He had parked the Golden Gull in the lush rainforest and found what the natives called grubworms. He had never been a fan of insects, but EDIS assured him it was a delicacy among the Pangaean people. Something she said stuck with him: in order to get around the armored shell, you must pierce the weakest part of the worm: the underbelly.

Silgryn dug into the slick mud at the intersection of the only opening into the pit. Aside from his sword, he only had two stims left, and he needed to use them wisely. Once the hole was deep enough, he plunged the sword—hilt first—a few feet in front of it. After getting stuck, he had learned the mud had different consistencies, some of it harder and more durable. He selected the toughest mud to hold the sword in place, hoping it would stay.

Up above, they broadcasted the conversation to the crowd, as if the King and Prince were commentators for an arena brawl.

"What's he doing?" the King asked.

"He's building a trap," Kalec said.

The crowd gasped. Some cheered at his ingenuity, while others booed - likely the ones who bet against his life.

Back during a mission to the Pyros Nebula, Silgryn was smuggling medical grade supplies to the highest bidder, who happened to be the Vraxed. They filled half of the crates on his ship with healing stims to be used by field medics when soldiers had taken battle wounds. EDIS droned on and on about them: medical grade healing stims are preferred in the field due to their rapid onset of action. Once administered, a wound is patched up in minutes, preventing the need for hospitalization or nano-sutures.

"Here goes nothing," Silgryn said, running his arm across the top of the blade. His skin split open, and blood welled in rivulets as it dripped to the floor. He ventured back through the tunnel leading into the pit, creating a trail of blood for the worm to smell. He cracked open the healing stim and applied it to his wound. It would only be a matter of time before the cut would seal up, effectively making him invisible again.

It was only then when he realized the crowd had gone silent. But they fixated all of their eyes on him. Where was the worm?

Then, Kalec's voice shattered through the silence. "TO YOUR RIGHT!"

Silgryn tried to move away to gain some distance, but the wall behind him exploded. Bolts of heat rushed through him as the sharp scales of the worm sliced through his left side, scraping the skin raw from his shoulder down to his calf muscle. He screamed in pain as he crashed into a nearby wall of mud. He dropped the remainder of the healing stim, now crushed underneath the beast as it gnashed its way toward him.

He cracked open the speed stim and drank from the phial. This was it. He pushed himself through the pain and lunged forward. The surrounding walls blurred as he ran, the adrenaline his only source of fuel as he moved toward the pit. He took a sharp turn, ignoring the chomping sounds behind him as the worm chased in a frenzy of hunger. Another turn, and his left leg screamed from the blood loss. No longer invisible, he would eventually end up in the pit without an exit.

The mouth of the pit loomed, and when Silgryn caught sight of the sword, he leaped. He didn't have time to think, except that it had to work. Back when he was on a mission in The Far Rim to smuggle mistmantle gems out of the planet's casino, he was working with a team of thieves. The leader had taught him one of the most valuable lessons: always have a plan B, because plan A never goes right. Silgryn hit the ground, squatting into the dugout he had created right behind the sword. It was large enough for him to curl inside, but not big enough for the worm to swallow him whole. And if the worm wanted to eat him, it had to deal with the sword sticking up from the rigid mud.

Darkness covered him, followed by chomping. Then a crash, along with a screeching sound. Silgryn kept his head down, eyes shut, waiting for the worm to devour him. An oozy liquid crawled into the dugout, the stench overwhelming his senses. Silgryn vomited inside his little hole. A wet, crunching noise sounded out above him, followed by silence.

The worm was on top of him, but it wasn't moving.

He inhaled gulps of air to calm himself, then pushed out of the hole, maneuvering around the sharp carapace of the lifeless worm. Pain replaced the adrenaline. Blood as dark as crimson stained the left half of his clothes, turning his gray pilot outfit into a shade of black. Somehow, he defeated the worm, even though he'd never considered himself a fighter by any stretch of the imagination. Lightness filled his head as the arena spun around him.

The King opened his mouth, but Silgryn could not make out the words. He crashed into the slick mud. The last thing he remembered was the smell of vomit in his mouth mixed with the metallic taste of blood before darkness consumed him.

\#

Terms

Silgryn emerged from strange dreams of crash landing on an unknown planet and gigantic mud worms. His room was colder than he remembered. Maybe he forgot to switch on the arclight radiator before retiring to his bunk.

Yet, something was not right. Golden lanterns floated around the room, one beside each cot. Voices filtered from the outside, in a language he did not understand.

He pushed himself up, and bolts of pain ignited on his left side. No, it hadn't been a dream. He wasn't lying in the Golden Gull. He was on Vanir.

"Lie back down." Kalec sat beside him, the same concerned frown he remembered seeing from the arena. "Give me room to work."

Kalec passed his hands over Silgryn's eviscerated flesh. Golden light radiated from his palms, hovering in the space between them. The skin around the reddened cuts turned to pink, leaving etch marks on Silgryn's entire left side.

"So, you're some kind of healer?" Silgryn asked.

"And you're either very smart or lucky."

"Ouch." Whether it was his ego or his body injured with that remark, he could not be sure. A faint buzz radiated from the glowing lanterns, reminding him of the Golden Gull and the navigation console. It was the last thing he remembered before crash landing on Vanir to complete his mission.

"You're going to be weak for a quarter moon," Kalec said. He placed a hand on Silgryn's bicep, and a burning sensation pricked his skin. "And it's going to leave several scars. I'm sorry."

Silgryn chuckled. "It's alright. What kind of space pirate doesn't have tattoos and scars, right?" He had

been teased in the space ports of Ismar, especially inside
cantinas where seasoned smugglers would celebrate
after successful hauls. At first, he chalked it up to being
young, but ten years later, he couldn't use that excuse
any longer. Especially when the worry lines replaced the
bad teenager acne on his forehead.

Truth be told, he always accepted the safe jobs.
The ones that paid just enough for him to get by with
food. Lucrative missions often came with greater risk,
and he had no interest in putting his life on the line.
No amount of money was worth his death. But when
his parents got sick, he had depleted his meager savings.
Suddenly, he had to take the tough missions, like the
Vraxed smuggling job. But at what cost?

Kalec frowned. "I suppose it will appeal to the
ladies."

"And what about Vaniren Princes?" he asked.

Kalec's pale face flushed red, breaking his otherwise
stoic demeanor. He cleared his throat. "You should rest."

"I don't understand." When Silgryn had set the
trap for the worm, Kalec warned him of the worm's
location. Without the intervention, it would have been
more than just his left side—he'd be dead. Kalec had no
reason to help him. At least—not a clear one.

"What?"

"Why'd you help me?"

Kalec stared at him for a long moment. The angular planes of his face differed from his own people back on Earth. His eyes held a golden color, illuminated by the floating lanterns in the room.

"Kalec." The King strode into the room, dressed in royal Vaniren regalia. A stark contrast compared to the simple robes donned by the Prince. "Ich mekindfra lund."

Kalec frowned. "Prutyndrea quchwanda est."

"Uh, where I come from, it's considered rude to speak another language in front of someone."

"Name your terms," the King said.

"What do you mean?"

"According to Vaniren tradition, if someone survives the Dar Mataan, we grant them a boon," Kalec said. "My father is asking what you want."

Silgryn inhaled a deep breath, then exhaled slowly. How would any rational person answer a question like that? The obvious answer would be money—loads of it—to repair the ship and take care of his parents. But it also felt… cheap. He couldn't imagine a life where he sat in a palace all day with stuffy dignitaries. No, he needed to be flying amidst the stars, seeking the next adventure. He needed to be free.

"I'm in no condition to fix my ship." He pointed to his scarred arm. "If you help me repair the Golden Gull, I'll get out of here."

"Proightwend," the King said.

"Father, you can't be serious." Kalec pinched his lips into a thin line.

The King turned on his heels and exited the infirmary without another word.

"Translation?"

Kalec sighed. "It appears I'm stuck with you a little longer."

\#

Conflict

Remnants of the Golden Gull lay scattered around him. Though the pilot's station remained intact, the exterior suffered from deep gashes. Nevermind the gaping hole in the ship's roof. Without the help of Kalec and his father, it would cost him a year's worth of credits from odd jobs to repair the ship.

"EDIS? You there?"

"Who's that?" Kalec pressed his lips into a thin line.

"The ship's AI. I had her installed to help me navigate smuggling missions."

"I see."

Before Silgryn could probe further into Kalec's questioning, a faint buzz from the ship's navigation console replied. A faint silhouette crackled in front of them before cutting itself off. Damaged, along with the rest of the Golden Gull.

Over the next several days, Vaniren engineers worked day and night to repair the ship. Since Silgryn was still recovering from his wounds, he took to the sidelines with Kalec to supervise the work. Though, he often intervened if he saw something amiss, especially for the welfare of the Golden Gull.

"Careful with that nanodrive spanner!" he yelled at someone tinkering inside the ship's mainframe. "You're going to short-circuit something."

Kalec tilted his head to one side. "These are the

best engineers in all of Vanir. They're responsible for all the planet's infrastructure with a millennia of combined experience. Relax."

Silgryn joined the engineers. He rummaged for the toolbox amidst the rubble. Perhaps if he could get the ship's motherboard functional again, he could activate EDIS and send an update to his broker.

"Fine. We're due for a break, anyway." Kalec motioned for the engineers to follow him back to the palace for lunch. "Coming?"

Silgryn sighed, then rubbed the back of his neck, ignoring him.

Kalec muttered something in his native language, and though he couldn't understand what it meant, the Prince's tone said it all. Had the circumstances been different, Silgryn could see himself getting along with Kalec. But he had a job to do, and there was no use getting attached.

The Golden Gull laid at the end of a skid. It had leveled a field of dreamleaf trees, sliding to an abrupt halt from the crash, where it laid half-overturned on a steep hill overlooking an enormous valley. He traced a finger along the blast marks on the hull, left behind by the attack.

As he searched for a replacement power capacitor, his breath hitched from a low, guttural growl. Behind him, a beast with glowing red eyes glared. The animal was the size of a bear, covered in fur around its face and paws. But the rest of its body was covered in serpent scales.

Silgryn straightened himself, standing upright with his hands in front of him. "Who's a good boy?"

The animal let out a screeching roar, then charged.

Silgryn dodged out of its path, tumbling into the grass. A crash resounded in the ship's hull from the impact, shattering crates containing the remaining cargo he had stolen.

The animal thrashed in the rubble. Perhaps it was stuck, but Silgryn's stomach sank at the thought of how many credits he had just lost. The traders back home would not buy damaged goods, especially anything to be sold on the underground market.

"No! Not the contraband. Go maul something else."

The beast whipped around, its red eyes now focused on Silgryn. He searched his belt for a weapon to defend himself, only equipped with a small hyperdrive wrench.

Hardly a match for the beast three times his size.

"Alright. No more Mister Nice Smuggler." He had defeated a giant mud worm in the Dar Mataan. Surely, a bear serpent would be no match for him, even in his wounded state. Right?

With newfound courage, Silgryn charged, landing blunt blows on the animal's ferocious snout. The spanner sang like crystal when its edge clashed against the scaled hide of the beast. He pushed his luck, but on an upswing, the animal used the opportunity to swipe at him with its enormous paw.

Silgryn catapulted into the air, losing his weapon and landing on the ground with a painful thud. Before he could regain his composure and push himself up, the beast was already charging at him in full force. In a few seconds, the fight would be over. He gasped, then closed his eyes shut, bracing for the impact.

"Stop."

The voice was singsong in quality. Gentle, yet firm.

When Silgryn opened his eyes, Kalec stood between them, both arms outstretched. Motes of magic drifted through the air, weaving around them and casting everything in shades of blue and green. The earth seemed different under their feet, as if changed. Calm.

The animal huffed at him, thrashing its head left and right, like it was resisting.

"It's all right," Kalec said. He turned to look at Silgryn. "Give me your hand."

Silgryn suppressed a quiver in his stomach. "Wait, what?"

"Do you want to live?" Kalec grabbed him by the forearm, then placed his hand on the beast's snout.

The animal sniffed at him, then sneezed, coating him with a layer of clear mucus.

"Aww, that's just mean," he said.

The hint of a smile broke through Kalec's otherwise rigid face. "He likes you."

With one last gentle nudge, the beast turned away, retreating into the forest. Silgryn wiped the snot off his tunic, then cast a sidelong glance at the Prince.

"What?" Kalec asked.

He rubbed against the goosebumps along the back of his neck. "I've been to lots of places, and I've never seen an animal like that before."

Kalec wrinkled his nose. "It must be nice, traveling all around the galaxy."

"Don't get out much?"

Kalec shook his head.

"Huh. I thought princes got to travel wherever you wanted. You know, with all that royal snobbery."

"And I thought smugglers could hold their own in a fight, with all those street smarts."

"We don't get gigantic worms on the streets of Earth." He poked at his bandaged arm, and a jolt of pain shot through him.

Kalec frowned. "Let me see."

Silgryn pulled away. "It's fine. Nothing a medpac won't fix."

Kalec grabbed his arm, then removed the bandages for a closer inspection. "Hmm. Needs peacebloom."

The prince led him away from the crash site, venturing deeper into the surrounding forest. Vanir felt so different from Earth—it was as if the air lived and breathed. Tiny flowers sprouted in Kalec's footprints on the grass as he walked. The bushes rustled in greeting as they passed. The forest was alive, like it was its own person. A friend, as much as a place.

Kalec stopped at the base of a large tree. He collected small flowers surrounding it. "When the first settlers of Vanir landed on this planet, these flowers were abundant." He pulled a mortar and pestle out of his satchel, crushing the flowers into dust. "We later learned they also carried healing properties."

Kalec opened a flask and poured it into the mortar, mixing everything into a tincture.

"That burns," Silgryn said, jerking his arm away. "Is this supposed to help?"

"Stay still."

Golden light radiated from Kalec's palm. Everywhere he touched, Silgryn could feel a tingling flow, as if a thousand tiny pinpricks tickled him, streaming into his blood. Kalec's fingers gently brushed over his arm, and whether the sparks were from the magic or from something else between them, he could not say.

Suddenly, the pain was gone.

"Better?" Kalec asked.

The Prince's face was inches away from him. So close he could smell the moonberry juice from lunch on his breath.

Silgryn opened his mouth to make a sharp retort, but the words wouldn't come. Something in the prince's face stopped him. Just a flicker—maybe imagined—but…

"Your highness!"

Kalec pulled away, turning to the voice of the knight calling after him. "What is it?"

"You're needed at once. Several villagers have fallen ill."

\#

Reversal

Day after day, more and more villagers fell ill. The castle infirmary was overwhelmed, and Kalec, as the chief healer, left his supervision of the Golden Gull's repairs to take care of the sick. On the bright side, the ship's mainframe computer had finally been repaired, giving Silgryn access to EDIS.

"There's gotta be a record of it somewhere. Keep looking," he said.

EDIS stared into the distance, something she often

did whenever scanning the intergalactic archives for information. "Negative."

Silgryn entered a series of search phrases.

Vraxed plague… no results.

Vraxed illness… no results.

Vraxed bioterrorism… no results.

Silgryn's chest tightened. Perhaps the Vraxed had all entries blocked from general inquiry. "Run another search on the symptoms, then."

The Vaniren had dubbed the sickness the outlander plague. Signs and symptoms included low energy, feelings of hopelessness, decreased appetite, and unexplainable pain. The healers had not pinpointed the cause, thus unable to control its spread.

"Inquiry." EDIS blinked. "Why do you care so much about helping? Our mission is proceeding as planned."

Back when he was an apprentice smuggler—a teenager scraping by on scraps of bread and false hopes of a brighter tomorrow—his late Captain Daelin had taught him a valuable lesson. During a treasure hunt gone wrong, they faced two options: kill and sail away with riches, or spare the innocent and forfeit their payout. All the money in the galaxy can't build meaning in a life that has none, he had said. And as much as his parents needed their medpacs, he couldn't shake the lump in his gut.

"How long until repairs are complete?" he asked, ignoring her question.

"According to my calculations, the ship will be fully functional in forty-eight hours."

"Find me a cure, EDIS. Holocall me as soon as you do." Silgryn exited the ship, mounting a horse to head towards the royal castle. As the trees of the forest swayed to guide his path, his mind retreated to the nagging thoughts hiding in the background. The ones revolving around Kalec.

He approached the village surrounding the royal castle, and his stomach churned. Clusters of villagers huddled around the portcullis, slowing his entry. Rows of cots lined the cobblestone streets, each filled with the blank stares of Vaniren citizens. Mere days ago, these were the same people cheering for a gigantic worm to kill him for sport, now struggling to stay alive themselves.

Silgryn stopped at the infirmary where he had been

treated as a patient not too long ago, tying the horse to a nearby post. The golden lanterns hummed softly, floating beside each cot. They were among the first to contract the plague and their advanced illness made them completely unresponsive, needing the most care to survive.

"How are the ship repairs coming along?" asked Kalec. He stood over a cot, wiping the sweat from his brow.

Silgryn shrugged. "EDIS tells me she'll be ready to fly in forty-eight hours."

"Wonderful."

The silence lingered between them, as if beckoning the other to speak. Silgryn eventually gave in to the awkwardness.

"Anything helping?" he asked. It struck him odd that Kalec could heal his wounds from the worm with ease, yet struggled with this.

Kalec shook his head. "My father has enlisted the best healers in Vaniren, but to no avail." He held his hand over the chest of a sick villager. The golden glow washed over her, permeating throughout like a force field. "I believe this is otherworldly."

"How so?"

Instead of answering his question, Kalec took him by the hand, leading him out of the infirmary. He could not deny the tingly sensation traveling from his palm and up toward his chest. Whether it was the Prince's magic—or something else—he could not say.

They weaved in-between crowds. The inner courtyard buzzed with activity. Servants swarmed like worker droids, carrying supplies in and out of the castle, moving at a frenzied pace. Silgryn wondered why Vanir existed in a vacuum compared to the rest of the universe, as if they still lived thousands of years in the past. No advanced tech compared to the other planets he had visited.

A wave of animal noises greeted them when they entered a stable. Kalec slid into a stall while Silgryn waded through the chickens to the small pen with the goats. A strong odor wafted up to Silgryn's nose, and once he had realized what he stepped in, he rubbed his boot against the compact stable floor, cursing.

He followed Kalec, who was now kneeling in the stall beside a horse.

"A wolf attacked him in the forest," Kalec said. Along the horse's side, reddened bite marks were crusted over with dried blood.

Kalec rested his hand over the horse's wounds, then closed his eyes. The gentle, golden glow returned, washing over the horse and stitched the wounds together, turning them pink as they healed. The horse neighed.

Silgryn sat beside Kalec as he worked, unable to find the right words.

When Kalec was done, he brushed the horse's hair and fed him a carrot. A faint smile returned to the Prince's face as the horse chewed loudly.

"Why did that work?" His left arm tingled with a phantom reminder of the worm's sharp scales.

"All magic on Vanir is just the transfer of energy from one form to another."

His thoughts froze. "I'm not following."

"The Vaniren call it ether." He placed his hand on Silgryn's arm. "These cuts. When the worm sliced through you, it harnessed its own ether to do so."

Motes of shimmering magic swirled around them as Kalec traced the scar tissue, sending a tingly sensation through him.

"Those of us who can harness the ambient ether

simply transfer it from one form to another," Kalec continued. "Nothing is created, simply borrowed."

"So… you're saying whatever the plague is, it's not natural?"

Kalec nodded. "Foreign to this world. Like you."

His mouth went dry. "You say that as if it's a bad thing."

"Perhaps." Kalec fixed him with a cool blue stare, every second passing between them imposing. Unsettling.

In a galaxy that's evolving too quickly, the only plan guaranteed to fail is not taking risks. The voice of Captain Daelin echoed in his mind. Silgryn didn't know the rules of courtship on Vanir, but he knew one thing for certain: he wanted to kiss Kalec.

"Everything alright?" Kalec asked.

Instead of answering with words, he leaned in and closed his eyes, thinking back to the kisses of his past. Childish pecks during the midsummer holidays of his youth. Nothing evoking a reaction like the rattling of his heartbeat trapped in his chest. Their mouths clung together for an endless moment, leaving them both breathless.

When he pulled away, Kalec just blinked at him.

"Was that alright?" he asked.

But before Kalec could respond, the Prince collapsed backwards onto the stable floor.

#

Revelation

Rescue efforts intensified once Kalec fell ill with the outlander plague. The King summoned healers from across the galaxy—shamans, ritualists, priests—anyone with the slightest inclination to ethereal manipulation who could help.

Silgryn oversaw repairs to the Golden Gull and sold off Vraxed cargo to get enough credits for six months of medpacs.

"Are you eating alright?" Silgryn's mother flickered over the holocall. "You look thin, honey."

"I'm fine, ma. Really."

The translucent blue projection of his father's image flickered. "What happened to your arm?" The tone of his father's voice was sharp, just like every other time he's called home. They grew up in Sector Seven. It's not like job prospects were abound when Silgryn became of age, and smuggling was low on the list of honorable professions. Perhaps his father would have more respect if he called himself a trader instead.

"It's just a scratch. Nothing to worry about."

"When are you coming home, sweetie?"

Silgryn's stomach flipped in a somersault. "Come on, ma. You know how much I hate sitting still." The truth of the matter was they couldn't afford for him to come home. If he wasn't working, they weren't eating.

"You'll still be home in time for the Lunar Festival, right?" she asked.

"I'm transferring credits to your account. Should be enough to last a few months." Silgryn entered his authorization code into the console. "Don't spend it all on Neptune Silver Ale, Dad."

His father huffed, then crossed his arms over his chest. "Don't get killed gallivanting all over the galaxy, kid."

Before he could argue, EDIS flashed onto the ship's interface. "Interruption: requested."

"Gotta go." He flipped the holocall off as his parents both opened their mouths to say something. "Nice save."

"I've salvaged a broadcast transmitted between two Vraxed ships. It was recorded right before impact on Vanir."

"Okay, let's hear it."

EDIS switched the screen to audio transmission. Two soundwaves appeared on the screen, each one fluctuating with a different Vraxed voice.

"I've got a lock on the target. Want me to take him out?"

"No, let him go."

"Captain?"

"I don't understand." Silgryn ran a hand through his hair. "They spared us?"

EDIS flipped the screen over, revealing a blueprint of the Golden Gull. "Tritanium is composed of three different metals, manufactured by ancient Vraxed technology."

"What's so special about it?" he asked.

EDIS blinked as she searched the intergalactic archives. "There are records of certain planets falling to the Vraxed Empire, namely those in the Ismar Cluster, due to ancient technology capable of enslaving its captives through neurochemical assimilation."

"Uh, dumb it down."

"This metal has been used by the Vraxed to enslave other planets through infection. Symptoms include: lethargy, depression, delirium, decreased appetite, and pain."

"I don't understand. How come I haven't gotten sick, then?"

"According to the archives, infection occurs through assimilation. Alien races with magical properties are particularly susceptible."

Silgryn's body tensed with the sudden realization of what he had done.

EDIS tilted her head. "Inquiry: is everything alright? Your vital signs have gone erratic."

He shook his head. "Nevermind me. What's the cure?"

EDIS blinked as she scanned the intergalactic archives. "Symptoms will resolve when the source is destroyed."

Silgryn rested his hand on the ship's console. When he had purchased the Golden Gull all those years ago on the intergalactic trade network, he hadn't considered it had been stolen from the Vraxed. "How do we destroy tritanium?"

"This metal is the first of its kind." EDIS frowned. "According to the archives, tritanium is indestructible."

\#

Deception

Repairs to the Golden Gull were completed the following morning. Silgryn tinkered with the mainframe, setting the coordinates back home. Truth be told, he'd been avoiding the royal palace. Aside from the rows of stretchers lining the village—like a fleet of corpses—he dreaded the thought of facing Kalec again. How would he confess he brought an incurable disease to Vanir?

EDIS flickered onto the console screen. "Incoming: Vraxed fleet transmission. Permission to broadcast?"

Silgryn's chest tightened. "Patch them through."

"Captain Kand'ros of the Vraxed Military Command. Your little trick bought you some time, but we knew you'd come back online, eventually."

Perhaps his parents were right. Getting caught up in the smuggling business was dangerous, especially in dealings with the most powerful alien force in the galaxy. "What do you want? I'm transporting the cargo you gave me, remember?"

"After you left, our analysts reviewed the scan logs and discovered a high concentration of tritanium on your ship. Have you heard of it?"

"No."

Kand'ros chuckled. "You have something of ours, and since you're such a talented barterer of goods, we're willing to strike you a deal."

"Not interested." He concentrated on keeping his voice flat.

"What if you never had to take another smuggling mission again? Have enough credits to pay for a lifetime of medpacs for your dear mother?"

The thought intrigued him. What would life be like, not having to worry about when his next meal would be, or whether he would get the call from the apothecary for past due payments. What would he do with his time then? Would Kalec accept him if he knew the truth?

"I'll give you back the Golden Gull, in exchange for the antidote."

Captain Kand'ros chuckled. "There is no cure."

"So they'll just die?"

"You only have yourself to blame. You brought this technology to the Vaniren."

"And if I don't turn over the ship?"

Captain Kand'ros grimaced. "Then we take it by force. You have twenty-four hours."

The transmission cut, and bright lights illuminated the map display as Vraxed ships entered the Vanir atmosphere. He had heard of Vraxed invasions before. It started with holding the economy hostage, preventing the entry and exit of trade ships for vital goods and supplies. Then, they would draft a treaty—often one-sided—giving them control over the planet for trade to resume. Ultimately, governments would be overthrown, and the planet would be another casualty in the Vraxed's goal for dominance over the entire galaxy. It had happened on Earth when he was a child, but he had never seen the takeover initiated. Until now.

"So my father was right." Kalec leaned against the hull door. His skin took on a pale, pearlescent color, one of the characteristic symptoms of the infection. "You brought this."

"No, I can explain." He moved towards Kalec, closing the distance between them.

But before he could say another word, the Prince held up a hand. Vines erupted from the ground below them, wrapping around Silgryn's body, suspending him in the air. "I trusted you."

He pulled against the force of the plants, which aggravated them further, tightening their grip on him. "It's not what you think!"

"You brought this upon us. And now the Vraxed are on our doorstep to finish the job. Did I miss anything?"

Silgryn opened his mouth to say something, then closed it. From the Prince's vantage point, he was just an off-worlder who didn't belong. Any goodwill he may have gained was shattered in an instant.

Kalec grimaced, then his eyes rolled upward as he crashed into the ground.

He pulled against the vines, which remained taut.

"EDIS, a little help here?"

"Affirmative." The Golden Gull's blasters fired at the plants binding him in place. He rushed towards Kalec, who had lost consciousness, likely due to fatigue from the plague. He scooped the Prince up, then rode back towards the Royal Palace. His mind raced with all the information swirling around in his head. When he crested the rise, the bodies of hundreds of Vaniren greeted him at the village entrance. They wouldn't stand a chance against a Vraxed invasion.

The King aided the healers in the infirmary, his attention turning to his son when they arrived. "What happened?"

"We were on my ship. He lost consciousness."

The King's expression tightened. "Why was he there?"

Silgryn had no answer. He did not know why—in his current state—Kalec would have risked coming out there to see him. The Vaniren held up their end of the bargain. They repaired his ship, and he had promised he would leave as soon as he could. Perhaps there were words left unsaid… on both sides.

"Sir." A royal knight saluted. "Vraxed ships have

breached the atmosphere."

The King looked at Silgryn. An older version of Kalec, with the same scowl. But his eyes were not filled with the betrayal of his son's, but the fury of a ruler running out of options.

"I know how to fix this," Silgryn said.

The healers attended to Kalec, placing him on a stretcher and holding their hands over him. They chanted in their native language, and the glow of the planet's ether washed over his body. The Vaniren were powerful, and had the plague not ravaged their planet, they could hold their own against the Vraxed. Silgryn just had to buy them some time.

"See that you do." The King turned his back to Silgryn, then rested a hand on Kalec's forehead.

\#

Trade

Silgryn stopped the recording.

"Are you certain about this plan?" EDIS asked.

"One hundred percent." Silgryn activated the Golden Gull's jet blasters, launching them back into

Vanir's atmosphere.

"There is a seventeen percent chance of success." EDIS said.

He sighed. "Better than zero. We have to try."

The Golden Gull hovered amidst the Vraxed fleet, surrounded by black, armed warships. The irony of putting the ship so close to danger after all the effort to repair it was not lost on Silgryn, but he needed to make things right again. Sure, he was a space smuggler with little to no honor to his name. And though he was a Vraxed accomplice, he wasn't a killer. Truth be told, he drifted around the galaxy, following the credits. Up to this point, he hadn't known who he was, what he believed in, or where his loyalties lied.

EDIS opened the communication line to Captain Kand'ros.

The image of the Vraxed leader materialized onto the display. "It's so good to see you again, Silgryn. Do we have a deal?"

"Yes." Time seemed to slow as he replayed the parts of the plan in his mind. "But I have terms."

"Let's hear them." Button sounds came through the other end of the holocall. "You have clearance to board."

"No. You will board the Golden Gull. Alone."

Captain Kand'ros raised an eyebrow. "You expect me to board your ship?"

"I'm on a survey ship in the middle of a battle fleet. Wouldn't take much to take me down."

"And if I refuse?"

Silgryn was gambling, hopeful the Vraxed would play the game with him. "I've got another buyer."

"Who?"

"We can discuss aboard my ship." Silgryn cut the communication line.

His old man hadn't taught him much, but there was one useful lesson amidst the drunken nights sitting around the table and a smoke-filled room. One of the first rules of Starship Triad was not to show all one's cards on the first hand. Play strategically, his father had said to him back when he was but a boy. Before his father had lost it all in one game, forcing their family to Sector Seven where the gangs ruled the streets and the stealthy survived. That was when Silgryn had resolved himself to get off the planet. Free to fly in open space, no longer tethered to the confines of a world that had abandoned them.

EDIS opened the teleportation channel into the Golden Gull.

Captain Kand'ros materialized in the primary hull, near where Silgryn stood. He had seen the aliens before, but only at a distance. Close enough to smuggle their goods away, but far enough to know they would be trouble. The alien was humanoid, yet with reptilian features. Five fingers on each hand, though the middle finger and index finger were fused together. And two sets of eyelids, the outer of which closed from bottom to top when he blinked.

"Cozy." Kand'ros peered around the ship, one eyebrow raised.

"She ain't got a lot of bite, but she makes up for it with her personality."

EDIS flickered onto the main display, a slight frown on her face. "My primary responsibility is maintaining optimal ship function."

"You installed artificial intelligence." Captain Kand'ros paced around the hull, his hands folded behind his back. "A nice addition."

"Before I return the ship, I have questions."

"Fine."

"What happens to Vanir?"

Kand'ros shrugged. "Left on their own, they don't stand a chance."

"So they fall in line with the Vraxed, or die?"

The Captain shrugged.

All his life, Silgryn had fought for survival, whether it was rummaging for food in the streets of Sector Seven or taking odd jobs here and there. He could save his own hide now by handing over the ship and returning home. Yet, there would be no guarantee that the Vraxed wouldn't just kill him after the exchange. He'd not only lose his life, but surrender an innocent planet in the process and guarantee the deaths of his own parents. Thoughts of Kalec swirled in his mind, like the ether that had surrounded them in the forest, a sinking feeling now lodged in his stomach.

"Supposedly, if I destroy the ship, the plague goes away. True?"

Kand'ros kept a blank stare. "Yet another fairy tale spun by humans."

"EDIS?" Silgryn asked.

"The Captain's heart rate increased by twenty-one

percent."

He was lying.

"Activate the jump drive."

The Golden Gull shifted to warp speed, moving past the Vraxed fleet to its pre-plotted destination.

The Captain's face warped, exposing two rows of sharp teeth as he lunged. Silgryn opened fire, missing and providing an opening for Kand'ros to tackle him to the ground. The alien bit into his neck, sending shock-waves of pain through him.

"NOW, EDIS!"

Two apertures opened from above the alien, enclosing the Captain in a web of fibers. The lattice lifted him upward, suspending him in the air as the wire prison encased him from the neck down.

Silgryn pushed himself up onto his elbows. His vision blurred from the blood loss, and his pulse pounded in his head as he crawled toward the main console.

The Captain snarled. "It will only be a matter of time before my brethren track you down. Just like we did on Vanir."

Silgryn pressed buttons on the directional display,

confirming the ship's course into the sun. According to the readouts, he had about three minutes. Lights flashed as he initiated override sequences, shutting off the automatic defensive mechanisms EDIS had built into the Golden Gull.

"You think you can destroy tritanium? It's never been done before, boy," the Captain said.

"Confirming automation sequence. All shields deactivated." EDIS flickered onto the screen. "Inquiry: are you sure about this, Silgryn?" The artificial intelligence had always been smarter than him, which was why he had saved enough credits to install her onto the Golden Gull. She'd gotten him out of many sticky situations, her calm demeanor and questioning steering him out of harm every time.

"Yes. Send the holo-recordings. Save the last one for right before impact, straight to the Alliance."

"Understood." EDIS blinked, transmitting the recordings: one to his parents to say goodbye, and the other to Kalec, to apologize. Not that it mattered. Kalec was royalty, and the likelihood of anything serious with a smuggler was out of the question. Perhaps if the circumstances had been different, maybe they could have been something more. But he would never know, not in this life, anyway.

The temperature in the hull increased as they approached the sun's atmosphere. Crashing sounds rocked the Golden Gull as turbulence pushed against their trajectory. It would only be a matter of time.

"EDIS, make sure your upload file is transferred with the recording."

EDIS blinked, her eyes holding something, as if looking at him instead of past him. "You will be a hero, Silgryn. It has been an honor to serve with you."

He pressed the transfer button, confirming the upload into the holocall network. EDIS flashed away from the screen. The ship's hull brightened, illuminated by the sun's molten surface as they approached. The Captain snarled, wrestling to break free from the lattice of wires restricting him.

A holocall flashed onto the screen, its origin from Vanir. Perhaps it was Kalec, calling to stop him from making a stupid decision. Or maybe the prince was calling to thank him for saving them. Could he look Kalec in the face one last time? If so, what would he say? Even if he wanted to, the radiation damage to the Golden Gull was too severe, preventing a stable holocall connection. It was better to leave the universe with no doubts. He had said everything he needed in his message.

"This isn't over," the Captain growled. "The Vraxed will continue to develop new technologies, able to take down entire galaxies. This is but a minor blip."

The walls of the ship's hull tore open as the Golden Gull reached critical levels from the sun's atmosphere. Flames burst into the cockpit, roaring like a dragon as the fire engulfed them. The Captain's screams wailed with the whistling sound of the ship as it tore into pieces.

The communication button flashed, waiting for confirmation, but Silgryn let the call go. Pressure built up between Silgryn's eyes. He thought about his parents back on Earth, and the last conversation he had with them. How they would be taken care of with the remaining credits he sent home, at least long enough to live comfortably with medpacs until their natural deaths.

He closed his eyes, and memories of his brief time on Vanir flashed through his mind. The planet felt so different from any other, as if the ambient magic suffused him with a newfound sense of purpose. Perhaps it was his destiny that brought him to this moment. This decision was where he would either be a weapon for the Vraxed or the spark of hope for other alien races fighting for their own survival. He never set out to be a hero, but he understood what it meant to live under Vraxed control. If losing his life meant another world would have a fighting chance, then that seemed like the right trade to make.

Raama felt the heat wash over him, and the roar of the explosion fading away, leaving his ears ringing. His face was damp, either with tears or blood; he couldn't tell. The sacrifice Silgryn had made to give another world a fighting chance seemed like the right trade to make, even if it meant losing his life.

The familiar pain of wishing he could have traded places with Aanee, facing her tragic fate instead, came rushing back. As he pondered the story, he wrestled with an unsettling thought. Even if he could rewind time, would it truly erase his loss? Or would it would trap him in an endless cycle of grief, haunted by the tragedy forever? Could Silgryn's actions ever make Vanir truly safe if the iterations were infinite?

A profound realization dawned on Raama. Perhaps in one of these variations of time, there was a version of himself who didn't bear the burden of sorrow. A Raama untouched by such loss. The thought was both comforting and disconcerting, reflecting the complexity of life's journey.

It made him question his motives, his desire to bring Aanee back. Could it be that reversing time was not the answer? That the path to peace lay not in changing the past, but in accepting it, learning from it, and growing beyond it?

The Golden Gull
By Steve Drew

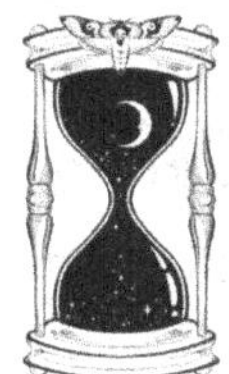

An elfish man walked out of the cave carrying a journal. Except for the scars, he looked identical to the elf that had walked in 30 years earlier. What had been wounds when he walked in were now long healed with scars barely visible. Fresh scars had been acquired along the way. Behind the eyes sat the weight of experiences. The tired wisdom only accrued over time as the soul gets burdened by the things you would redo differently.

While Raama did not live his life by regrets, each mistake added its own small load. Thus, the universe assured you the opportunity to learn from them and do things differently. Raama had learned much in the caves. While his soul would have been still relatively unburdened by 30 years' worth of experiences, he had, in that time, lived many lifetimes and carried the accumulated burden of all. The journal had his notes on those experiences and his experiments with magic. He fantasized he would someday pen a book about them.

After exiting the cave, he smiled at the remains of the spire upon which he had wrecked his beloved Golden Gull and killed the only love of that lifetime. He smiled wistfully as he walked towards the spire, touching small motes of blue floating in the air along the way. His hubris and his attempt to unwind fate had doomed the ship to be found, and floundered again and again for as long as time went on. Raama now understood how each decision spun off in multiple directions. He knew that versions of the Golden Gull would exist in ways completely unrelated to the original sea-faring vessel she had started as. As he brushed his fingers over one mote, he sensed the Gull floating through the vastness of space, and shuddered. Even after so many experiences, thinking of space still evoked a physical reaction in direct response to the memory of his first exposure. He sensed the pain in some orbs and wished he could more directly intervene to spare them the fate to which he had doomed them. He felt small moments of opportunity that he could twist in their favor, but that was the extent of his influence today.

Raama stopped walking when he reached the spire. He noticed that the orbs he had passed along the way were floating lazily behind him, as though compelled to follow him. He knew that at least one voyage could be set right. Taking a few breaths to center himself and drawing on the surrounding lei, Raama started weaving a complex blend, carefully picking from the surrounding particles. He drew the blue orbs into himself, absorbing them. Instead of shying away from the pain he had caused others, he acknowledged it and pledged to carry them with him, hoping that someday he would make amends.

He touched his weave to the spire, cave and shore, then watched the aging of time reverse at high speed. Waves crashing against the shore in reverse were mesmerizing to watch. At a high enough speed, he could almost imagine that it looked the same as the normal way. He could see the spire pieces reform as if the water deposited the rock upon the shore, piece by piece. He could then see them break off the shore and fall upwards along the spire, seating themselves firmly and making the spire larger.

As the sand formed a large dent in the shoreline, he knew he was getting close. He siphoned off some flows of air to create a shimmering shield around himself to avoid being seen. He crafted a small disc of stone and stepped upon it, floating towards the center of the depression in the sand. As he finished, time reached the point where the younger Raama had entered the cave. Raama felt a pang in his heart as he saw himself. Your body has a defense against remembering pain, but apparently that defense fails when you can see your younger self feeling that pain. It was no different watching it from the outside than it had been to live through it the first time. He set his mind resolutely and continued on, as he watched himself return to the shore, looking lost and forlorn. From this perspective, younger Raama seemed to give up and lay on the ground for a nap.

Raama shifted his focus to below his feet, waiting for the Golden Gull to reappear. He specifically could not watch what he knew his younger self was going to do, carrying the body of the one he loved to and from the cave. Instead, he watched pieces of driftwood and flotsam bob back and forth in the ocean, but eventually settle in the indentation. These must have been pieces that broke off. And then she was there. His beloved version of all time, the Golden Gull, was beneath his feet again.

During his time in the caves, Raama had spent at least a full lifetime in the presence of a young man named Micah. He could hear Micah's voice now, nagging him on the dangers of fracturing time. However, he knew with certainty that Micah would understand the need for what Raama was about to do. He must let this incarnation of the Golden Gull continue on its journey. That does not mean he could not fork its fate and let an earlier version have another chance.

He brought a flow of magic around like a hammer and struck it hard against the lei. It had the force of tiny hammers hitting every single particle and sub-particle simultaneously, shaking what Micah would call a quantum partner awake. He quickly latched onto the Golden Gull before those particles could resettle and, holding it apart, released his time magic everywhere except where it touched his Golden Gull. Now, in the same space, there were two Golden Gulls. One Gull was now continuing forward in time, and one going backwards. Raama rode the one going backwards as it slide up the spire, gathering more pieces of itself and bodies of the crew. As it departed the spire on a journey into the sky, it was whole again. Raama endured the torment of the ride back up into space. The worst part for him. Not only because of the physical or emotional suffering but also because there was now a third Raama which was created during the time fracture.

Unlike the presence of the younger Raama on the beach, which had always existed, this Raama was a new existence, both pulled from and bound to Raama and younger Raama. That pain would fade over time, but it did not make the lack of oxygen in space more tolerable. Raama knew he was close to the pinnacle of the journey, as the flames surrounded the ship, and body parts started reassembling into crew members outside the ship. With the ship in space again, Raama was surprised at how long it had floated there while the younger Raama had been unconscious. Raama knew every particle on this ship, as his magic touched everything. He allowed himself to focus on those particles that made up Aanee. He was glad younger Raama had never seen her this way. She was frozen by the exposure to space, but she had died reaching out for him. It was hard for Raama to see her now, and he remembered the madness he had worked to keep at bay in those first years. If the younger Raama had seen her, he likely would have been undone completely. At least he was saving Aanee now, in his way. As the ship started to sink, he felt tears stinging his eyes as he watched the stiff, frozen crew thaw and begin moving slowly. A long felt guilt eased partially in his chest.

It made enduring their suffering in reverse more bearable to know that they were alive again, almost. Raama watched over the side of the ship and gave other Raama space. The farther he could stay from him, the less discomfort he felt. As he looked over the side, he saw the ships of Citadel of Mages and felt an anger eons in the making. He held his magic, making time stop. He knew that nothing he did here would affect his reality, but he calmly brought his forefinger and thumb together. As he pulled them apart, a liquid arc of frozen lightning formed. He drew complex symbols over each of the ships with that liquid lightning, finally releasing it. He once again sundered the quantum state of the surrounding particles, resulting in two younger selves separating from each other. One younger Raama had experienced a brief existence but would never know. The other younger Raama stayed as Raama rolled the new Gull forward again in this timeline and left the old Gull to continue its original journey. That Raama would dissipate after the crash as he caught up with the original timeline. Original Raama channeled a flick at the latest Raama, and knocked him unconscious with a quick blow to the back of the head. While he was still collapsing, Raama let his lightning spell fly. From below, it looked like a separate web of lighting arced toward each of the Citadel ships. Raama did not release the lightning until the first contact was made with the ship, resulting in a lightning column, more than a ship wide, striking the ocean until long after what had been a ship was gone. Raama thought about how an evolved being does not let their anger get so out of hand that they do this much damage. He also felt slightly regressed in letting himself feel satisfaction that these mages were gone. He knew his response had been overblown and out of proportion. Yet, looking over the side, all he could think to say was, "Fuck them."

He guided the ship back to the ocean gently, as the crew set about helping the unconscious younger Raama. Raama could already feel his connection with this reality fading. He spent his last few moments looking at Aanee's face as she cared for the younger him. He wished younger Raama a lifetime of voyages upon the Golden Gull besides Aanee.

Then, he found himself floating in the middle of the ocean, back in his reality. Settling into a back-float and reaching out with his mage senses to see where the nearest ship was, he thought about the other things he needed to set right, and a war that was 30 years overdue.

Meet the Authors

Steve Drew is a master of tales. His work immerses readers into unforgettable worlds, leaving them eagerly anticipating the next adventure. Steve's creative talents and passion for storytelling captivate and inspire audiences across various mediums.

Seán McNicholl is an Irish GP who enjoys writing short stories in a variety of genres. He has had work published in Beyond Words Literary Magazine, Raw Lit, 34th Parallel, BarBar and two anthologies from Wicked Shadow Press. He has featured on the Blue Marble Storytellers Podcast and the Read Lots Write Lots podcast. For more: www.sean-mcnicholl.com

Redd Herring has taught English and coached for almost 30 years in middle and high school. His career choice was a natural given his love of reading, writing, and helping. He found out early that he liked working with young people, even when no one else - parents included - liked them. Redd is the creator of the Book of Choices, which evolved into a cooperative project with multiple authors. Several of the episodes have been featured on the Crossroads Cantina Podcast. He is currently working on a collection of these stories for a future anthology. Redd lives in Texas with his wife, an educator as well; his son who is in college and has plans to be a U.S. Marine, and his daughter who is a cosmetologist (the reason he started this past school year as a 56 year old teacher with purple hair!) He enjoys spending time with his best friend at their small property that is soon to become a family farm.

Riel Rosehill is an author of a wide range of short stories, with a passion for speculative fiction, a sprinkle of magic, and a healthy dash of queer romance, ranging from sweet to dark.
Her short stories have recently been featured in podcasts and anthologies, she was shortlisted in a short story contest on Reedsy and won a Fictionette short story contest in 2022. Currently, she is working on her debut novel, along with a few short story collections and an exciting, brand new novel-

ette for The Golden Gull anthology, titled Brave Soft Hearts, which she can't wait to share with the world! You can find out more about Riel's published work and literary achievements on her website, www.rielrosehill.com

Beth Connor is an accomplished author known for her imaginative and captivating storytelling. She has written books in a range of genres, including "Hollow City," a dystopian novel, and "Micah and the Candles of Time," a heartwarming fantasy story. Beth's upcoming releases include "Prodigy of Flame," which is eagerly anticipated by her fans. In addition to her writing, Beth is also the host of the popular podcast "Crossroads Cantina," where she explores the intersection of storytelling and imagination. Beth aims to inspire readers to explore new worlds and see the magic in everyday life through her work. For more info: www.bethconnor.com

Chris Morris is a writer from Dundee in Scotland. He has self-published a collection of short stories called "Which Way is North?" and two novels: "Dreams of a Damselfly" and "Joy's Lament." He is currently planning a horror/comedy novel that he hopes to publish traditionally. Chris is also the writer/producer of a fiction podcast called "The Finding North Podcast." In 2023, Chris had stories published by Wicked Shadow Press and Quillkeepers Press. When he's not writing, Chris teaches music, assists learning in a high school, and savours every moment of the best job of them all: being a father to a kind, brave, hilarious little girl.

J.C. Lovero is a (legal) drug dealer by day and writes in the cracks of his life, almost always with a cup of coffee. His work has been recognized online, spanning multiple genres set in the contemporary world, fantastical realms, or in galaxies beyond our imagination. For him, any setting works if it involves two men who fall in love. When not reading and writing, he enjoys holding the title of "favorite gay uncle" to his two nephews in Texas. More about him and his writing can be found at medium.com/@jc_lovero.